Sparking THE Vibe

a cozy fantasy romance

AMBER L. WERNER

Published by Werner Ink

Norristown, PA

Cover designed by Amber L. Werner

Map designed by Inkarnate

Paperback ISBN : 978-1-960073-13-6

Library of Congress Control Number: 2026912014

Contents

FAIRVALE
Crater Gorge
CARRAN
MAUDWIN
Wile Basin
FAIRVALE
Rubble Mines
Halwin Lake
Veil Ruins
LARKINGE
Jade River
EVERPASS
Avalon Shallows
PELOITH
Pelo Lake
Paradise Plains
FAVERSHAM
Windswept Woods
SOUTHHOLD
Tempest Isle
SEAHAVEN
Sunken Cove

Depraved

Ali

"Hey, wait up!" A bright floral perfume clung to the evening air as Ali hurried to catch her favorite surly half-troll. They'd just finished a few drinks at her best friend Nora's tavern, but the conversation she had in mind required a degree of secrecy that couldn't be guaranteed at Stellar Spirits. She drew a deep whiff of the spring breeze, steeling herself before plastering a cheery grin on her face. "You busy tonight, Maalik?"

He aimed a scowl up at her face. "Why?"

"I have a proposition for you." She tucked a strand of short black hair behind her ear. "Nothing we haven't done before."

"Quiet!" He snagged her elbow and carted her into an alley, his strength surprising, seeing as she towered over him by at least two heads. "Are you trying to ruin my reputation?"

As they halted in the narrow corridor, she lifted a brow and leaned in. "Funny, I thought being seen with me would be a boon to your reputation."

With thinning brown hair, pale freckled skin, and a short, stocky build, Maalik wasn't exactly a success with the village ladies. Whereas she'd never had much problem attracting members of the opposite sex—often to her detriment, regrettably.

Like most nymphs, Ali had always been fit, willowy, and more attractive than the average human—a blessing that she wasn't always thankful for. But right now, she didn't have a problem playing arm candy. Not when Maalik had already proven he possessed a very desirable skill that she desperately needed him to use again.

Too bad Maalik seemed more inclined to leave her in the lurch than march hand-in-hand with her through the streets of Everpass. "I told you already. Once was more than enough."

"Don't be like that, Mal. You had fun last time. Admit it." She inched closer, lowering her voice. "Aren't you dying for an excuse to put your talented hands to good use?"

His scowl deepened as he tugged the hem of his checkered tunic. "Of course it was fun. But I could lose my job if anyone found out what depravity you talked me into."

That was laying it on a little thick. Sure, what they'd done was a bit out of the norm. But depraved... No way. Still, she could see how the stiff suits down at Maalik's bank might be inclined to think differently.

"No one is going to find out." She smiled reassuringly. "Echo's sleeping over at her friend's house. We'll have the place to ourselves. You can pop up to my room and we'll be done before you know it."

She'd been so confident she could talk Maalik into coming, she'd already prepared, spreading out the goods on her bed. Of course, she'd locked her bedroom door afterwards. Always better to be careful when you live with a nosy preteen.

He pursed his lips. "I don't know..."

"Come on, Mal. You can't let your gift go to waste."

He scoffed. "Some gift."

"It *is* a gift." She grabbed his hand. "You can do such wonderful things. Just think of all the pleasure—"

Maalik tugged his hand back. "Don't remind me." He stepped away, heading for Main Street.

"Please." Her voice cracked. "I need this. You know I do. And you're the only one I can—"

"Aww, hell." He froze in place before slowly turning. "Fine. But this is the last time. I mean it."

Maybe strolling hand-in-hand wasn't out of the question after all...

The tension pooling in her shoulders subsided as a delighted smile crossed her face. "You don't know what this means to me, Mal. I swear, if there's anything you need from me—ever—I'm your girl."

She practically shouted the last bit, and looped her arm through Maalik's, earning curious glances from a pair of imps as they emerged on Main. *That ought to get the rumor mill swirling.* Pleased, she fell in step with Maalik, heading home.

"Did you have to announce that so loudly?" Maalik hissed under his breath.

"Darling, of course I did." She patted his arm lovingly, putting on a show for the looky-loos. With how pleasant the weather was, there was no shortage of villagers out for a stroll. "Can't I show a bit of appreciation for my main man?"

Maalik rolled his eyes. "If you think that act will fool the town gossips, you're bound to be disappointed. No one in their right mind would think you and me—"

"Fire! Our Glass is on fire!" a shout rang out from ahead. "Make way for the brigade!"

Ali's stomach dropped. "My shop!" She dropped Maalik's arm, all pretenses instantly forgotten. Her boots pounded the cobblestone road, each step reverberating through her body and ratcheting her anxiety higher.

As she raced forward, images bombarded her of flames engulfing the building, swallowing everything she'd worked for over the last decade. She couldn't stop picturing the roof caving in, burying all that she owned under charred wood and smoke.

Our Glass wasn't just Everpass's only glassblowing shop; it was her home. If her second-story apartment was caught in the inferno's path, she wouldn't just lose her business. She'd lose everything. All her belongings. Her daughter's treasures. The place where they'd finally set down roots after being abandoned by everyone in their lives who should've mattered most...

How did this happen? She was always so careful. The habit had been drilled into her from an early age. *One must be forever cautious when their gift is born of the underworld.*

She shook the old superstition out of her head. There wasn't time for it now. She had to get home and assess the damage. Maybe her shop could be saved. And at least no one had been there when the fire started. *Thank the goddess Echo's at that sleepover.*

"It doesn't look big," Maalik huffed from beside her as they neared the next turn. "We'd see smoke by now if it was big."

She swallowed heavily, Maalik's words doing little to ease her anxiety. Darkness shrouded the sky, which could disguise how bad things really were. She wouldn't relax until she saw her shop standing with her own eyes.

The acrid stench of char filled her nose as they careened down her block. Dozens of bodies blocked the way—mostly stunned villagers craning their necks up at the second story, mixed with a few strapping young men in suspenders, thick woolen pants, and the shiny black jackets of the fire brigade.

She shoved through the crowd, weaving nimbly around an orc carting a ladder, and losing Maalik somewhere in the process. "What's going on? Where's the fire?" she yelled.

"Excuse me, Ma'am." A lanky human wearing a helmet and brigade gear strode forward, blocking her path. "Step back and let us do our job."

"This is my shop. I deserve to know what's happening!" She crossed her arms and popped a hip, eyeing the front of her shop closely. A few curls of smoke seeped out of the upstairs windows, but thankfully, the building stood, seemingly still sound. "Is the fire contained? Can I go inside?"

She had to get closer. Inspect the damage. But the jerk in her way refused to budge, no matter how hard she glared at him.

"Ali," a familiar voice called. Kieran, the newest member of the brigade—a handsome half-elf former spy, who also happened to be the love of her bestie's life—appeared and clapped a hand on the shoulder of the man blocking her way. "Let me talk to her, Johan. We're friends."

She barely waited for Johan to step aside before asking Kieran, "What happened? How bad is it? Am I totally screwed or—"

"Hey, relax." Kieran squeezed her forearm. "I'll explain everything, I promise."

She forced out a shaky breath. "I am calm." Yeah, that was clearly a lie, but Kieran was either too nice or too wary of the steam currently pouring from her nostrils to call her out on it.

Kieran's green eyes narrowed as he gestured ahead with his other arm—which sported a hook attachment, the hand lost in service of the Crown. "The most important thing is that everyone is safe. We got Echo out before—"

"What?" she shouted, her heart dropping to her feet. "Echo wasn't supposed to be home!"

"Oh..." Kieran bit his lip. "Well, she was. But she's fine. Come on, I'll take you to her."

"You think?" she choked out, her pulse pounding so furiously she didn't even attempt to temper her tone. "Where is she? My baby!" Her voice warbled before turning downright icy. "Goddess, I could kill her!"

"You might wanna save the threats of murder for later. Too many witnesses," Kieran drawled.

Ali side-eyed him, a cutting retort on the tip of her tongue. But the words fled as she spotted Echo crouched on the front stoop of the blacksmith shop next door, her arms wrapped around her folded legs, making her look much smaller than her ten years.

"Echo!" She rushed forward, and scooped her daughter up in a tight embrace. "Are you all right? What were you doing at home? I thought you were at Gracie's house?"

"Mom? I'm okay." Echo groaned. "Jeez, quit squeezing so hard."

Ali's frantically fluttering pulse gradually slowed. She drew back, cupping Echo's cheek, examining her dark-brown skin for burns and finding none—thank the goddess. "What happened, baby? Tell me everything."

Echo's dark-brown eyes dropped to the ground. "I-I'm sorry, Mom. Gracie and I got into a fight, and I came home. Your bedroom door was locked, so I figured you were asleep... Th-then a fire started in the kitchen. It all happened so fast. I screamed for help, and Davos came."

Davos. Her eyes shot to the smithy door. If he'd burst into her apartment to put out the fire, then she owed him far more than she could ever repay.

Echo twisted her hands in her bright yellow skirt. "Lio was there, too. He must've been visiting Davos. He got the fire out fast. It's not that bad, Mom, I swear."

"Lio..." Great. She should be thankful. Having the fire brigade chief next door had clearly saved her home from ruin. And yet, she couldn't mistake the prickles that erupted down her spine.

"Did he get you out of your room?" Echo cocked her head.

Hold on... "My room?"

"The door was locked. I told them you were sleeping. Lio said he'd get you out, but that I had to wait outside."

Oh no. No, no, no!

"Baby," she began. Just then, Maalik appeared, huffing and slightly sweaty. She waved him over. "You remember my friend Mal, don't you?"

Echo nodded, her twin black plaits bouncing on her shoulders. "Yep."

"Stay with him while I go inside, all right?"

Echo's lips pursed. "I wanna go in, too."

"Not yet, sweetie. I... have to make sure it's safe." And make sure a certain nymph who was too sexy for his own good didn't just uncover the secret that might be the only thing that could save her family. She shifted her attention. "Mal, can you watch Echo while I check out the damage?"

Maalik frowned. "Are you certain that's wise? Surely it can wait."

She dragged him aside and hissed out the side of her mouth. "Everything's on my bed… you know, for tonight. And Echo told them I was in there, asleep."

Maalik blanched. "You mean… everything?"

She nodded.

"Go. I'll watch her."

"Thanks, Mal. You're my hero." She forced a smile and turned, praying for a miracle.

Yeah, Lio was hot, but he didn't strike her as the type of guy who bent the rules. He'd out her for sure. Tell the entire village exactly what she'd been doing in her home behind closed doors. And small towns like Everpass weren't the type of place where folk let so-called "lewd" behavior slide.

Forget losing her house to fire. If she didn't do something fast, she'd end up getting kicked out of town, with a permanent stain on her good name.

If Lio already broke down my door, I'll never be able to set foot on the streets of Everpass again.

Temptations

Lio

“**M**y mom's sleeping inside! Please, you have to save her!” Echo's plea rang in his ears long after he sent the little girl outside.

Lio's shoulder ached. He'd lost count of how many times he'd rammed it into the thick oak door. After making no headway, Davos had wandered off, muttering apologies. As the town blacksmith, he'd been the one to install the lock. One of his best, apparently. But while Davos returned to the smithy for his tools, Lio kept at it, determined to save the slumbering nymph.

"Ooof," he grunted as his shoulder made contact again. If only the woman inside would wake up and let him in. She must be a really heavy sleeper.

Granted, they'd gotten off on the wrong foot, but he didn't wish her ill. And there was no telling whether smoke had made its way through the door cracks. If Ali was sleeping deeply, she might be breathing in the dangerous fumes without even realizing.

"Hey, Chief." Johan appeared at his side, an axe in his hands. "Looks like you could use this."

Lio frowned. "I thought you were on crowd control." He snagged the axe.

"Kieran took over." Johan tilted his head. "Need a hand with that door?"

"This should do the trick." He nodded down the hall. "Do me a favor and double-check nothing's smoldering in the kitchen."

As Johan wandered off, a pang lodged in Lio's gut. He should've accepted the backup. On any other job, he likely would've. Hell, he wasn't even supposed to be on duty. Yet for some reason, he'd sent his second in command away when he was about to finally break down the stubborn barrier preventing him from saving the sleeping beauty.

Beauty or not, he had to stop thinking like that. Ali was just another villager in a bind. Soon he'd set her free, then he could go back to pretending she didn't exist. Like he didn't sneak glimpses of her whenever she popped into Davos's shop during one of his visits. Or that her clever quips didn't secretly amuse him when he overheard her talking with her friends on the days he walked his sister home from work.

Alsira Mikelli was a temptation better left alone. *Funny thought to have as I'm breaking down her door.*

The wood surrendered with a deafening thwack. With one last shove, he was inside, but the captivating dark-brown eyes he'd been expecting to find glaring at him were nowhere to be seen.

"Ali?" He shuffled into the bedroom, quickly taking in the homey décor. Woodland paintings hung on the walls. An oblong mirror flanked a modest dresser, the only furniture in the bright blue room besides the enormous four-poster bed.

But no Ali. He nearly turned back, ready to head outside and report to Echo that her mother most definitely was not sleeping in her room, when something strange caught his eye.

The multicolored starburst-patterned bedspread had camouflaged the odd trinkets at first glance, but as he inched closer, he realized Ali's bed was covered with the curiosities. About thirty strange glass tubes were spread out, fitted with metal bottoms similar to the dimmer switches on the lamps he owned.

He lifted one to eye level, marveling at the detailed craftsmanship. He'd never been inside Ali's shop, but he'd peeked inside the front window enough to recognize her art. The glass cylinder glimmered, shimmering with swirling purples and pinks.

Pretty. But what is it?

It must be a new type of light. Some kind of glow stick, he'd guess. Curiosity got the better of him. He twisted the metal bottom, expecting the glass to brighten with light magic the way his lamps did.

Hm. Nothing.

Strange indeed. But nothing he needed to worry about. Ali wasn't here, which meant she was safe. He ought to head out. Stop intruding on her privacy.

He set the cylinder on the bed. It rolled sideways and clanked into another, colored in varied shades of green. His brows pinched together. The second cylinder was much bigger, with a rounded, bulbous tip. The shape was almost... phallic.

Oh... Clarity hit him like a gut punch. He snagged the second cylinder off the bedspread, his stomach clenching and heart pounding out of control.

He wasn't a prude. He understood that women had... needs. And he'd seen the books Ali read at that book club she started. But most people kept things like this hidden in a closet or bedside drawer, not spread out on their mattress.

And there were so many. Why did she need so many?

"It's not what it looks like." Ali's voice came out of nowhere.

Panicked, Lio fumbled the cylinder. The green glass shot out of his hand, flew up, and whacked the bottom of his chin before careening back down toward the floor.

He wasn't sure how he caught it—years of training catching tools tossed his way, maybe—but somehow, he snagged it just before it dropped out of reach.

With the beefy glass beast clenched in one hand, and the axe held firmly in the other, he slowly spun. Ignoring his stinging chin, which was probably turning as red as his burning cheeks, he aimed a glare at the cringing woman hovering in the doorway.

"Not what it looks like," he repeated lamely.

She stepped inside, attempting to drag the ruined door closed behind her. Dressed as she always was, in a long-sleeved top and dark slacks that hugged her figure perfectly, she managed to look casual and downright gorgeous, despite the frantic wrestling match she was currently losing.

With a frown, she gave up after the splintered wood barely budged. "Yes, it's not what you think. I'm... well, I'm..."

He'd honestly never thought he'd see Ali at a loss for words. She was always so composed. Sure of herself and bursting full of positivity. It was strange to hear her stumbling, with a light sheen of sweat dotting her dark-brown forehead.

"I'm sorry." She plastered on an apologetic smile and waved at his chin. "That must've hurt. It's the biggest model I've got."

He scanned the bedspread. "So they are yours…"

"No." She hurried past him and ducked beside the bed. "Actually, yes. But not for long."

What in the realm? He blinked repeatedly as fabric whooshed across the wooden floor. "What are you doing?"

"I need to put these away before Echo sees them. Kids, they get into everything, you know what I mean?" She dropped a big black duffel bag on the bed and hurriedly began packing the glass tubes inside. "Now that my door is ruined—thanks for that, by the way—I have to figure out where to stash these."

"Am I just supposed to ignore what those… things… are?"

She smiled sweetly. "Yep. That'd be great."

"You can't be serious. Why in the realm do you have so many of those… those…"

Glass clanked in the duffel as she stuffed the last cylinder inside. "Personal massagers."

"What?" His brow furrowed as he stared at the green beast in his hand.

She rounded the bed and snatched the cylinder out of his hand. "Yep. This is the orc model. Very popular, I hear. You have good taste."

More heat rushed to his cheeks. "I do not—"

"Moooomm. Where are you?" Echo called from the hall.

"Shit," Ali muttered under her breath. She raced back to the duffel and stuffed the green monster inside, zipping it closed just as her daughter appeared in the doorway.

An out of breath troll—the barfly named Maalik that Ali always seemed so chummy with when he stopped by Stellar Spirits—popped into the room behind Echo. "Sorry. She's too fast. Got away from me."

"Yikes, what happened to your door?" Echo whistled. "Can we get something to eat, Mom? I'm starving."

Ali's hands shot to her shapely hips. "Really, Echo? Our apartment almost burned down, and all you care about is your stomach?"

Echo shrugged. "Can't help it. I'm always hungry."

Ali hurried forward. "Come on, baby, let's go to the kitchen."

He suspected Ali was willing to do anything to distract her daughter from the bag on her bed, but that wasn't happening. "Not that kitchen. I'd strongly advise you two find somewhere else to stay."

Ali pressed a splayed palm to her chest. "Is it really that bad?"

"I'm afraid so. You'll need a handful of repairs before you move back in. The place won't be safe otherwise."

Ali's face fell, and he fought the urge to comfort her. But it seemed her good buddy Maalik wasn't afraid to step up. He wrapped an arm around Ali's back. "It'll be all right, lass. You'll wind up back on your feet before you know it. Promise."

She sighed heavily. "I suppose we'll have to rent a room at the Golden Lark Inn for a while."

Echo perked up. "Is that what the bag is for? Ooo, can I see what you packed for me?"

Eyes widening, Ali reached for the bed, her lips twitching as if she were grasping for an excuse she couldn't summon. Echo's knees connected with the mattress, making the glass inside the duffel clink.

Goddess... Don't do it, Stelios. You're in too deep already.

Ali stuttered, taking a step forward, her hand outstretched.

Echo's little fingers pinched the zipper. She was a heartbeat away from discovering something that would undoubtedly change her opinion of her mother forever.

"Actually, that's mine." Rough fabric slid across his palm as he dragged the bag off the bed. The heavy weight settled on his shoulders like an anchor, rooting him in place. "Just some tools and debris from the fire. Nothing you need to see."

He was an idiot. He should've left well enough alone. Now he was stuck carrying the bag. One he wanted absolutely no part of.

Echo's dark-brown eyes narrowed suspiciously. "Really? Then how come you're using my mom's bag?"

Fantastic. Sweat pooled on his lower back. Barely a moment into the first lie he'd uttered in ages, and he'd been found out by a ten-year-old. *See what happens when you let temptation get the better of you?*

Ali finally found her voice. "He asked to borrow it. And it's always nice to share, right, baby?"

Echo lifted a single shoulder in a half-hearted shrug. "Yeah, right." She shot another suspicious glance at the bag, then bounced on her knees, turning in a semicircle, and gave her full attention to Maalik. "You wanna see my room, Mal?"

Maalik chuckled. "Sure. I'll help you pack, kid."

Echo bounded out of the room with a smile, and Ali spun to face him.

"Thank you. You didn't have to do that, but I'm really, really thankful that you did." The gratitude in her voice cut straight to his core.

In his profession, he was used to being looked at like a hero. Kind of came with the territory of extinguishing fires and rescuing kittens from trees. But something about having *this* woman look at him like that—like he was pure magic—struck on a deeper level. Goddess, what he wouldn't give to bask in that feeling for just a little longer... "It was nothing," he said gruffly.

She held his gaze as she moved closer. His breath caught in his throat.

"So does this mean..."—her gaze trailed down, lingering on his mouth as she stepped even closer— "you're going to do what you said earlier?"

He swallowed thickly. "Huh?" He'd said a lot of things. And he could hardly recall any of them with Ali standing so close, her bed spread out beside them, another enticing lure in a day filled with never-ending temptations.

He choked down a gasp as her warm touch slid across his wrist.

"Forget," she whispered. Then her fingers slipped off his hand and closed over the duffel strap. "I'll hide this. You can slip out before Echo gets back, no one the wiser."

He should've let go. If he'd been thinking clearly, he would've. But he wasn't.

Ali's scent washed over him, a strange mix of smells he couldn't quite put his finger on, likely from her shop, mixed with a heady floral sweetness. As he breathed it in, reveling in the unique aroma, his hand refused to move. Even after she tugged on the strap, and her shocked gaze shot back up, meeting his own.

They stood frozen for a tense moment that lasted forever and no time at all.

"Mom, I'm packed!"

Ali dropped the strap and backed away, heading for her closet. "Coming, sweetheart." She shoved clothes haphazardly into a small pack as Echo bounced into the room.

"Oh, you're still here." Echo clapped her hands and grinned. "Do you wanna see my room, too?"

Lio cleared his throat. "No. I was just leaving." He paused in the doorway. "I'll bring your bag to Stellar Spirits."

Ali replied hastily, a touch of panic in her tone, "Don't trouble yourself. I'll come pick it up from you."

Wonderful. Not sure why Ali wasn't a fan of that plan, but it was clear she wasn't. *Idiot. Looks like you're stuck with the bag of... massagers... until further notice.* With a nod and a sigh, he lifted his hand in a wave. "You got it. See you soon. I'll have my crew lock up when they're through with the investigation. Stay safe."

"We will. Thank you, Chief," Ali said, gifting him a carefree smile. "For everything."

THE STORY OF HER LIFE

Ali

She didn't know whether to laugh or cry. The last thing she'd expected when she arrived at her bedroom was to find Lio staring at an orc model massager like it was a puzzle he couldn't solve... or for him to clobber himself with it.

Good goddess! If he hadn't looked so affronted, with that displeased glower plastered to his stupidly handsome tanned face, she'd have laughed at that. Thankfully, she hadn't. He probably wouldn't have felt inclined to save her when Echo was about to dig into that duffel if she'd cackled at his misfortune.

But why in the realm did he have to take the bag? Now she had no choice but to see him again. A task she was loath to undertake, especially after that charged moment they shared.

Was she destined to always fall for the wrong man? It was the story of her life. Her traitorous heart seemed determined to flutter for the most inappropriate choice of partner, time and again.

Yeah, he was drop-dead gorgeous, tall, dark-haired, and a nymph to boot, but that didn't change the fact that Lio wasn't right for her. She'd known that on the first day they met, when he took one look at Echo—and scowled.

She refused to court anyone who treated her daughter like an inconvenience they couldn't stand to be around. And from everything she'd seen, she suspected Lio wasn't a fan of kids. That was one deal-breaker she couldn't ignore, no matter how much the man made her pulse quicken.

"Come on, Mom." Echo tugged her sleeve. "Let's go. I'm starving, remember?"

"How could I forget?" She grinned, shouldering her bag.

Maalik cleared his throat. "Is that all you're packing? Thought you had more stuff you'd want to bring along."

It was clear from the wiggle of his brow what he was referring to. But she couldn't exactly tell Maalik that the glass she needed him to imbue with magic had already left the building in Lio's hands. Not without curious ears catching wind. "This is it. You mind if I bring the books you wanted to borrow to your place later in the week?"

"Not a problem." Maalik leaned back on his heels. "Well, suppose we should head down."

Soon they found themselves on the road again. Maalik bade them goodbye, and as they began the trek across town, a frantic voice stopped them.

"Ali, oh my goddess! I closed up and came as quickly as I could. Are you all right?" Nora—the owner of Stellar Spirits and her dearest friend—pulled her into a hug.

Ali sighed, squeezing Nora back tightly. "Yeah, we're fine. The fire was contained in the kitchen, and no one got hurt."

Nora broke the embrace, glanced down at the bags they carried, and a soft smile crossed her tanned face. "Let me guess, you need somewhere to stay for a few days?"

"Mom says we get to stay at the inn," Echo chimed in.

Face pinching in an exaggerated expression of disgust, Nora bent to Echo's height, which required little effort, since Nora was on the petite side and Echo took after her, tall and willowy, even at ten. "Say it isn't so. You know I used to work at the Golden Lark, right?"

Echo's eyes popped wide. "You did?" Her eyes narrowed, and her head tilted. "Oh yeah, I remember."

"Let me tell you, the owner of that inn is an old stick in the mud. You won't have a lick of fun if you stay there."

"Nora..." Ali rubbed her temples. Sure, they were bound to be walking on eggshells unless they wanted about a dozen knocks on the door asking them to keep it down, but there was nothing to do but grin and bear it. The Golden Lark was the only inn in Everpass.

Nora's golden-brown eyes twinkled in the moonlight. "If you ask me, Echo, you ought to convince your mom to stay at Stellar Spirits instead. Heck, I won't even charge you, so long as you promise to play with Roo every afternoon after school."

Echo giggled and clapped her hands. "Can we, Mom? Can we?"

Ali's eyes watered. "Nora, you don't have to—"

"Of course I do." Nora flicked her dark-brown curls over the shoulder of her plain black dress. "The upstairs apartment is sitting idle. It's my turn to help you. After everything you did for me last fall, I owe you this much. Please say you'll stay."

Nora suffered through a few problems of her own recently, nearly losing her tavern in the process. But now her business was thriving, so much so that she'd just purchased a cottage in town, allowing her and Kieran to move out of the bar's upstairs apartment.

Still, Nora was wrong about one thing. She didn't *owe* her anything. After learning she was a witch, the first magic Nora mastered was light magic—so she could imbue the lamps in Our Glass free of charge. It was a handsome deal, more than making up for the glasses and jars Ali had supplied Stellar Spirits with.

But if her bestie wanted to save her some funds, she wasn't about to complain. She desperately needed every coin she could get her hands on, now more than ever.

"Well... if you insist." Ali grinned. "So long as I get to play with Roo, too."

Echo giggled again. "Mom, you're too old to play."

Ali scoffed. "Am not!" She leaned closer to her daughter and stage-whispered, "Shhh... Miss Nora's a year older than me. You'll hurt her feelings. And she can't handle more pain, what with her old lady hips."

"Oh... right." Echo nodded sagely.

Nora arched a brow. "Thirty is not old. And my hips are amazing... or so I'm told." A dreamy look passed over her face, as if she were recollecting something particularly steamy.

Good for her! At least one of us is putting their hips to good use. She straightened and sent Nora a saucy wink. "I stand corrected. Shall we?"

They ambled through the village streets, heading for the tavern. Weariness plagued Ali, and she took no note of the mismatched architecture they passed. As the last stop before the mountain pass leading to the capital, Everpass was a hodgepodge town, filled with many species who'd brought their unique building styles with them.

It was one thing that first drew her to the village. After growing up surrounded by folk who weren't the friendliest, she'd longed for a place to fit in. Everpass undoubtedly exceeded her expectations. Here she wasn't the lone fire nymph, sticking out among a sea of water, earth, and wind nymphs. She was just another person, running her business and raising her daughter in relative anonymity.

Ali had settled in Everpass when Echo was a toddler. She'd taken a job with the local glassblower, who taught her everything he knew, while she fantasized of one day owning a shop all her own. Then, a few years back, her mentor retired and sold her the shop.

It was a dream come true, especially for her, a single mother who had no family in Everpass to rely on. Having the means to support Echo and give her the childhood she deserved was all that she could ask for. Getting to do something she loved on top of it? It was more than she'd ever imagined possible when she left home with an infant and barely two coins to pinch together.

And everything had been going so well until recently. Strangely enough, the fire was far from the biggest disaster in her life.

But that was a problem for another day. She had a pillow inside Stellar Spirits calling her name.

She sighed as Nora opened the door to her second favorite building in Everpass. It wasn't just that her bestie owned the place and was nice enough to let her host her book club meetings there every month. Every time she slid onto a stool at the L-shaped marble-topped bar, she felt at home.

Echo hurried inside first, her footsteps clacking across the black-and-white hexagon-patterned tiles as she circled behind the bar. "Roo! Guess what? I get to play with you every day after school!"

Nora's familiar, a tiny brown-furred kangaroo mouse, looked adorable as ever as her beady black eyes locked on Echo, her extra-long tail and ears lifting with excitement. Echo plucked Roo from her bed, a cozy box that lived between bottles on the bar shelves, and set her down on the bar top.

"You can't play for long, Echo. We really ought to get you to bed soon." It was the weekend, so there was no school to worry about in the morning, but after escaping a fire, she was bound to need a good night's rest.

"But Mooomm, what about dinner?" Echo pouted as she rolled up a paper napkin, making a makeshift ball.

Nora chuckled. "Don't worry. I've got that handled." She ducked into the attached kitchenette, which was walled off on the bottom-half only, allowing Nora to chat with her customers while she cooked the delicious meals she served. "How's pulled pork with mac and cheese sound?"

Echo squealed. "That sounds amaaazing!"

Ali sank onto her favorite stool. "You sure this isn't too much, Nor?"

"Don't be silly. How could feeding two of my absolute favorite people be too much?" She scooped a serving onto two plates. "Besides, this was left over from the dinner rush. Can't have it go to waste."

Ali lowered her voice. "We're not keeping you from hanging out with lover boy, are we?"

Echo giggled as she rolled the paper ball across the bar, and Roo bounced after it.

Nora waved the ladle in a circle. "Nope. He'll be busy with the brigade until morning. I swear, if I'd known the odd hours he'd be working, I might not have encouraged him to go after that job so soon."

Ali pursed her lips. She seriously doubted that. Nora was the type of friend who always put others first. "Yeah... but it would've been a shame to miss out on that uniform." She wiggled her brows and smirked, eliciting the giggle from her bestie she'd been angling for.

But the smirk fell off her face as she suddenly recalled a different man in uniform. Ugh. She needed sleep. Maybe then she'd stop being plagued with thoughts of the man she definitely should not be ogling.

"Something wrong?" Nora asked as she set the plates on the bar.

The savory aroma of salted pork and rich, cheesy noodles wafted through the air, and Ali's stomach rumbled. Echo tucked into her portion immediately, doing a little happy dance as the first bite hit her tongue.

Ali speared a chunk of pork with her fork. "It's nothing. Just tired, I guess."

"Don't worry. You'll love the bed upstairs. It's so comfortable I begged Kieran to take it with us when we moved, but he insisted we needed to upgrade to a bigger mattress." Nora's face fell. "Oh... I hope you don't mind sharing? I can hunt down a cot for Echo if you need me to."

Ali waved a hand. "Not a problem. I'm used to it. She ends up climbing into bed with me at least once a week."

"Mooomm," Echo said, seeming not to care that her mouthful of noodles was dangerously close to spraying out. "Don't tell people that! They'll think I'm a baby."

"Naw. Babies know better than to speak with their mouths full," she retorted. *Wow, I really must be tired. That doesn't even make sense.*

Luckily, Echo didn't call her out for it. She just shoved another forkful of noodles into her mouth and chewed aggressively.

"On that note, I'm gonna head home. You still have your spare key, right?" Nora asked.

Ali patted her pocket, making the keys jingle. "You bet."

"Okay. I'll see you two in the morning. Can you tuck Roo in when you're done playing, Echo?"

"I will, Ms. Nora. Thanks for the food. It's really yummy!" Echo replied happily. The door swung closed, and it felt like barely a moment passed before Echo announced, "Done!"

"Good. If you're done, it's time to wash up for bed." She pushed off the bar, taking her half-filled plate with her before scooping up Echo's, which had been practically licked clean.

Echo pouted. "Aww. Can't I play with Roo a little longer?"

Ali chuckled, spotting Roo's little head tilt as if she were silently urging for more playtime, too. Sure, the magical critter might be older than any mouse had a right to be, and so intelligent she could hold full-blown conversations with Nora in her mind, but she clearly loved to play as much as any pet. "Not tonight. Head upstairs with your bag and wash up. Brush your teeth. You know the drill."

Echo sighed. "Fine. Come on, Roo." She gently lifted the mouse onto her palm and deposited her back in her bed. "You coming too, Mom?"

"I'll be up soon. I'm just gonna wash these plates and double-check the locks."

"Okay." Echo's steps slapped the stairs on her way to the upstairs loft.

As Ali got to work on the dishes, her stomach flip-flopped. She could've convinced herself that it was just the delicious food settling in her belly. But that would've been a lie. Truth be told, she was dreading the conversation she'd put off since the first moment she realized Echo had been at home when the fire started.

After double-checking the locks—twice—she forced herself to stop avoiding the inevitable. The loft stairs creaked as she ascended, and her frayed nerves tightened further.

Echo was already under the covers, her adorable face peeking out from the top of a purple comforter. Ali didn't bother scanning the room. She'd been in the loft before. There wasn't much to see. The double bed dominated the small space, along with a couple of dressers and a rocking chair that perched beside the large octagon window.

"Honey? Can we talk?" Ali perched on the edge of the bed.

Echo chewed on her lip. "About what?"

Her heart sped. "I'd like it if you told me more about what happened tonight. Can you do that for me, please?"

"Um... okay, I guess."

"Why did you leave Gracie's house? You said, you two got into a fight?"

Echo's nose scrunched, and her voice warbled. "Not like a fight, fight. She... yelled at me. So I left."

Ali drew a deep breath through her nose. The part of her that never wanted her daughter to experience the loneliness and hurt that she'd been through as a child raged with injustice. That part of her longed to march over to that kid's house and scream right back in her face. But she tamped down the urge and merely said, "That doesn't sound like Gracie. You two are usually twined together like ivy. What happened before the yelling?"

Echo picked at the comforter. "I was helping Gracie's dad make some fishing lures. He asked us both to do it, and it looked like fun. Gracie didn't wanna, but I did. Then after we got done, she said... she said..."

Ali grabbed Echo's hand and squeezed.

"She said, 'He's my dad, not yours.'" Echo's lower lip quivered. "She said I was just hogging him 'cause I don't have one."

Ali's heart shattered like a broken glass in her shop, only she knew this mess wouldn't be so easy to sweep away. "Baby, I'm so sorry."

"I-I didn't want to sleep over anymore after that. S-so I came home. And then... and then..." Echo's eyes turned glassy, her words choking up as if she was living through the memory—and the pain—all over again. "I don't know what happened. I was just so... so mad. And then..." Echo lifted her hand, staring at her palm with horror before turning her tortured gaze back to Ali. "I did it, Mom. I started the fire," she finished in a whisper. "I didn't mean to do it, but I-I did."

Goddess... It was exactly what she'd been afraid of.

Echo burst into tears, and Ali pulled her into her arms.

"Oh honey. Of course you didn't mean it. I believe you. And I promise everything is going to be all right."

She ran a soothing hand down her daughter's back, praying she hadn't just told Echo the biggest lie she'd ever uttered.

Trust Me

Lio

He stalked through the darkened house, taking care with each step. Lio held his breath, praying that Tini wouldn't awaken as the duffel clanked softly at his side.

He'd held off returning home until after his sister went to bed. Well, after he *hoped* she'd gone to bed. She'd begun keeping later hours in the last year or so, after taking a job as a barmaid at Stellar Spirits. He'd never complained. Especially since every step Tini took toward independence was another step closer to his eventual freedom. But tonight, he suddenly wished he'd been stricter with her curfew. It would've been much less stressful sneaking a bag of objects he hoped his teen sister didn't know existed into his room, if he could be certain she was fast asleep.

Shadows danced along the walls from the dim light seeping through the living room windows. He hadn't bothered turning on any lamps when he arrived at their modest cottage. The portrait of his late parents hanging over the mantle stared at him as he inched closer to his bedroom door, their smiling faces seeming particularly disapproving tonight.

Perhaps that was just his guilty conscience talking. What would his parents think if they knew what he was sneaking into their home, where their baby daughter might discover it? Somehow, he doubted they'd be pleased.

Not that he could change things now. Not unless he wanted to march across town to the Golden Lark and wake the whole inn by banging on Ali's door in the middle of the night.

Yeah... That was definitely not happening. Certainly not while a much younger, infinitely more annoying female might be the one to answer.

Why did the one woman who'd interested him in ages have to be a mother? Terrible luck, that. He ought to be used to it by now. Luck had never been one to bless him. At least not since before that terrible night over a decade ago, when everything changed.

He forced aside his morbid thoughts. *Concentrate, Stelios. You're almost there.*

The knob turned slowly under his fingers, the latch surrendering with a barely audible click. He eased through the doorway, turned on the lamp, and shuffled to his bed. There weren't many places to hide something so large in his room. His closet was already bursting, full of everyday clothes and brigade gear.

Under the bed would have to do. He lifted the bottom of his navy-blue comforter, sliding the noisy duffel underneath. And not a moment too soon.

"Lio?"

"Tini!" he squeaked, his typical baritone escaping a few octaves higher than usual. He cleared his throat as he spun to face her. "What are you doing up so late?"

His sister hovered in the doorway, her dark-brown curls obscuring her face, her chest lightly heaving beneath her long-sleeved cotton nightgown. He took one look at her, instantly regretting the accusation infusing his tone.

"Hey, come here." He threw out his arms wide. "It's all right. I'm here, Runt."

Her nose wrinkled, just like he knew it would—using her old childhood nickname always got that reaction—but her chest settled a bit as her watery blue eyes lifted from the floor and connected with his. Then she hurried forward and sank into his arms.

"I'm okay." She hugged him tightly and released a deep sigh. "Big Butt."

Normally, he wasn't shy about teasing Tini for the idiotic nickname she'd given him when he started calling her Runt—in her defense, she was only five at the time—but he always let it slide on nights like tonight. "Another nightmare?"

She nodded against his chest before backing away. "Yeah."

"Same as last time?"

"Same as always." Tini's gaze turned downcast. "Why does this keep happening to me?"

He grabbed her hand and tugged until they both settled on the edge of his bed. "I wish I knew. Do you want to talk about it?"

She shook her head. "Not tonight."

Tini had been plagued with nightmares nearly her whole life. Over the years, he'd tried everything he could think of to help her, to no avail. Well… almost everything. But some things were better left unexplored.

"I've been thinking…" Tini peeked at him through the curtain of her hair.

"About what?" he asked warily.

"I want to go back."

"We've been through this. After everything that happened, I don't think it's wise—"

"What if I do think it's wise?" She straightened. "You've always said I was too young, but surely now that's not the case. I'll be eighteen in a few weeks."

Like that would make a difference. He knew better than anyone how dangerous that place could be to someone on the cusp of adulthood. "Absolutely not. There's nothing left for us in Paradise Plains. Trust me on this, Tini."

Her fingers tangled in the hem of her nightgown. "I need answers, Lio. Maybe going back will help me get over these nightmares."

"It won't."

"How can you know that?" She met his gaze, her blue eyes still glossy. "And what about my power?"

He stood, unable to remain sitting calmly while his sister was talking about upending their peaceful existence. About returning to the one place he refused to go back to—one filled with painful memories he couldn't bear to revisit. "What about it?"

"You know what." She huffed, crossing her arms. "I'm practically the only nymph in existence that hasn't discovered their power at my age."

He waved a hand, pacing. "There's nothing wrong with that. You're just a late-bloomer. It's not uncommon—"

"The book about nymph magic I just bought says differently."

"You bought a book about nymphs?" His pitch rose once more. "Why would you do that?"

She lifted a brow. "Why do you think? Maybe if you'd told me more than the bare minimum about our heritage, I wouldn't have to."

"Trust me, Tini. You're better off not knowing."

Another sigh spilled out of her lips, much heavier than the last. "Trust *you*. I wish you'd trust *me* enough to tell me the truth." Tini rose from the bed and marched into the hall. "Good night, big brother."

"Good night..." He trailed off as her door slammed shut.

It was better that way. Because no amount of nightmares were worth the trouble that would plague him if he gave in to her request.

And yet, worries niggled at him, refusing to let him fall asleep long after his head hit the pillow.

If I don't take her back, will she go without me? The thought should've brought him comfort. After all, he'd been waiting for the day Tini would strike out on her own for over a decade. Only it didn't comfort him in the slightest. *She'll see reason. Tini's always listened to me before. She's always trusted me... She'll trust me on this.*

After repeating the reassurance in his mind enough times that he finally began to believe it, Lio drifted off to sleep.

SACRIFICE

Ali

Ali hurried forward with an apologetic smile as Stellar Spirit's front door swung closed behind her. "Sorry I'm late. What did I miss?"

Her day had passed in a blur. She couldn't afford to take off on one of her busiest weekend days, so she'd opened up Our Glass in the morning after calling in a favor from Mrs. Pilbeck to watch Echo. Normally, Echo hung out with Gracie on the weekends, but after the argument they'd had, she wouldn't force her daughter to face her so-called friend until she was ready.

It meant stretching her budget even thinner. Mrs. Pilbeck was the best sitter in Everpass, which meant she wasn't exactly cheap. But

Echo's happiness had to come first. Even if it meant trekking to the far side of Everpass and back instead of simply dropping her off at Gracie's house two blocks away.

She'd been swamped with customers all day. Then after closing, she'd had an appointment with the builder she hoped to hire to complete the repairs on her kitchen. At least now the workday was through, and she could finally relax at her favorite gathering—book club.

"Hey, Ali," Paige called, patting the empty stool between her and Maalik. "Glad you finally made it."

Nora grabbed a pitcher and poured red liquid into a glass. "You missed a lot. Everyone left just before you got here. But I saved you a drink."

"Oh…" They'd held the meeting without her. Guess she wouldn't be relaxing at book club after all. She plopped onto the stool with a sigh, nodding hello to Maalik, the only other book club member besides Paige and Nora who'd stuck around.

Paige tilted her head, setting her honey-blonde streaked brown hair bobbing across the shoulders of her light-blue dress. "Hope you don't mind, we picked next month's selection. Here's your copy." She slid a paperback across the bar.

Ali's stomach clenched as she scanned the cover. On it, a beefy man wearing a brigade coat and helmet carried a woman in a singed dress. "Who picked this one?"

"Me," Paige announced cheerily. "Figured Nora would get a kick out of it."

Nora's cheeks pinked. "I'm looking forward to it."

Paige giggled. "Maybe you can talk Kieran into leaving his helmet on one night."

Maalik's mug slammed on the bar top a little too loudly. "Please spare me the details."

Ali's pulse fluttered. She'd read her share of firefighter romances, but something told her this one would be hard to pick up. At least not without thoughts of a certain fire brigade chief intruding on the story.

"What's wrong?" Paige asked. "Have you read it already? Was it terrible?"

She forced a smile. "No, I haven't. I just wasn't expecting to read about a fire so soon after my kitchen was destroyed."

"Oh, goddess. How insensitive of me. I didn't even consider—"

Ali snagged Paige's hand as she attempted to pull the book back. "No, it's fine. And this looks like a great read."

Nora's rag halted its scrubbing on the already pristine bar top. "Are you sure, Ali? We can easily choose another."

"Don't." Ali placed the book on her lap. "But I'd love to talk about something else. Mrs. Pilbeck is dropping off Echo soon, and I'm dying for an adult conversation." She lifted her glass, finally taking a sip of the mystery mocktail. "Wow, Nora. What is this? You've outdone yourself."

Nora's cheeks pinked again. "Actually, I can't take credit for that concoction. It's something Kieran whipped up for me."

Maalik snorted. "Tell her the name." He nudged Ali with his shoulder. "You'll love this."

"Kieran's infinite bliss," Nora muttered.

Ali sniggered. "Wow. Hope he's as good at making drinks as he is at more important things."

"Moving on," Nora said curtly as she turned to Paige. "I want to hear more about your new man."

Ali's eyes widened. "You've been courting someone?"

"Yeah." Paige sighed dreamily. "I don't want to jinx it, but... I really like him. I think he might be the one."

Something in Ali's gut curdled at the news. Of course, she was happy for Paige. While she hadn't known the pretty country witch as long as she'd known Nora, Ali had quickly grown close to Paige after inviting her and her mother, Opal, to join book club a few months back. Paige was an amazing person, kind enough to help Nora when she was at her lowest. If anyone deserved happiness, she did.

Yet deep down, Ali couldn't escape the truth. Her friends were pairing off, finding the partners they deserved, while she was stuck in a loveless rut that seemed doomed to never end.

But the last thing she wanted was to wallow in her own misery during the brief window of time she had with her friends. So she pasted on a bright smile and said, "Don't stop there. Tell us all about him!"

"His name is Emil. I met him in Fairvale a few weeks back. He's living there now, but get this—his uncle owns the bookshop here in Everpass."

"You mean Ever Bound?" Nora asked. "I love that shop."

"Me too." Paige grinned. "Emil's in the grocery business now. That's how we met. I sold him a few bushels of corn from the farm. But he's been hinting that what he really wants to do is move to Everpass and take over Ever Bound when his uncle retires."

Maalik swigged some ale from his mug. "I like him already. Think you can get the book club a friends and family discount?"

Nora rolled her eyes playfully. "Really, Mal?"

Maalik shrugged. "What? Doesn't hurt to be frugal." His gaze connected with Ali's briefly before returning to his mug.

"So what makes you think he's the one?" Nora asked.

"I've only seen him twice so far, but he's just so… sweet. Pulling out chairs, opening doors. A proper gentleman, you know?" Paige flashed a little half-smile. "And we have a lot in common. We both want a big family. And he loves to *read*."

"We all know how hard that is to find," Ali mused. She'd been trying to get more male members to join their book club for ages.

"He sounds great. When do we get to meet him?" Nora asked. "Ooo, you could invite him to book club."

"Actually… you'll meet him before that. He asked me to accompany him to the spring dance next weekend."

The dance was an annual tradition in Everpass, which happened during the evening hours of the spring festival. Though much tamer than the giant dances and masquerades held in the capital, all the villagers and folk from the surrounding farmland looked forward to it. For some of them, it was their only break to relax during the grueling planting season.

Ali took Echo to the festival every year, but she'd never stuck around for the dancing portion, preferring to get Echo home before the dancers inevitably ended up a bit too tipsy on celebratory drinks. She'd assumed this year would be no exception, but it seemed now she had a reason to stick around a little later.

"That's so exciting! I can't wait to meet him." Ali sent Paige a smile.

"Me too," Nora chimed in.

Paige's answering smile came out somewhat pinched.

"What is it?" Ali asked. "Afraid we're going to scare him off?"

The sigh Paige released was so full of angst Ali feared she'd hit the mark. "I'm not worried about you… But I am worried something else might scare him."

Nora leaned in. "What?"

Paige traced the rim of her mug with her forefinger. "Well, he's human, and... I haven't told him I'm a witch yet."

The back door slammed open before any of them could persuade Paige that her worries were unfounded. Frankly, it was probably better they'd been interrupted. With how feared witches were by the common-folk in the realm, any reassurances would be wishful thinking at best.

"Hey, Nor." A huge half-orc burst in, his auburn hair wind-tousled and bright blue eyes shining. "Ma burned dinner again. I'm gonna need some grub to go."

"Sure, Seth. Coming right up," Nora replied with a chuckle as she ducked into the kitchen.

Nora was Seth's sister—though foster sister was more accurate. But Seth never let the fact that she'd shown up in a basket on his mother's doorstep stop him from treating Nora like blood.

"Mal, fancy meeting you here," Seth greeted with a wink. "Ali, good to see you." He grinned at her, but his smile faded away when his gaze trailed to the last stool. "Paige."

Paige swiveled forward, a barely discernible nod her only return greeting.

Ali wasn't surprised. Paige and Seth had gotten off on the wrong foot from the start, due to a misunderstanding that she'd found especially hilarious. And it appeared they hadn't gotten chummy quite yet, despite their mother's becoming fast friends.

"Hope I'm not intruding on your discussion." Seth leaned against the bar, his green skin contrasting nicely with the short-sleeved white tunic plastered to his muscular chest.

Maalik's nose twitched. "Nope."

"You don't have to intrude if you're involved." Ali slid the paperback across the bar. "Plenty of time to join the next round."

Seth squinted at the cover before shaking his head. "Naw. Reading's not my thing. If I stare too long at all those words, I always end up with a headache."

Paige scoffed before lifting her drink to her lips.

Seth slid the book back to Ali. "I heard about the fire. Anything I can do to help?"

"That's sweet of you to offer." She'd always liked Seth, and not just because he was Nora's brother. He'd been nothing but kind to her since they'd met, and never hesitated to help around the tavern when Nora was short-staffed. Of course, it didn't hurt that he was easy on the eyes, too. "I think I've got everything under control. I had a meeting with a builder earlier, who promised to start repairs next week."

"That's good." Seth's grin returned with a vengeance. "So... I hear there's a dance next weekend."

Beside her, Paige stiffened.

Ali's gaze flicked to the open back windows. Had Seth caught wind of their conversation on his way in? "Should be a fun night. You planning to go?" she asked casually, hoping to diffuse some of the tension brewing in the tavern.

"Yep. I'm a big fan of dancing. Love it, really. It's one of the few things I miss about Fairvale." Seth shifted from one foot to the other as he rambled on. "You know, in the capital they have a dance nearly every other week. Or at the least, once a month. But here, we get what? One or two a year. It's a damn shame."

"Sure," Ali agreed easily.

Sweat beaded on Seth's forehead. "So you like dancing too, then?"

"Yep, who doesn't?" she replied.

Maalik raised his hand. "Won't catch me prancing around in circles, stuffed in some fancy suit. You lot look like a bunch of painted pigs caught in a whirlpool."

Laughter spilled out of Ali's chest. "Really, Mal?"

"Who paints their pigs?" Paige asked.

"No one does. Mal's just a fan of colorful insults," Seth insisted.

Maalik lifted his chin. "That I am. But you're wrong about the pigs. Ever been to Larkinge? Those idiots think it's hilarious to paint piglets and race them against each other."

"Goddess, that's awful." Paige shook her head.

"Dunno. It was kinda funny when I saw it," Maalik replied.

Paige gasped and slapped Maalik's shoulder. "Mal!"

"What? I'm not gonna lie to you, lass." Maalik shrugged. "It was pretty entertaining."

Seth gritted his teeth. "Anyway—"

"Entertaining? Spare me." Paige crossed her arms, clearly disinclined to let the topic drop. "Why in the realm would anyone spill paint on a cute little pig? And then force them to race? That's just plain cruel, if you ask me."

"No one asked you, did they?" Seth palmed his forehead.

The glare Paige leveled at Seth was so icy it even made Ali chilled.

Nora popped out of the kitchen holding two paper containers. "I've never heard of pig painting. Or racing. You sure that's even a thing?"

Maalik nodded sagely. "Yep. In Larkinge."

Seth grabbed the boxes from Nora. "Thanks." Then he heaved a heavy sigh before aiming a rueful smile in Ali's direction. "Well, as I was saying—"

The tavern door swung open, and Echo darted inside. "Mom. I'm back!" Barely a moment passed before she collided with Ali, nearly toppling her off the stool.

"Hey, baby. Did you have a good day?" Ali smoothed Echo's hair as the familiar warmth from her daughter's unconditional love spread through her chest.

Mrs. Pilbeck, a plump woman dressed in a black-and-white checkered dress with a halo of white curls encircling her pale face, shuffled inside a few moments later, her gait slow and breathing labored. "Ms. Mikelli. May I have a word with you in private?"

Seth shot Echo a grin. "Hey, good to see you, kid. You promised to show me the trick you taught Roo, remember? No time like the present."

"Okay." Echo launched herself off Ali's lap. "You're gonna love this!"

Ali mouthed a silent 'thank you' to Seth as she hopped down from the bar stool and joined Mrs. Pilbeck at the table closest to the front door. "Is something wrong? Did Echo—"

Mrs. Pilbeck held up her hand. "Your daughter was a delight, as always." She pulled out a chair and sank onto it heavily. "I'm afraid we have a different issue."

"We do?" Ali sat across from her.

Nora bustled over and set a glass of water on the table.

"Thank you." Mrs. Pilbeck chugged half the water as Nora returned to her spot at the bar. "You know I adore Echo, but I can't keep making the trek across town. Not at my age."

"Oh... I didn't realize."

A wrinkled hand closed over Ali's on the tabletop. "Not your fault, dear. I've been living in denial." She waved at the door, her chest still pumping far more heavily than it should. "That walk just now proved that I can't keep pretending that I'm still the spry young thing I once was."

Ali's heart twinged. It had been months since the last time she'd brought Echo by Mrs. Pilbecks. And even longer than that since she'd asked her to walk Echo home. She would've never made the request if she'd known the old woman couldn't handle the exercise. "I'm so sorry. Let me hire a wagon to take you home."

There she went again, stretching her budget to the max. She bit back a sigh.

"That would be most appreciated. And I'm afraid I must ask that when you bring Echo by again, you handle both the pick-up and drop-off."

"Of course." Ali forced a smile while internally groaning. That meant she'd end up putting in longer hours or closing the shop early. But it couldn't be helped. Not if she wanted to keep her daughter safe. While some parents might be comfortable leaving their ten-year-olds home alone, Ali wasn't one of them. Especially not after the fire. And letting her hang out in the shop wasn't ideal either. Echo's boundless energy had led to her accidentally smashing display items in the past.

"Thank you for understanding." Mrs. Pilbeck patted her hand gently.

"Sure. I'll go find you a wagon."

The sound of her daughter's laughter rang in Ali's ears as she headed for the door. *At least she's happy.* She'd sacrifice anything to keep her daughter smiling. That was all that mattered in the end.

Ali yawned as the kettle's mournful whistle steadily increased. "Echo, quit fooling around with Roo and finish your breakfast." Sunshine filtered into the tavern windows and glistened on the bar, where her daughter's untouched plate of fruit and eggs grew cold.

She never understood how Echo could be positively ravenous in the afternoon and evening, but only picked at her food in the morning. Normally, she had more patience for her dawdling. Not today. She had to walk Echo to school, then open up her shop, where not just one, but three custom orders were waiting to be started.

The kettle cried out, its piercing call dragging her back to the moment. Before Ali hauled herself into motion, Nora stepped in, flicking the burner off and pulling the kettle off the heat.

"Why don't you let me handle the drinks around here, hm?"

"Thanks, Nor," Ali said, hiding another yawn behind her hand.

"An extra-strong cup of tea, coming right up." Nora chuckled. "Long night?"

Ali leaned against the wall. "You could say that. I stayed up later than I should have reading." To tell the truth, that wasn't unusual. Her nightly routine consisted of putting Echo to bed, then reading, more often than not.

"Been there before." Nora peered out of the kitchen, her gaze zeroing in on Roo and Echo, as if to check that they were still occupied. Then she lowered her voice. "I'm glad I caught you before you left this morning."

"Really? Why?"

"I have a favor to ask." Steam curled through the air, and a pleasant aroma redolent with honey and lemon wafted out of the mug Nora placed in front of her. "It's about Seth."

Ali lifted a brow. "What about him?"

"He stuck around for a while after you and Echo went upstairs last night. And he told me something very interesting." A coy smile tilted Nora's lips.

"Which was?"

"Seems he was pretty upset he kept getting interrupted while chatting with you."

"Who knew pigs were so fascinating?" She chuckled.

"Yep. The painted pigs." Nora grabbed an apron and tied it around the waist of her navy-blue dress. "Apparently, before all the pig drama unfolded, he was trying to ask you to go to the dance with him."

Ali blinked, shock spreading through her core. "Really?" No wonder he'd been nervously rambling and acting out of sorts.

"So do you want to?" Nora asked, her tone earnest, her eyes alight with the pure hope of a woman who wanted only the best for her brother and her best friend. "Seth needs a win. He's been feeling down about being beaten out for all the houses he's put an offer on. And I can tell he's still not over the fact that I found out I have a sister. A night at the dance with good company would do so much to lift his spirits."

Ali's stomach churned. "I don't know, Nor. He's your brother. What if things go horribly wrong?"

Nora waved her hand. "They won't. He's not some skirt-chaser who will just use you and break your heart. I can vouch for that."

Ouch... Nora doesn't realize how much that comment stings. Not that she could blame her. She hadn't been forthcoming with all the sad details of her past—even with her bestie. "I know that... but what if it goes well for a while, and then suddenly it doesn't? Won't that be awkward?" Ali lifted the steaming mug. "I don't want things to become awkward between us, Nora. Ever."

"Then we won't let it. Promise. Besides, we're getting ahead of ourselves. This is just one dance. You deserve a chance to let off some steam, too. I've seen how hard you've been working. When was the last time you took a little time just to have fun?" She leaned in and lowered her voice further. "*Adult* fun."

Ali sighed into her cup. Truth was, she couldn't even remember the last time she'd been out with a man. The only thing she'd hired a sitter for in *years* was book club.

Like Nora had read her mind, she said, "I'll even keep an eye on Echo for you, so you don't have to bother Mrs. Pilbeck."

She frowned. "What about you and Kieran? Don't you want to dance the night away with him?"

"Kieran has to work, so I rented a booth at the festival. You can bring Echo by just before the dance starts, and I'll put her to work until I close up for the day."

"That stinks. It would be more fun if you were there." Might make the outing feel a little less like a date, too.

Of course, she was flattered that Seth was interested, but if she were being honest, she'd never considered courting him before. Probably because he was Nora's brother, and she'd rather swallow broken glass than ruin their relationship over a guy. Although it seemed Nora had no problem with her and Seth going out. Maybe she ought to stop letting the association bother her.

"Kieran's taking me to a masquerade in the capital next month to make up for it." Nora lifted a shoulder in a lopsided shrug. "Hey, who knows? If this dance goes well with you and Seth, maybe you two can join us at the masquerade. Wouldn't that be fun?"

"What would be fun?" Echo chimed in.

Ali flinched, nearly spilling her tea. "Hey, little gremlin. What did I tell you about sneaking up on me?"

Echo blatantly ignored her. "Ms. Nora, I like fun! Tell me!"

Nora grinned. "I know you do. That's why I asked your mom if you could work for me at the spring festival. How would you like to be my official cider slinger?"

Echo's nose wrinkled. "Work? That doesn't sound like fun."

Nora wrapped an arm around Echo's shoulder. "I'd send you out into the crowd with a tray full of cider to sell. And you'd get to keep *all* the tips."

"Ooo, tips..." Echo's eyes lit up. "Can I, Mom?"

Ali sighed heavily. "I'll think about it. But only if you eat your breakfast."

Echo hurried off, and a few moments later she was shoveling eggs into her mouth.

"So..." Nora grinned. "What do you think? Sounds like Echo is in."

"I don't know..."

"Come on, Ali. It's just one dance." Nora grinned. "I know you're worried about what could go wrong... But imagine what could happen if things go right. Seth is a great guy—and I'm not just saying that because he's my brother. And you already know Echo loves him."

That fact was certainly undeniable. Seth never treated Echo like a burden. He enjoyed spending time with her, and vice versa.

Hell, what are you so scared of, Ali? Go for it.

"All right. You convinced me. Tell Seth I'd be delighted to be his date for the dance."

Nora squealed. "This is going to be great, Ali! You'll see."

The front door swung open as Echo's fork scraped her empty plate. "Goft morphfing, Teeni!" Echo blurted, her mouth stuffed so full it was a miracle she managed to get the greeting out at all.

Tini shuffled inside, pulling the door closed softly behind her. "Good morning to you too, Echo." Lio's sister was everything he was not. Petite where he was hulking. A bright ray of sunshine that stood out against her brother's perpetual scowls. But this morning, Tini's expression was dimmer than usual.

Ali's chest clenched. She couldn't help feeling a kinship with her as one of the few nymphs in Everpass. Maybe she could help... "How're you doing, Tini?" Ali asked.

"Oh, I'm fine. Just got a rotten night's sleep." Tini unbuttoned her white shawl, revealing a bright yellow dress hemmed in white.

Nora ducked back into the kitchen. "Let me make you a cup of tea. Ali will tell you, it does the trick."

"She's right." Ali lifted her mug to her lips and swallowed the last mouthful. "This stuff always wakes me up."

"Good to know." Tini smiled, but Ali suspected it was more than a little forced.

Not sure what possessed her, but Ali stopped at Tini's side and said quietly, "Hey, if you ever need to talk, I'm here, kay?"

Tini's brow creased. "Um... Thanks."

Great. Now she probably thinks I'm crazy. Just another weird nymph full of superstitions, letting their illogical feelings lead their lives. She'd moved halfway around the realm to escape them. Yet here she was, falling right back into that pattern with the first nymph she got close to.

Better get a move on before she said something else she regretted. "Come on, Echo. Time to go."

Insults and Favors

Lio

"Hey, beef stew," Lio called out loudly as he weaved around a half-finished sword in the smithy. "Where are you?"

Davos's shop was a marvel. The oblong showroom featured red-brick walls and silver accents, giving it a warm elegance that perfectly complemented his expertly crafted pieces. Weapons and tools of all shapes and sizes decorated the walls, showcasing his skill at a glance to anyone wandering in off the street.

But Lio wasn't there to shop. He desperately needed advice from the one person in Everpass he considered a friend.

Odd that Davos would be out. He was practically chained to his forge; a loner who couldn't stand being gawked at. And seeing as he was the only one of his kind in the village—and worse, one of the few of his kind in the entire realm—staring was basically guaranteed when he ventured out of the smithy.

He followed the muted hum of voices out back. There he finally spotted Davos, his burly frame blocking Lio's view of the forge, a rectangular brick hearth that dominated the fenced-in space he shared with Our Glass. "What's cooking today, hoof daddy?"

"Aqua twit. You here to rain on my picnic?" Davos whipped around, a wide smile painting his bovine lips, his large curved horns gleaming in the morning sunshine. His leather apron rustled as he crossed one brawny brown arm over the other.

A feminine giggle intruded on their typical routine insults. "I know you guys love poking fun at each other, but you really ought to be more creative. Does every joke have to revolve around you chuckle-heads being a minotaur and a water nymph?"

Davos sidestepped, and Lio finally spotted the source of the interruption. Not that he needed the visual to attach the voice to a name. He'd been cursed with the recollection of Ali's husky laugh since the first moment he'd heard it.

Ah, hell. Finding her bent over stoking the forge's flames wasn't helping matters. His pulse ratcheted up in record time as fire magic streamed from her hands—an impressive show that nearly everyone would be too awed to look away from. Not him. He couldn't tear his eyes off the tight-fitting trousers molded to her curves.

"I don't make the rules."

Davos's lighthearted reply snapped Lio out of his trance just before she finished conjuring. Ali straightened and turned to face him. *Thank the goddess for small favors.* If Ali had caught him staring at her rear, he was sure she'd never let him hear the end of it.

Lio jabbed his thumb at Davos. "Cleverness isn't in the cards for this one. If he traded in all his brute strength for brains, he'd still owe a massive debt."

Davos chortled out a huge, hearty laugh that echoed through the yard nearly as loud as his hammer striking iron. Lio glanced at Ali, a peculiar stab of disappointment hitting his chest when she didn't join the laughter.

"Me?" Davos wiped a tear from one of his deep-set, dark-brown eyes. "You have all the depth of a tide pool, my friend. Shallow"—he smirked—"and full of crabs."

Ali's melodic chuckles joined in with Davos's delighted guffaws.

Lio couldn't help it. He scowled.

"Think you're set for the day, Dav," Ali announced after their laughter naturally tapered off. "Let me know if you need a top-up."

"Wait, Ali. I have something for you." Davos's steps pounded the ground as he headed for his back door. "Be right back."

What luck! He'd come here, planning to ask Davos for advice on how to approach Ali about taking back the bag he'd unintentionally borrowed. He couldn't exactly storm into her shop and demand she take it. Not without coming off like an insensitive jerk. Which, for some odd reason, he didn't want her thinking in the slightest.

Now here she was, alone and looking for something to talk about. But why did he suddenly feel so tongue-tied?

Ali rocked back on her heels. "So... hope those crabs aren't being too pinchy."

"Huh?"

"You know, like Davos mentioned. In your tide pool." She ran her gaze down his frame, lingering on his trousers. "Sounds mighty uncomfortable."

His discomfort was becoming a theme where Ali was concerned. "Very funny."

She chuckled sweetly, pacing closer. "You ought to lighten up, Lio. I would think a guy who comes up with so many inventive insults would be more inclined to crack a smile every now and then."

She stopped within arm's reach, a coy tilt to her full lips. Her eyes twinkled with mirth.

Goddess. Being near her was like standing too close to the forge; warm at first, until the fear of being burned consumed him. *No one's getting burned. You can't let it happen, Stelios. Never again.* His fingers twitched at his side, and he held them steady with the sheer force of his will.

"Hey. You all right?" Ali's gaze captured him, still smoldering, but softer somehow, like dark coals cooling in a fire's wake.

It was enough to snap him out of the memory he should never have allowed himself to get lost in. "Fine," he spat out just as Davos stomped back into sight.

"Here it is," Davos announced, holding an oblong metal tube aloft. Another phallic cylinder, made of bronze instead of glass.

Lio nearly groaned as a stomach-churning sensation of déjà vu washed over him. It was like he was back in Ali's bedroom, wondering what depths of artistic depravity he'd just stumbled upon. "Not you too, Davos!"

"Huh?" Davos halted in place, the metal shining under the morning sun. "What are you blathering on about?" Then he turned, revealing the interior of the piece. The object was hollow, with a distinctive honeycomb pattern chiseled inside.

"Yeah, Chief. What *are* you thinking?" Ali shot him a smirk before taking the cylinder out of Davos's hands. "Thanks for the mold, Dav. This ought to do the trick."

"Mold?" Lio rubbed the back of his neck as his cheeks heated.

"A tool in the glassblowing trade. Some folk claim it's cheating, but my old mentor always used to say, 'All good artists cheat. Great artists cheat with style.'" Ali backed away, still smirking. "I'll leave you guys to your insults. I'm gonna go test this out."

Davos waited for the backdoor to Ali's shop to swing shut before pinning him with an amused stare. "Do I even want to ask?"

Lio sighed. "Not sure you do."

"Hm." Davos leaned back on a massive anvil perched in front of the forge. "You sure about that?"

"Fine. I need your advice."

"Go on..."

He nodded to Our Glass. "How'd you get so chummy with her?"

Davos laughed. "You're kidding, right?"

If only. He shook his head.

"She didn't give me much choice. I swear that woman could befriend a lich if she had a mind to." Davos turned his head, eyes narrowing. "Why do you ask?"

He probably should've spilled the whole sorry tale, but something held him back from sharing the full scope of his idiocy. "We may have gotten off on the wrong foot the night of the fire. Ran into her when I was clearing out her apartment." He crossed his arms. "Where did you end up? Thought you were heading down for your tools and coming right back?"

"You can blame your brigade for that. They refused to let me back upstairs." Davos's eyes narrowed. "So... how'd you tick her off?"

"Rather not say."

"That bad, huh?"

"Pretty much."

Davos chuckled. "Since she didn't immediately attempt to roast you to a crisp when she spotted you, I'm willing to bet it's not as bad as you think. Lucky for you, I know how you can get back in her good graces."

"Yeah?"

Davos pushed off the anvil and paced closer. "Easy. Take an interest in her art. There's nothing Ali likes more than talking my ear off about her craft. Well, except for Echo."

Glassblowing it is. He couldn't exactly bond with Ali over Echo when the last thing he wanted in his life was another kid to take care of.

"Here." Davos dug in his pocket. "Go over there and give her this. Tell her I sent you." He tossed another metal contraption into the air.

Lio caught it and lifted it to eye level, examining what appeared to be a smaller version of the piece Davos had given Ali earlier. "Another mold?"

"That one turned out a bit warped. I was planning to melt it and use it for something else, but maybe you'll both find it useful." Davos winked. "Go on. You got this."

Lio shook the mold at him. "I'm just keeping the peace."

"Sure you are. Later, you damp dandy."

"Buh-bye, beefcake." Lio dragged in a breath, then strode through Our Glass's backdoor. "Ali? Davos asked me to bring you this." The last word escaped in a hush as he gaped at Ali's workshop.

Heat pulsed in the air, escaping from the furnace mounted on the side wall. A smooth metal table stood prominently in the center of the clean, sparse workspace. Curious tools, like wooden paddles topped with different-sized half-formed bowls, were stacked neatly on a rack. Dim humming echoed in his ears, which appeared to be coming from a series of boxes tacked just below the ceiling.

Ali stood in front of the furnace, a long metal pole in her gloved hands. "You might want to put on a mask. The ventilation system removes the fumes, but some folks are more sensitive to them than others." Ali wasn't wearing a mask, though she had donned an oversized set of spectacles.

But he wasn't planning on getting close to that furnace. And whatever fumes were floating around were nothing compared to the air quality he was subjected to working for the brigade. "I've dealt with worse."

"Suppose you have." She shrugged before dragging the pole out with a glob of molten glass affixed to the end. "You can drop whatever Davos sent you with on the marver."

"Marver?"

"The table behind you."

He lifted a brow. "Why do you call it that?"

"I'll show you." She strolled up to it and began rolling the red-hot glass against the smooth surface. "Marvers are just one tool used to shape glass."

Lio watched, fascinated, as the mass of glowing goo smoothed out under her expert handling. It was clear she was in her element, a skilled crafter who moved with precision and confidence. He couldn't help but be impressed.

Ali met his gaze briefly before returning her attention to her task. "What did Davos send over?"

"You two help each other a lot, I take it." He held out the metal piece. "Do you light his forge for him every day?"

"Yep. And he makes me tools when I need them. It's a good trade." Her eyes twinkled and a crooked smirk crossed her lips. "He makes all the repairs to my glory hole, too."

His eyes bulged. "Your *what*?"

"Why do you look so scandalized, Lio? That's just what we glass-blowers call our reheating furnaces." She chuckled merrily. "Whatever were you thinking?"

Nope. He wasn't about to answer *that* question. Lio placed the mold on the edge of the table. "Davos made you another mold. He said it was slightly warped, but he hoped you'd find it useful."

She grinned. "I'm sure I will. Tell him thanks."

He drummed his fingers on his leg. "While I'm here—"

"You want to know when I'll pick up my bag. Right?" She turned on her heel, taking the pole with her and plunging the hot end back into the flames.

Was he that easy to read? "The thought had crossed my mind."

"I have a favor to ask…" She slowly spun the pole. "Think you can hang onto it for a few more days?"

"I'd rather not." He crossed his arms. "You aren't the only one with a nosy teen under your roof."

Ali winced. "I'm sorry, but I had to ask. I don't have anywhere to hide it right now. We're staying in a room the size of a shoebox." She sighed heavily. "But I'll figure something out. It's not your problem."

The hint of defeat in her tone sliced through his chest and made him blurt out something he'd likely live to regret. "Fine. I'll keep it for a few more days. A week, tops."

"Really?" The smile that flashed across her pretty face was so full of relief, it almost made the threat of his sister finding Ali's stash worth shouldering. "Thank you, Lio. You know, when we first met, I thought you had the heart of a frost giant and the humor of a tombstone, but I couldn't have been more wrong. You're a good friend."

Great. He should've probably been insulted by that comparison. Yet all that seemed to register in his head was Ali's last declaration. He was a good *friend*. If only things were different, he'd show her just how wrong she was. He didn't want to be her friend... not even close.

But for Tini's sake, he could play along. His sister wanted a connection to their heritage. Maybe befriending the only other nymph family in the village would be enough to slake that desire.

Ali glanced back at him. "You don't have to stick around. I'll make sure to pick up the bag soon. Promise."

"What if I want to see how the sausage is cooked?" He buried a wince at his dumb choice of words. With her quick wit, no doubt she'd find a way to make him regret it.

Ali's stare turned incredulous. "You really want to watch me work?"

"Yep." Taking an interest might be the quickest way to win Ali over, but even if he hadn't been given that advice, he'd still have found the process fascinating. "I've always wondered how glassblowing works."

"Aren't you just full of surprises?" Ali grinned. "My assistant has the day off. You wanna be my stand-in?"

She wanted him to hang around a fire he wasn't expected to put out? The thought should've made him uncomfortable, but oddly, it didn't. He shrugged. "Okay."

Her grin turned positively luminous. "Great. Let's get cooking." She chuckled and shot him a wink. "You'll never look at a breakfast platter the same way again."

His brow furrowed. "Huh?"

"Your sausage, of course. I'll show you how it's made, but fair warning: last time someone fainted and another ran off with the butcher. It was quite the day."

The corner of Lio's lips quirked up. "I'll take my chances."

Lies of Omission

Ali

Her heart pounded, thumping in her chest even louder than her fist on the schoolroom door.

"Come in," a pleasant voice called from within.

While the quaint red brick school was likely welcoming to most, Ali's childhood learning environment had been very different from this. The walls festooned with children's artwork, neatly lined-up desks, and the faint aroma of chalk never ceased to make her feel out of place. Especially not after she'd been called in out of the blue by Echo's instructor regarding a matter most urgent.

Ms. Crowley, a perpetually perky middle-aged elf with pale skin, bright blue eyes, and cornflower yellow hair she'd piled atop her head in a tight chignon, rose from her desk as Ali shuffled inside. "Please have a seat. Thank you for making the time to drop by."

"Of course. I always have time for Echo." Ali sank into a chair, wishing she'd changed out of her work-rumpled shirt and trousers and slipped into one of the few dresses she rarely donned. Perhaps then she wouldn't have felt so shabby next to Ms. Crowley's pleated skirt and flowy white blouse.

Ms. Crowley retook her seat. "I'm afraid there's been another incident in class. It happened during lunch between Echo and a group of boys. I stepped in when it became apparent that the conversation was becoming too heated for them to resolve among themselves."

Her stomach dropped. "Do you have any idea why this happened?"

She shook her head sadly. "I'm afraid not. The boys blamed Echo, though they were tight-lipped about what exactly started the argument. They claimed she began insulting them—repeatedly and quite... colorfully."

Oh no. That doesn't sound good at all. She had a sinking feeling that was Ms. Crowley's roundabout way of telling her that her daughter swore worse than a pirate on the high seas. "I'm so sorry." She gulped. "May I ask... What did Echo say happened?"

"That's the thing." Ms. Crowley steepled her hands on her desk. "She refused to say anything at all."

Ali groaned internally. This wasn't the first time Echo had been in trouble at school. Far from it. Refusing to come clean about what happened—or apologize for that matter—was something she continued to struggle with. "I'll speak with her about her behavior as soon as I see her."

"I appreciate that. As I'm sure you're aware, disruptions like this are not tolerated here. And with Echo's history... I'm afraid if she has another outburst this year, we may be forced to expel her." Ms.

Crowley leaned back in her chair. "Of course, if she were to apologize, we might be more inclined to leniency."

"I understand." Ali's stomach dropped. The last thing she needed was Echo getting kicked out of Everpass's only school. There was no way she could afford a private tutor. And she refused to deny Echo the education she deserved.

Ms. Crowley leaned forward, her kind expression at odds with the harsh words she'd just uttered. "Did you reach out to the specialist I recommended after Echo's last incident?"

That incident had been a doozy. Echo and a girl a few years her senior had burst into a full-blown brawl just before winter break. She still hadn't explained what started that fight—even after months of gentle coaxing, demands, and outright bribery.

"Yes, I've arranged for him to meet with Echo once a month." Much to her purse's despair. The children's wellness guru Ms. Crowley recommended was one of the best in the realm—with a fee to match.

"Perhaps you should make it bi-monthly. Or weekly even," Ms. Crowley suggested. "Investing in your children's health is always coin well spent."

Echo *had* been behaving better since she started seeing the specialist. Until today. But at least this incident hadn't resulted in violence. Or worse... flames. "You're probably right. I'll see if he can meet with her more often."

"I'm happy to hear that." Ms. Crowley rose again, and Ali followed suit. "I truly hope it helps. Echo has a bright future ahead of her, so long as she discovers a way to temper her emotions."

"Thank you, Ms. Crowley. And I'm sorry again about Echo's behavior."

After a quick goodbye, she emerged into a sunny afternoon. But the chirping birds and delightful spring breeze couldn't fully lift her spirits. Not when her daughter was one step away from becoming a delinquent.

Honestly, the swearing wasn't the worst of it. After all, it was far better than throwing fists. That wasn't what made her stomach clench and a cold sweat break out on her skin. It was Echo's lies—or more accurately, her lies of omission.

Why was she keeping everything bottled up inside? Refusing to explain what happened to Ms. Crowley was bad enough, but she suspected Echo would keep her lips sealed when she spoke to her, just like she had after that brawl months ago.

Didn't her own daughter trust her enough to let her in?

"Hi, honey. I'm home!" Ali called out as she entered Stellar Spirits with Echo in tow. Echo darted behind the bar with a happy squeal and lifted Roo out of her nest.

Kieran chuckled from his spot behind the bar. "Fantastic. Mal was starting to get tired of my flirting. I'm tagging you in."

"You say that like it's a chore." She shot Maalik a steamy stare. "Hey there, hot stuff."

Maalik blinked slowly, clearly unimpressed, before taking a swig of his ale. "You're here earlier than usual."

In the week since the fire, they'd developed a routine. Echo headed to Mrs. Pilbeck's after school until she closed up the shop. Then Ali made the trek to collect her, just after dusk. They'd arrive at Stellar Spirits together and scarf down one of Nora's delicious meals before heading upstairs to bed. But after the meeting at school, she picked up Echo early rather than head back to work. They had a lot to talk about before she could handle chatting pleasantly with customers again.

"Closed up early today." She glanced around the tavern as she plopped onto her favorite stool. She really ought to drag Echo up and start the inquisition, but she couldn't bear to tear her away from Roo while she was clearly enjoying herself. "Where's Nora?"

Footsteps clattered on the stairs leading down from the loft, and Nora emerged with linen stacked in her hands. "Oh, hey, Ali. I was just upstairs straightening up and changing the sheets."

Ali's chest tightened. "You didn't have to go to any trouble on our account. I would've—"

"Don't be silly." Nora dumped the pile of cloth into a basket behind the bar. "This is good practice for me. If we're going to rent that room out to travelers after you and Echo move back home, then I'll be doing this kind of thing all the time."

"Well... thanks. The kitchen repairs are underway. The builder told me he'd have everything fixed by this time next week." Ali dragged a hand through her hair. "Then you can start giving old man Lark another reason to grind his teeth."

"Good. I hope he grinds them so loud I can hear it from here." Nora giggled. "Did I tell you he tried to talk the town council into shutting us down last month?"

"No... Really? On what grounds?" Ali asked.

Kieran chimed in, "He claimed the upstairs was a fire hazard. But luckily, we'd already built the new emergency exit stairs." He leaned closer, lowering his voice, though he probably didn't need to bother. All the other patrons were seated at tables far out of earshot and engrossed in their own conversations. "What's worse, the weasel tried to say Nora wasn't fit to serve food or drinks on account of her newfound heritage."

Maalik snorted. "Idiotic fool."

Nora grabbed a rag and started polishing the bar. "We're lucky the council isn't as superstitious as he is. And it's a good thing I didn't find out I was a witch while I was still working there. I bet he would've fired me on the spot."

Mention of the council had Ali's stomach churning for an altogether different reason. It was true, they were plenty accommodating to business owners of all races—it was hard not to be in a town with such varied species living in it—but a few of their rules weren't nearly as lenient as larger cities, like Fairvale. Rules that might lead to her ruin if someone like Phineus Lark discovered exactly what she'd been crafting in her workshop.

Goddess, she'd been so lucky that Lio hadn't turned her in. But Nora's tale reminded her she wasn't in the clear just yet.

Lio won't rat me out. He would've done it by now if he'd planned to... right? She buried the thought before anxiety overwhelmed her. "Echo, I need to talk to you upstairs."

She braced herself for the inevitable "But Mooom..." that would surely follow. Only it never appeared. Echo sighed heavily, returned Roo to her bed, and marched forward with heavy steps, her head hanging and eyes downcast.

Nora side-eyed Ali and whispered, "What's that all about?" They both turned to watch Echo as she made her way toward the loft stairs.

Ali hopped off her stool. "Not sure. But I'm going to find out."

"I'll save you both a dinner plate." Nora called out loudly, "Thanks for playing with Roo, Echo."

Echo nodded curtly before disappearing into the stairwell.

"Good luck." Maalik tipped his mug in her direction.

"Thanks. I'm gonna need it." Ali followed her daughter up the stairs, every creak of the wood under her soles ratcheting her unease higher.

Echo plopped onto the bed and dragged a pillow into her lap, clenching the fabric tightly. "I guess you heard about what happened at school."

The mattress groaned as Ali sank beside her. "Ms. Crowley called me in. She said you got into an argument with some boys."

"Yeah." Echo's face fell, her voice colored with anguish.

"What happened? You can tell me. I promise I won't be mad." Ali softened her voice, praying that the reassurance would be what Echo needed to feel safe enough to share.

Clearly, something had set her off. Echo wouldn't just curse at those boys for no reason... would she?

Echo bit her lip. "I-I..." She shook her head.

"Honey, you can't keep bottling everything up inside. You'll feel better if you get it off your chest."

She shook her head again, so hard that her pigtails whacked her cheeks. "No, I won't."

Time to try a different tactic. "What about doing what's right? I know you, Echo. You're a good kid. Caring. Honest. Why wouldn't you tell Ms. Crowley the truth about what started the argument?" Ali's voice cracked. "Why won't you tell me, baby?"

Echo sniffled. "Because it'll make you sad, Mama."

Mama... Echo hadn't called her that for years. "I can handle it. Promise. Even if it makes me sad." She grabbed Echo's hand. "At least we'll be sad together."

Echo drew shaky breath after shaky breath. But just as Ali began to despair that she'd burst into tears—or worse, pull herself together and don a stoic mask of indifference—Echo lifted her gaze from her lap and met Ali's eyes.

"They were making fun of me. They're always making fun of me, Mama. Sometimes they'll tease me about being a nymph." She shrugged. "That's not so bad. Everyone teases everybody about what they are. But today…"

Ali squeezed her hand. "Today?"

"They said I don't have a dad because male nymphs are dirty cheaters. That… that I probably have a dozen brothers and sisters who can't stand to be around me—just like him."

"Oh, baby, that's not true." Ali's heart twisted. What's worse—there was an inkling of truth in that bald claim. Just not in Echo's case. She'd saved her daughter from that fate, only to rope her into an equally disappointing situation. "Your father wasn't even a nymph. You're half-human, remember?"

Echo's lip quivered. "I remember. But… why won't you tell me anything else about him? Why don't we ever visit our family? Do I even have a grandma and grandpa?"

Ali sighed deeply. "There's a reason that I left and never went back. A good reason, I promise. But… it's complicated. And very sad." She rubbed Echo's back. "I don't want to make you sad either, honey."

Echo stared up at her with glossy eyes. "Then we'll be sad together. Like you said."

Goddess… Why did I have to say that? Sure, she wanted to tell her daughter the truth. And she would…eventually. But at ten years old? She refused to lay the burden of her past at her daughter's feet. "I'll tell you when you're older, baby. I promise."

Echo's expression hardened, her jaw tightening, eyes dimming. "Okay." She pulled her hand out of Ali's grasp. "I'm starving. I'm going back down to get something to eat."

Ali watched her go, her stomach sinking. *Please tell me I didn't just make a terrible mistake.*

Ill Intentions

Lio

"Come on, Lio. I don't want to miss the first dance!" Tini grabbed his hand, dragging him through the crowded village streets.

Orbs of light magic twinkled in the night sky, giving Everpass's annual spring festival a charming ambiance. Countless delicious aromas drifted past his nose. Vendors lorded over pop-up booths, hawking homemade wares. Children chased each other through the crowds, giggling—hopped up on sugar from one of the many sweets stands, no doubt.

He hadn't been sure what to expect—it was the first festival they'd attended since moving to the small-town last fall—but he'd been pleased to discover the event wasn't at all like the gigantic balls rife with debauchery held in the capital.

At least, not yet. He'd insisted on accompanying Tini to the evening dance, intending to guarantee it stayed debauchery-free. Always best to be cautious when teens were given free rein to get up close and personal.

The last thing he wanted was some horny bloke getting the wrong idea about his baby sister. Yeah, Tini was almost eighteen. He would have to get used to the idea of her courting. If not now, then soon. But at least he could stick around and make sure she didn't get dragged off to some shadowed alcove by an idiot with ill intentions.

Speaking of ill intentions... He nearly choked on his own tongue as he spotted a vision in silver silk standing outside the dance hall.

Hell... he was in trouble. It was hard enough keeping his attraction hidden when she was just dressed in her usual work shirt and trousers, but in a dress that molded to her curves and strappy heels, Ali was utterly stunning.

To make matters worse, the short black locks he was so used to seeing straight and sleek were curled tonight, leaving her elegant neck on display and making him long for things he shouldn't. Like asking her to dance so he could dip his nose into that curve to discover if she smelled half as wonderful as she looked...

Look away, Stelios. You're staring. Yet even after chiding himself, he couldn't tear his eyes off her.

"Oh wow. Ali's dress is gorgeous," Tini exclaimed.

They were too far from the entrance for Ali to catch his sister's statement. A fact that he was exceedingly grateful for when a tall, auburn-haired orc wrapped his arm around Ali's shoulders and led her inside.

A spike of ice stabbed him in the gut, and he had a sudden, irrational urge to rip a certain burly green arm out of its socket.

"That's funny. I didn't know Seth and Ali were courting." Tini tilted her head.

"Why would that be funny?" he asked gruffly.

Tini shrugged, sending the chestnut curls she'd fashioned into a fancy updo bouncing. "I thought she was already courting someone else."

He should've left it at that. No reason to clue his sister into how intensely curious he was to know who that person was. "And who's that?"

She leaned closer. "Word around town is that she was strolling with Maalik a few nights back. Apparently, she loudly proclaimed she was his girl." She shrugged again. "Could be a rumor, I suppose."

So, Ali dates trolls and orcs. Fantastic. "You really shouldn't treat everything you hear working at that tavern like gospel."

His sister's squeal stole his attention as they strolled through the entrance. "They're here!" She waved at a trio of young ladies decked out in colorful frocks, her face lit with delight. "Mind if I go hang out with my friends?"

"Go on." He shooed her away. "I'll be around if you need me."

Tini was already sprinting across the dance floor before he'd finished speaking, leaving him alone, feeling increasingly out of place.

The dance was being held in the village council house, but it looked far different tonight than when he delivered the brigade's quarterly reports. The benches had been pushed aside, the wooden floor lacquered to a near mirror shine. Planters full of spring blooms perched on every table. Daisy chains and wreaths festooned the walls, nearly rivaling the ladies in their colorful dresses.

Lio shuffled toward the closest bench, keeping his eyes on the floor, hoping to avoid drawing said ladies' attention. He knew how these things worked. If he accepted one invitation to dance, he wouldn't rest all night. And that was the last thing he needed when he'd only come to keep an eye on Tini.

So he ignored the music ringing out from the band—even though the lively tune made him feel like tapping his toes—and plopped down in a spot with a clear view of his sister.

All was well for now. Which was unfortunate, in a way, since that was likely why his attention kept drifting away from Tini giggling with her friends and returning to the temptation he just couldn't ignore.

It was no surprise Ali wasn't content to hang along the dance floor's edges and chat. He found her in the thick of the revelry, her skirt whipping around her legs as Seth swung her to the lively melody.

Goddess... why did she have to be so distracting? His hands curled into fists. And why did she have to be with *him*?

Suddenly, the merry tune shifted, slowing to a soft waltz.

He stole glimpses through the crowd, gritting his teeth as Ali placed a palm on Seth's chest, the other swallowed up in his massive green grip. They swayed slowly while murmuring to each other. Far too quietly for him to listen in, especially with the music and the crowd. But it didn't stop him from wishing he could hear what they were saying. Was it just banal chitchat, or something more? Something deeper, perhaps... even personal?

The pair shifted, turning in time with the beat. Ali glanced up, her dark gaze burning into his as it caught—and held.

His pulse thundered, the deafening rhythm defeating the band for dominance, at least in his own head. Thank the goddess no one else could hear it. They didn't need to know how one look from that woman turned his blood molten and made his heart ache.

They shifted again, breaking the connection. Lio pulled a deep breath into his lungs and stood. *Stop. Just... shut it down. She's not right for you, and you know it.* He needed to stop staring before the whole town pegged him for a creep.

After a quick glance to make sure Tini was still chatting happily, Lio strode outside. Some fresh air would do the trick. He hoped...

Moonlight shone down on the square. Dozens of townsfolk still lingered, though the crowd had thinned, and many of the vendors were breaking down their stands. Though not all. The drink stand Nora manned still had a large line. Her hands were a blur, mixing and shaking while she kept an amiable smile on her face.

Huh... That's interesting. A familiar figure wove through the crowd, balancing a tray half-full of drinks. Echo stopped beside a family of trolls, waited for the father to drop a few coins on the tray, then deftly handed out two cups to the children.

Guess that explained what Ali had done with her daughter while she danced the night away. Echo was a bit young to be a serving girl. She'd never be permitted to maintain a full-time position, but the council turned a blind eye to children helping during festival days.

But just because it was legal didn't mean he agreed with it. He couldn't stop picturing Tini at the same age, working in the evening hours while the village crawled with tipsy strangers. His parents would have loathed the mere thought.

He ought to head back in. Spotting Echo—working in a crowd where anything could happen—had been the sobering reminder he needed. It wasn't his responsibility to keep her safe. His sister was the first and last child he intended to raise.

And yet, an odd twinge of premonition sent tingles coursing down his spine and rooted his boots to the cobblestones. Mere moments later, a trio of young men descended on Echo's position, approaching from her back as she finished handing a cup to an elderly couple.

Goddess, help me. I knew it.

Echo flipped to face the men, hiding her expression from his view. But Lio could see the men's faces clearly. They took turns shooting smirks at each other—and leering at Echo.

Leave it alone, Stelios. She's not your responsibility. Before he realized what was happening, he'd shoved through the crowd. Anger pulsed in his chest as he closed in enough to eavesdrop.

"What do ya' mean, you don't wanna?" The tallest of the trio bellowed, leaning so close to Echo she was forced to back up a pace. "I'll have you know that's a pretty offer you just turned down."

"Pretty offer for a pretty lady," drawled the pockmarked bloke standing beside him. It might've been enough to make a young girl blush, if not for his slurred speech and lustful grin.

Lio barreled between them, sliding to a stop facing the trio of perverts. "Are you as blind as you are drunk? She's not a lady. You're speaking to a child. Leave her alone. Now."

"You her Da or something?" the third fellow asked, a hint of bravery in his tone—until he dragged his gaze off Echo and looked Lio's way. Then he blanched, backing away. "We didn't mean anything by it. I swear."

The rest of the cowards fled on his heels, seeming eager to escape Lio's wrath.

Behind him, Echo clicked her tongue. "You just lost me a big tip."

He whipped around, frowning as he spotted the amused half-smile painting her face. She looked so much like her mother—especially while wearing that inappropriate expression. Didn't she realize men like that were dangerous?

"You need to be more careful, especially as a nymph."

Echo's head cocked sideways. "What does me being a nymph have to do with those creeps?"

"You look older than you should. Mature on the outside, when you're still a kid." Most nymphs looked a few years older than a human would during their teenage years. With Echo's height, she could easily pass for fourteen or fifteen, especially to a fool who'd had more than his share of celebratory wine. "Didn't your mother ever warn you to be wary around humans who don't bother to ask your age?"

"That's funny. Cause I once heard Mom say I ought to stay away from you. Pretty sure she said an imp would be better company." She giggled.

Funny. He recalled the conversation all too well. Ali threw that insult at him the first day they met, after he caught Echo spying on him when he first moved to Everpass.

But that didn't change the facts. Protecting their youth was the main reason nymphs isolated themselves from other races, sticking with their own.

The problem was one he knew well. He'd chased well-intentioned—and even some ill-intentioned—young men away from his sister over the years. Now that Tini's outer appearance had finally caught up with her real age, he was supposed to be off the hook. Yet here he was, playing guard dog for another girl when he'd sworn to himself he was through.

He gritted his teeth and drew a calming breath through his nose. "Just go home, Echo."

"Who made you the boss of me?" Echo rolled her eyes. "Now, if you aren't here to buy a cup of cider, I have tips to earn."

Yep. Frustrating as hell. Just like her mother. "If you won't leave, then at least stay out of trouble," he called to her retreating back.

With a sigh, he wove through the crowd again and headed inside. The dance was in full swing. He forced himself to ignore the flash of silver silk he spotted in the corner of his eye, searching for Tini. But she wasn't where he'd left her.

His pulse sped. If some idiot had dragged her off while he was outside butting into business he didn't belong in...

A huge whoosh of relief wheezed out of his lungs.

Tini twirled on the dance floor, her eyes lit with joy, a laugh on her lips. And thank the goddess, her dance partner wasn't some horny bloke, but one of the young ladies Tini had been so excited to chat with—her best friend, Sera.

He sank back in his chair, just as Sera dipped Tini and leaned down with her, their faces drawing so close they had to be sharing the same breath. They stared into each other's eyes, holding the pose longer than he'd expected. Much longer than two friends would.

Lio rubbed his temples as awareness stole over him. He'd been so vigilant in chasing off all his sister's would-be suitors over the years. How could he have been so blind?

Guess he never had to worry about horny *blokes* after all...

Plain and Simple

Ali

She twirled, near breathless and half-exhausted from dancing her fourth country jig in a row. "How are you not tired yet?" Ali asked Seth as she wiped the sweat gathering on her brow.

He chuckled. "I got plenty of practice dancing the night away when I lived in the capital. Need a break?"

She nodded gratefully. "And a drink."

"Come on, then." His massive green hand nearly swallowed hers whole as Seth led her across the packed dance floor.

Sure, her shoes pinched her feet, and she couldn't quite escape the feeling of eyes on her back, but she was happy she'd let Nora talk her into coming. Getting lost in the rhythm of music for a little while had been exactly what she needed.

Seth had been the perfect gentleman. His hands never strayed where they shouldn't, and he'd showered her with compliments about her dress and dance skills. But since they'd scarcely paused dancing since they'd arrived, she couldn't help feeling like they'd barely scratched the surface of getting to know one another.

She owed it to Nora to give her brother a chance. Perhaps now that they'd found seats on the dance floor's perimeter, she could finally remedy that.

Seth left her alone and swiftly returned with drinks in hand-labeled wooden mugs. He lifted the first close to his face and squinted. "Would you like lemonade?" He repeated the lifting and squinting with the second. "Or fruit punch?"

"Lemonade sounds lovely." She accepted the mug and took a sip. The tart liquid was far from the best she'd tasted—that honor would always be reserved for Nora's—but it wasn't terrible. "Do you mind if I ask a personal question?"

She braced herself, unsure what to expect. If her past with men had taught her anything, it was best to be cautious when broaching delicate topics.

She released a tiny sigh when Seth merely smiled nonchalantly and said, "Sure. I'm an open book."

"It's about books, actually. You said you weren't much of a reader... Do you think that might have something to do with the way you squint when you read?"

"Dunno. I've never given it much thought."

"Have you ever tried wearing a pair of spectacles?" She braced herself again. Her ex had been notorious for blowing up at her whenever she suggested a way for him to better himself. As if he couldn't stand the mere mention that he might be less than perfect.

Seth's brow pinched. "No. I haven't. Do you think that's my problem?"

She nodded carefully. "Could be. If you're open to it, stop by my shop one day. I'll let you try some out. See if they help." The old owner of Our Glass had been quite skilled at crafting spectacle glass. A skill she'd made certain to carry on.

"Didn't realize you were so observant."

Her stomach knotted. Was that a compliment or a dig? She shrugged. "Attention to detail is a necessity in my trade."

"Thanks for the offer. Don't be surprised when I take you up on it." He winked. "Would be nice to give the old peepers a break from everyone's fuzzy scrawl."

"Of course." That comment made her certain her guess was correct. Especially after she peeked at the perfectly straight handwriting on her mug. "You really ought to treat your peepers well in your old age."

Seth let out an affronted gasp. "Old age? Exactly how old do you think I am?"

But the smile on his face finally set Ali at ease. Seth was nothing like her ex. He'd *thanked* her for her suggestion, and he clearly wasn't opposed to a little teasing. She needed to stop comparing every man in her life to the no-good scoundrel whom she'd had the misfortune of meeting first.

She leaned in with a smirk. "Old enough that your body is beginning to betray you."

He laughed merrily. "I promise you there's nothing wrong with this body." Then he lifted an arm, flexing his muscles and wiggling his brows.

She joined in his laughter until Seth's gaze lifted from his arm and caught on someone in the crowd. She followed his line of sight and spotted Paige whirling past in a bright purple dress, her arms wrapped around a handsome fellow she didn't recognize. *Not so blind after all, I see.*

It wasn't the first time she'd noticed Seth's gaze lingering on the pretty country witch. And she suspected it wouldn't be the last.

"See something you like?" she asked bluntly.

Seth dropped his arm. "No. The opposite, actually."

Her eyes narrowed. "You don't mean Paige, do you? Because if the number of times I've caught you sneaking a glance at her are any sign—"

"You've got the wrong idea." He thumped his empty mug against his chest. "I don't court witches. Learned that lesson long ago."

Interesting... "Well, I would never court a nymph, so I understand." It was an odd thing to have in common with a date. Were they really bonding over their mutual dislike of entire groups of people?

"Sounds like there's a story there."

She drew in a breath and released it slowly. "You'd be correct on that count. But seeing how we're trying to have a pleasant evening, I'd rather not get into it."

He nodded. "Fair enough."

"How about you? Are you ever going to spill what happened that made you loathe witches so much?" she asked. Nora had been at a loss to explain Seth's peculiar aversion. Maybe she could finally wiggle the truth out of him.

"I'm going to have to decline for the same reason."

"Fair enough," she echoed. "Will you at least share what made you clam up just now? If it wasn't Paige, then..." She lifted her brows imploringly.

Seth stood. "I'll do better than that." He held out a hand. "If you care to join me."

"Of course." Ali allowed him to help her out of her seat. Then they strolled around the edge of the dance floor until they ran right into Paige and her date.

"Ali!" Paige's face lit up, dimming a touch as her gaze trailed to Seth. But she pulled herself together swiftly and motioned to the man at her side. "I've been hoping I'd run into you. I want to introduce you to someone. This is Emil."

She smiled warmly and shook his proffered hand. "Nice to meet you." The smile fell off her face when she noticed something strange. Emil—who was even more handsome up close, with hazel eyes and curly brown hair framing his deeply tanned, chiseled face—had barely looked at her. He was too busy staring at Seth like he'd seen a ghost.

As Ali dropped Emil's hand, Paige waved at Seth with an obligatory smile plastered on her face. "And this is—"

Emil spoke before she could finish. "Seth. Nice to see you. It's been ages, hasn't it?" He stuck out a hand, only to stuff it in his pocket after Seth blatantly ignored the gesture.

Paige's gaze darted between the pair, her mouth falling open.

For half a heartbeat, Ali feared they were about to witness a brawl. But then Seth schooled his expression, adopting a casual air that seemed forced.

"Yeah, it has been ages." Seth smirked. "Guess I shouldn't be surprised you graduated from befriending witches to courting them."

Emil blanched. Then he turned to Paige and cleared his throat. "Excuse me. I-I need to…" He gulped. "Bathroom."

Ali's stomach dropped as Emil hightailed it across the room like his ass was on fire.

Paige's lower lip wobbled as she watched him disappear. Then she spun on her heel and faced Seth, her voice venomous. "What gave you the right to say that?"

Seth glared down at her. "How was I supposed to know you didn't tell him?"

"Ugh!" Paige jabbed a finger into Seth's chest. "I hate you, Seth Rowen. Stay the hell out of my life!"

Ali punched Seth's shoulder after Paige marched away. "Hey, you didn't have to out her like that."

Seth didn't even give her the courtesy of flinching, he was so wrapped up in watching Paige's skirt swish as she retreated. When Paige dipped out of sight, he finally met Ali's eyes. "Maybe she shouldn't be lying to the men she courts. Besides, I did her a favor, chasing off that prick." His lips curled into a sneer. "Emil is bad news. Trust me."

Ali opened her mouth, but before she could force out another question, Seth grabbed her hand and tugged her into a spin.

"Come on, Ali. Let's dance."

With a sigh, she gave in, letting the music carry her away and lift her spirits. She'd let the topic drop for now, but eventually, she would find out exactly what that interaction had been all about.

Soon she was breathless again and having a wonderful time. Maybe this thing between her and Seth *could* turn into something. If they had this much fun together, that was a good sign, right?

But suddenly, the notion was completely wiped from her mind. Because at that moment she spotted a different man across the dance floor. One that made her heart stutter and left no question that the way she felt toward the right man would *not* feel the way she felt when she was with Seth.

Sure, Lio wasn't the right man—at all. But when she spotted him dancing with his sister, devotion and love lighting his gaze, she almost wished that he was.

She'd felt nothing remotely as intense toward Seth. Only friendship, plain and simple. The spark just wasn't there. And she had to stop kidding herself that it ever would be.

Ali slipped out of the loft bedroom, easing the door closed with a barely discernible click. She'd left Echo sleeping in bed, a rarity that hardly ever happened—her daughter was notorious for being an early riser—but she clearly needed the rest after hours on her feet helping Nora yesterday evening.

Her brows lifted in surprise when she descended into the tavern and found Nora there, wide awake and humming behind the bar, a huge spread of yellow weeds covering it.

"Am I still dreaming? What in the realm are you doing?" she asked.

Nora grinned. "Good morning. Decided to get an early start today. I've been dying to make a batch of dandelion wine."

That was why Stellar Spirits was such a smashing success. Nora clearly loved her job. Who else would wake up at the crack of dawn to harvest something nearly everyone else considered a nuisance, so they could turn it into something extraordinary?

"Dandelion wine. Huh. I didn't know that was a thing."

"I tracked down a recipe last winter, and I've been itching to test it out." Nora pinched her lips together. "Didn't realize it would be quite so labor intensive. But when the key ingredient is free, who am I to complain?"

Ali plunked onto a stool. "Can I help?"

"Sure." Nora held the flower in her hand aloft. "I have to pull all the petals off. Apparently, the stems will turn the wine bitter."

Ali watched as Nora plucked the petals and deposited them into a large glass jar. Seemed simple enough. "Got it." Then she lifted a flower and joined in.

"So..." Nora shot her a grin. "How was the dance?"

She should've guessed Nora wouldn't be able to resist asking for long. "It was... nice."

Nora frowned. "Just nice?"

"Yeah." She sighed heavily. "I know you were hoping for more. And your brother was the perfect gentleman... well, for the most part."

Nora's eyes narrowed. "What did he do? I swear I'll wring his big neck if he—"

"Relax, Nor. Honestly, it wasn't that big of a deal for me. Paige, on the other hand..."

"What happened with Paige?"

She plucked the next petal a little too forcefully, tearing it in two. "Seems Seth and Paige's new flame have a history together, and I don't think it's pleasant. When Paige introduced us to Emil, Seth chased him off. Right after he mentioned Paige was a witch."

Nora gasped. "Oh, that's awful! And she was so worried about telling him."

"Seth said Emil was bad news. I'm not sure why, though. He distracted me with dancing before I could ask."

Nora shook her head. "I'm not surprised. My brother can be frustratingly secretive when he wants to be." Her eyes widened, like she had just realized she'd said too much. "But we all have our failings, don't we?"

"Nor, you can stop trying to butter him up on my account. I'm sorry to say, but Seth and I are going to stay just friends."

"Really?" Nora pouted. "Drat. I honestly thought you two would make a good match."

"It's not that I don't like him. I just don't like him like *that*." She shrugged. "The spark wasn't there."

"Hmm. Too bad."

"Yep. It's a shame. And don't worry, I already had a chat with him about my feelings when he walked me home." She'd barely dredged up the courage, but thankfully, Seth had taken the news much better than she'd expected. "He even agreed we were better suited as friends."

"I hope he wasn't too disappointed..."

"Trust me, Nora. Seth was *not* that into me." If he had been, he wouldn't have spent half the night sneaking glances at someone else.

The front door swung on its hinges, and in walked Tini, with a soft smile on her lips. "Good morning. I'm here for my shift, and I brought you a present."

Ali's pulse sped as Lio strolled in, carrying an enormous basket overflowing with dandelions.

Nora clapped her hands. "Tini, you are a gem! Thank you so much."

Tini's cheeks flushed a pretty pink. "I remembered you were planning to make wine today, so I enlisted Lio to help me pick every dandelion we saw on our way here from our place."

Nora beamed at Lio. "Have I told you lately how amazing your sister is? Best barmaid ever. And I'm not just talking about the flowers. All the customers love her—especially the ones who wander in looking for a kind ear. She has an uncanny knack for easing their worries."

"Glad to hear it." Lio dropped the basket on the bar, the smile one would expect to see after hearing their sister was doing a bang-up job at their chosen career nowhere to be seen.

Nora grabbed the basket and turned to Tini. "Come with me. I'll show you how to clean them."

Ali crossed her arms as the pair headed into the kitchenette. "Looks like someone woke up on the wrong side of the bed."

Lio lowered his voice, his deep baritone whisper tickling Ali's ears and making her breath catch. "Thanks to you. There's been a lump under my mattress for the better part of a week."

She winced. "Sorry about that. I've just been so busy. But I promise I'll find the time to—" The words snagged in her throat as Nora slid back behind the bar. She swallowed. "Um. I'll close up early tomorrow night so that we can meet to go over your report on the fire investigation."

Nora grabbed a dandelion off the bar. "Why don't you go tonight after work? Tini will be here holding down the fort, and Kieran has the day off. I bet he wouldn't mind taking a stroll with me to collect Echo from Mrs. Pilbeck's."

Ali waved a hand. "Oh, I don't want to trouble you guys."

"Don't be silly. Kieran's always nagging me to go for a stroll. This way he gets the fresh air he's been begging for, and it'll save you from having to close up early tomorrow."

Something told her that Kieran wasn't really *that* into fresh air. He was probably more interested in peeling Nora away from the tavern for a bit of alone time. And Nora just invited her daughter along to be the third wheel. "Are you sure, Nor?"

"Definitely. This is important stuff. You need all the information about the fire so your builder knows exactly what to fix." Nora narrowed her eyes at Lio. "Be sure to tell her every detail. I refuse to let my two favorite girls move out until their place is safe."

Her heart quivered with guilt. She'd never intended to keep Nora in the dark for so long. It felt increasingly awful every time she stacked another lie on the heaping pile of falsehoods she'd woven.

But even she had to admit the timing was perfect. What better time to sneak out the bag than when both Echo and Tini would be occupied elsewhere?

Lio nodded curtly. Then he turned to her, lifting a brow. "See you tonight?"

"Sure."

The door creaked as it swung closed behind him. Ali watched it swinging, her mind swimming with worries. She'd just agreed to meet with Lio. Tonight. In his house. Alone. What could possibly go wrong? *I don't know... How about anything?*

Nora's chuckle drew her from her thoughts. Ali spun on her stool, frowning. "What?"

"Oh... nothing. Let's just say I have a sneaking suspicion I discovered where that spark you were missing last night is. And whoo, baby. Boy, is it smoldering." She grabbed the neck of her frock, using it to puff air into her face.

Ali pursed her lips. "Smoldering my as—" the loft door slammed open, "—tonishing! That's simply astonishing, Nor." Ali blew out a shaky breath before plastering a motherly smile on her face. "Good morning, Echo."

"What's astonishing? Tell me, tell me!"

She grinned as Echo bounced over, thanking the goddess for her quick reflexes. "This dandelion wine recipe Nora's making. I had no idea you could make wine out of dandelions, did you?"

Echo's eyes widened. "Me either. Cool!"

Nora chuckled and ruffled the top of Echo's head. "That's not all. You can turn dandelions into tea, too. You want to help me make a batch?"

"Okay!"

Ali released a sigh as Echo darted behind the bar, an eager grin on her face.

Maybe tonight wouldn't be so bad. If she could handle a precocious kid with ears like a hawk, surely she could handle one brief encounter with a sexy as sin nymph, right?

Contagious

Lio

Lio paced in his living room, at a loss for why he was so nervous. *Stop kidding yourself, Stelios. You know exactly why.*

He'd cleaned the place until it was spotless, which had taken little effort. Tini teased him relentlessly for being a neat freak, but he couldn't help it. Having everything in order just felt right.

So now he had nothing to do but wait. He took deep breaths as his socks sank into the carpet. It was a wonder he hadn't worn a path in the rug, but the movement helped. If he sat down and allowed his mind to wander, he knew it would linger on the wrong things. Like the fact that Ali was headed over there at any moment. They'd be together. All alone.

His pulse whooshed through his veins like a tsunami when her knock finally rattled his front door. With a deep breath, he eased it open, glancing up and down the road behind her.

She brushed past him, not waiting for an invitation. "Don't look so worried. No one saw me. Your reputation as the most eligible bachelor on the brigade won't be called into question by the village gossips."

He lifted a brow as he pulled the door closed. "I would've thought the gossips had more exciting things to talk about than me." Like how Ali had been out on a date with two different men in the last week. The memory made his scowl deepen as he spun from the doorway and found Ali standing before the fireplace, her gaze locked on his parent's portrait.

"Oh, you know how gossips are. Can't keep their mouths shut about anything." She jerked her thumb at the wall. "Friends of yours?"

He groaned internally. "Something like that." He wasn't in the mood to spill the sad story behind that painting. Time to change the subject. "Come with me. I'll get your bag."

The hair on the back of his neck lifted as she followed him down the hall to his room. *Idiot.* Why had he invited her with him? He should've asked her to take a seat and wait out there.

No, then she might have had more questions about the painting. It was better this way. He'd just grab the bag and send her off on her merry way. His stomach churned as if the thought hadn't digested well. He shook off the strange sensation as he pushed open his bedroom door.

Ali's husky chuckle rang out, doing dangerous things to his libido. That tempting sound didn't belong here—so close to his big empty bed. "You weren't kidding about the lump, I see."

He dragged the bag out from under the foot of his bed, and his mattress dipped slightly. "I rarely make a habit of lying." He held out the bag, his biceps straining as Ali allowed it to hang in mid-air without reaching for it.

She lifted her gaze to meet his, and he spied a hint of emotion there. One he couldn't quite put his finger on. Was she... sad?

"I realize that. And I'm sorry I made you break your habit. But I'm really thankful you did. Your little white lie really saved my ass."

Ah... not sad, then. Contrite. "Don't mention it." He shook the bag slightly, drawing her attention to it as the glass inside jangled. "You do want this back, don't you?"

She flashed a wobbly smile. "Sorry." Then she snagged the bag and backed up a pace. "Guess... I'll be going then."

That was it? All his worries about being alone with her were completely unfounded. Ali couldn't get out of his room fast enough.

"Wait," he blurted.

She froze, her gaze snapping back to his. "Okay... What is it?"

Yeah, Stelios. What is it? Goddess, he didn't have a clue. He'd just seen her leaving, and something inside him screamed, *No. Not yet.*

Ali's hands clenched on the bag's straps, and she shifted from one foot to the other. Time ticked slowly, his heart hammering louder with every passing moment. Ali bit her lip. She eyed the door.

Say something, you idiot! "Why do you have so many of those... things?" *Ugh. Not that.* He didn't need to know. He really didn't need more unwanted images of that woman driving him insane when he climbed into bed at night.

A smirk spread across her lips. "Do you really want to know?"

No. Definitely not. "Yes."

"Well, if that's the case, we're going to need to go on a little field trip." She sashayed through the door back into the hall. "Grab your shoes and come with me. Cute socks, by the way. They're very... colorful."

Lio glanced down and cringed. He hadn't even realized until that very moment, but he was wearing the pair Tini had embroidered and given to him on his last name day as a joke.

They were bright yellow and covered in animals—but not of the cute variety. Quite the opposite, in fact… She'd embroidered nearly every half inch with a sketch of an animal's rear—sheep, cows, pigs, you name it, each with a raised tail making it blatantly obvious which end was on display—on account of her pet name, of course. They'd both laughed so hard when he'd torn open the gift wrap.

And now Ali had seen them. *You clean the whole damn house but forget to change your socks? Real smart, Stelios.*

"They were a gag gift. From my sister," he explained as he hurried after her into the living room.

"Sure they were." She leaned against the couch as he scooped his boots from their spot in the front closet. "Guess now I know why you haven't been courting any of the village ladies. I mean, I'm not one to judge, but normally when people have a fondness for farm animals, they tend to fixate on their faces. Just saying."

He groaned, and not just internally this time. "You're not gonna let this go, are you?"

She smiled sweetly. "Nope. Don't think I will."

I can't believe I'm about to tell her this… "She calls me Big Butt," he muttered.

"Excuse me? What did you just say?"

He shoved his feet into his boots. "Tini. It's her nickname for me. She's been calling me Big Butt since she was five." He tugged the laces hard, more than a little surprised when they didn't snap in half. "There? You happy?"

"That's the best thing I've heard all day!" She cackled, clutching her stomach and absolutely exploding with mirth.

A smile fought to surface, but he swallowed it down. "At least someone finds it funny."

"Aww, come on, Big Butt." Ali wiped a tear from her eye. "Don't tell me you're sore?" She exploded with laughter again.

Lio's lips twitched. His spine tingled. And then something unexpected happened. He joined in, unable to hold back his amusement, no matter how hard he tried. The situation was just so utterly... ludicrous.

Why did he keep those stupid socks?

Why did he wear them, today of all days?

And why was Ali's laughter so ridiculously contagious?

But as his big belly roar tapered off into soft chuckles, he spotted Ali staring at him, her gaze softer than he'd ever seen before. Then she smiled, but it wasn't her usual smirk, or even the teasing grin filled with amusement that she flashed so often. This smile was something else entirely—and seeing that soft curve directed at him made his fingers itch and his heart flip-flop like a beached fish gasping for breath.

All the air in the room escaped. Or at least it felt like it had. He was about half a heartbeat away from dragging her into his arms and kissing her senseless when she broke the tension by stepping toward the door.

"You should laugh more often, Lio. You're really great at it."

They strode through the cobblestone streets in silence. After they turned the first corner, Lio insisted on carrying the bag, and Ali handed it over without complaint.

He wasn't sure what had made her clam up, but he wasn't complaining. He'd never been much of a talker. If Ali was content to walk in silence, he'd happily oblige.

Where were they going? It wasn't to her shop, or Nora's tavern. He'd figured that out as soon as she headed for Westpass—the neighborhood where the more affluent families in Everpass lived—instead of turning down Main.

Was he about to be introduced to yet another man she'd been courting? If she sidled up to some rich jerk's front door and asked the bloke to explain what all those glass phalluses were for, Lio was going to scream. Then the guy was probably going to end up getting punched in the throat. Or maybe with a ridiculous sock shoved up his—

"Here we are," Ali announced as she stopped in front of a tall building just before they reached the swanky manors of Westpass. At a house that had been converted into apartments, he guessed, judging by the amount of doorbells on the doorframe. "Come on. He'll be happy I brought you with me. It'll look more like a friendly get-together if there's two of us stopping by."

So it *was* a man. And what was all that talk about what things looked like? What were they really up to if they were so concerned about appearances? *Don't be stupid. She wouldn't bring you along if they were planning on doing anything weird...*

As if she sensed the direction his thoughts had taken, Ali flashed him a smile and squeezed his forearm before pressing the bell. "Relax. This won't take long. And you'll have all your questions answered."

His gut rankled as they waited on the stoop. There was no way to even guess which races lived inside. Often, the architecture in Everpass hinted at who had built the abode. Giant stone houses of orcs. Tiny wooden imp cabins. The meticulously maintained homes of elves. But while this building appeared to have been built by human hands, anyone could've moved in once it was converted. So it was a complete surprise when the door swung open, and Lio was met with a scowl that rivaled his own.

"Oh great. It's you," Maalik said, his sarcastic tone completely at odds with his words. He shot Lio a contemptuous glare before waving them in. "What are you waiting for? Get inside before somebody sees you."

The surly troll's squat legs wobbled slightly as he led them to the third floor. Lio gritted his teeth, unable to halt the less-than-friendly thoughts flickering through his mind.

What did Ali see in him? Maalik had to be the grumpiest person he'd ever met—and yes, he was including himself in that assessment. Hell, he'd just laughed, hadn't he? Bet Maalik hadn't cracked a smile in ages.

Maybe Ali had a thing for grumpy guys. That would certainly explain a few things.

Maalik slammed the door. "Have a seat."

Lio glanced around the sparsely decorated living room, his gaze landing on the only piece of furniture in it: a checkered couch built to troll proportions, which meant it'd likely break if he tried to sit on it.

Ali didn't let that stop her. "Thanks, Mal." She perched on one side, taking up an entire cushion and a half. Then she waved him forward and patted the seat beside her. "Get over here, Lio."

He frowned. "I'll stand."

"Suit yourself." Maalik plopped down beside Ali, leaning on the armrest and looking entirely too comfortable with Ali squeezed beside him in such close quarters. "Why did you bring him anyway?"

Lio fumed internally, biting his tongue.

Ali laughed. "He insisted on carrying my bag." She waved him forward again. "If you won't sit, then at least put that down on the table."

He bent, dumping the bag onto the small glass table that sat in front of the couch.

"Careful!" Ali exclaimed as the glass clinked loudly within. "I can't sell them if you break them."

"You're planning to sell them." Relief washed over him like a tidal wave.

Ali smirked. "Course I am. Why else would I need so many?"

Maalik snorted. "He probably thought you were leading him into some perverted tryst."

Honestly, that guess hadn't been too far off. Lio's cheeks warmed.

"Don't be silly. Maalik and I save the perversions for special occasions, don't we, honey bear?"

Maalik rolled his eyes. "You can cool the act with this one, lass. He doesn't look like the gossiping type."

Lio stuffed his hands into his trouser pockets. "What act?"

Ali snagged the bag and inched open the zipper. "I promised to help Mal improve his chances with the village ladies if he helped me."

"A promise no one asked you for," Maalik cut in.

Ali continued on, undeterred. "It's working, by the way. Just yesterday I overheard Mrs. Munchouser in the market whispering to one of her gaggle of gossips. She didn't realize I was listening when she said, and I quote, 'Wonder what that horrid troll is hiding in his trousers to keep her interested?'"

Maalik tossed a hand in the air. "Bah! Who cares what that old bat thinks?"

"You will when the ladies line up to see for themselves," she retorted.

"I'll believe it when I see it." He rolled his eyes again. "Mark my words. No woman in her right mind is going to approach me angling for a peek in my trousers."

Lio's gaze darted between them. He suddenly felt like the biggest idiot in the realm. There were clearly no romantic feelings between the pair. They acted more like squabbling siblings than lovers.

Ali chuckled. "So long as they don't ask to see your socks, you'll be fine."

He buried another groan.

"I'll have you know my footwear is top of the line." Maalik lifted a foot and wiggled his toes, drawing Lio's attention to a perfectly normal pair of tan socks.

Good for him...

"Since I've kept up my end of the bargain—"

Maalik spoke over her again. "That no one asked for."

"—it's time for you to keep up yours." Ali pulled out a glass cylinder and deposited it in Maalik's lap. "Go on, Mal. Put those talented hands to good use."

Maalik's eyes widened as he stared down at the green glass. "The hell is this?" He held it aloft, and Lio's chin ached with a phantom pain as he recognized his attacker. "If this is what the ladies are after, they'll be sorely disappointed when they find out what I'm working with."

"That's the orc model." Ali giggled. "It's Lio's favorite."

Lio dragged a hand down his face.

Maalik snorted. "That right? Suppose I ought to get it working so you can have your fun with it."

Lio glared at Ali, but she only leaned back on the couch with a mischievous grin. He really ought to say something to clear his good name. But he had a sneaking suspicion Ali would end up twisting his words and making him look like even more of a fool. And he was beyond ready to discover what Maalik was planning to do with the curious device.

"That would be fantastic." He forced a smile that likely looked more like a grimace.

"Here, I'll help." Ali plucked the cylinder out of Maalik's hands and twisted off the metal attachment at the bottom. "You've probably seen these dimmer switches before. They're an essential piece in any crafted item that's imbued with magic."

Lio nodded. "Like lamps."

As Ali handed the glass back, he spied a thin opening in the center of the glass.

"Yes, exactly. But Mal's talent isn't in light magic." Ali grinned.

Maalik placed his finger on the opening's edge, and the room erupted with a gentle hum as the glass began vibrating. He handed it to Ali with a sigh. "Still wish I had enough quake to break through rock, like a full-blooded troll would."

Ali twisted the dimmer switch back on the bottom, and the vibrations stopped. "Well, I'm certainly glad that you have the talent you do. After I sell these in Fairvale, I'll be set for funds for a while."

"You're not selling them at Our Glass?" Lio asked.

She shook her head. "Can't. The town council won't allow it. But there are different rules in the capital."

"You never told me what happened with the last batch," Maalik said as he began imbuing another decorated with swirling shades of pink and purple.

"They practically flew off the shelves from what I've heard." Ali twisted the switch on the next. "They've been outselling the old models like crazy."

Lio lifted a brow. "Old models?"

Ali explained, "I didn't just wake up one day and decide to become the chief supplier of the adult boutiques in Fairvale. My mentor already had a contract in place when I took over Our Glass. But the old models were stationary. Still got the job done, but not like this." She grinned as she plucked a third from Maalik's hands.

Lio stood there, stunned, as they worked in silence. He couldn't help but be impressed. Ali saw a way to improve an existing product and made it happen. Sure, it wasn't exactly a respectable product, at least by Everpass's standards, but he couldn't fault her for doing what she needed to ensure her business stayed afloat.

Though that did beg the question... why was Ali hurting for funds? Our Glass wasn't some rundown shop that no one frequented. He always spotted folk coming in and out when he visited the smithy. What did she need the coin for so badly?

"When are these headed to the city?" Maalik asked.

"Tomorrow. I scheduled my assistant to work a cashier shift at the shop. Figure I ought to make the trip on a slow day, when I won't have many folks stopping in to ask for custom orders."

Lio's stomach turned. "You don't hire a runner for that?"

Ali refilled her bag with the imbued glass. "A runner can't haggle with the shop owners for a better cut of the sale price."

He really didn't like the idea of her traveling to the capital and visiting a bunch of adult boutiques all alone. But he could sense there would be no talking her out of it.

Unwanted images bombarded him, like Ali being accosted on the mountain pass by ruffians who'd take one look at what was in her bag and get the wrong idea. Her being propositioned by a slimy customer in one of those shops. Or worst of all, by the deviant owner who held the key to her money woes in his hands.

So it came as no surprise when a sentence he hadn't planned to utter spilled out of his lips. "When are you leaving? I need to pick up a few things in the city."

Ali froze, her gaze the only thing moving as it lifted to his face. "Do you really?"

Nope. Not a thing. He leaned back on his heels. "Yep. Been meaning to make a trip there for a few weeks now."

"Don't you have work?" she asked.

"Day off." It wasn't, but he'd trade with Johan.

Maalik sniffed. "Aren't you lucky?"

Ali patted Maalik's knee. "If these babies take off the way I think they will, you might be able to quit that banker job and have all the days off you want."

Maalik's hand closed over hers. "Naw. I already told ya, lass. I don't want to be cut in. You're the one doing all the work. Just keep my name out of it, and we're square."

Ali smiled warmly, her voice full of gratitude. "Thank you, Mal. You're my hero. You know that, don't you?"

Maalik's eyes glistened. "Bah! Get out of here. Both of you. I need a nightcap. And my bed."

"Next round at Stellar Spirits is on me," Ali called over her shoulder as she headed for the door.

Lio followed on her heels, touched and slightly confused by what he'd just witnessed. As they exited onto the street, he grabbed the bag out of her hands. "So, when are we leaving?"

She eyed him suspiciously. "I'll tell you as soon as you tell me what you need in the city."

"Oh, you know. Things."

"Things?" She lifted a brow.

Goddess, what was he getting himself into? "Socks," he blurted.

She giggled. "Hmm. That tracks."

"Meet you at Stellar Spirits? Tini has a shift in the morning."

"I suppose..." She nodded at the bag. "You mind sleeping on a lump for one more night?"

It seemed there was no end to the insanity he'd agree to when she asked. "Fine. But we'll have to swing back to grab it after I drop my sister off."

Ali grinned. "Good plan. Your house is on the way to the mountain pass from Stellar Spirits." With a wave, she strode off. "See you tomorrow, Lio."

Off Her Game

Ali

"Are you sure you don't want to get your shopping done while I'm conducting my business?" she asked Lio as they approached the first stop on her list.

They'd shared a pleasant stroll through the mountain pass that morning, chatting about nothing of importance and nibbling on breakfast sandwiches she'd purchased from Nora. Ali had wondered if Lio would peel off once they arrived in Fairvale; instead, he'd clung to her side like glue.

"Shopping won't take me long. Besides, I've never been to a pleasure shop before. Could be fun to browse."

She couldn't resist teasing him a little. It was quickly becoming one of her favorite hobbies. "Got plans to dole out a lot of pleasure in the future?"

He met her gaze directly. "I'm sure that would be fun, too."

Good goddess. Her face burned. Did he have to say that in such a sultry tone, and with such intense, unwavering eye contact?

Suppose she deserved it after how many jokes she'd made at his expense over those ridiculous socks. He was clearly trying to get back at her by making her equally uncomfortable. And it might've worked—if she didn't find the idea of Lio meting out pleasure to some eager recipient more titillating than she should've.

"Good luck with that. I'll leave you to your browsing." She pushed open the door, hoping the chiming bells disguised how loudly her heart rattled in her chest.

The Passionate Parlor was always her first stop when she visited the capital. Delicate lamps hung on the walls, the refined décor more reminiscent of something you'd expect to find in a fancy manor house, and not a shop in the bustling streets of Fairvale.

Shelves filled with all manner of curiosities dotted the store. Ali didn't have much personal experience with the items sold in the Parlor, but she recognized some from her novels. A few others were completely foreign to her. But that wasn't what made this the preeminent adult boutique in her eyes. She happened to get along with the owner of this shop much better than the proprietor of the second shop on her list.

Like her thoughts had summoned her, Ivana appeared, her long floral-print skirt swishing as she ducked out of the back room, a huge smile plastered to her wrinkled face. "Alsira, darling. I'm so happy to see you!"

"Good to see you, too, Ivana." She heaved out a breath as Ivana wrapped her in a hug, trying to avoid sucking in a whiff of her powerful scent.

Ivana was human, but she didn't let that stop her from catering to all races who frequented the capital—going so far as habitually wearing the pungent perfumes laden with sour notes that were considered an aphrodisiac to imps, but most other races found slightly off-putting.

"Well, hello there." Ivana fluffed her long black curls and adjusted her skin-tight white top, tugging it down to show off her ample tanned cleavage. "Can I help you?"

Ali flinched when she spotted Lio standing just behind her. "Aren't you here to browse?" she asked him.

He held out the bag. "Thought you might need this."

Yikes, how did she forget that? He'd definitely thrown her off her game with that comment outside. "Thanks." She grabbed the strap, shivering involuntarily as their fingers made contact.

"New assistant?" Ivana asked. "Or new flame?"

Ali smiled. "We're friends. He just wanted to look around."

"Mm hmm," Ivana said, her tone making it clear she suspected either one or both of those statements were a lie.

"Lio's never visited an adult boutique before," she added. At least *that* was true.

"A virgin. My favorite," Ivana purred. "I'll show you all my best wares after Ali and I catch up."

Lio backed up a pace. "I can handle browsing on my own. But thanks for the offer."

He disappeared down an aisle, and Ivana watched him go with an appreciative gleam in her dark-brown eyes. "Some friend you've got there."

It was lucky Lio wasn't more than her friend, or she'd have been insulted by the amount of ogling she'd just witnessed. "Yep. Ready to talk shop?"

"Of course, darling. What did you bring me?" She waved at the front counter. "Let's see all the pretties."

"Sure." She carefully placed the bag on the counter. "They're the same model as last time."

Ivana didn't even wait for the zipper to ring out before she said, "I'll take them all."

Ali worked overtime to hide her smile. "I can't do that. Not without a signed contract giving your shop the exclusive sales rights."

"And at a premium cost, I'd wager."

Ali shrugged. "It's the only way I can justify not diversifying my bets. But if you aren't interested, I can give you half at our original—"

"Let's talk numbers." Ivana leaned in. "I might have enough room in my budget to save you a trip to that rundown cesspit across the street."

Ali left the Parlor a half hour later with an empty bag, a heavy coin purse, a signed contract, and a smile on her face.

Lio nodded across the street at the Passionate Parlor's main competitor, the huge Adult Only sign in the window making it impossible to miss. "Do you need to stop in there?"

"Nope. Not anymore." She squinted and stopped short, her gaze catching on a familiar figure across the road. A tall, handsome, dark-haired man strolled into the shop in question, turning his face as he entered. But the recognition she'd expected to find in his gaze was suspiciously absent.

"Something wrong?" Lio asked.

"Just thought I spotted someone I knew a lifetime ago." She blew out a relieved breath. *Thank the goddess it's not him.* "But I was wrong." She resumed her walk, shaking off the unwelcome false familiarity.

He frowned, keeping pace with her as she strode deeper into the city. "I don't get it. Wouldn't you make more profit if you sold to both shops?"

"I might. But I value my time more than I value squeezing them for all that they're worth. By giving Ivana the exclusive rights, I only have one shop to resupply, saving me time, and I get a much larger cut of each sale. It's a win-win, the way I see it."

"Hmm. I didn't think about it that way…"

"Besides, the other owner gives me the creeps. Last year, when I told him off after one too many rude comments, he started using a different glassblower for the old models, so it will be easy to cut ties. I'd much rather only deal with Ivana." She shuddered. "I barely made it out of there without punching his slimy face when I stopped by last month to show off the new model. If I didn't want Ivana desperate to sign an exclusive deal, I wouldn't have bothered."

Lio fell silent, his fists clenching and unclenching at his sides.

"You all right?"

"I don't like that you have to deal with guys who give you the creeps."

She smirked. "Look, I know you like playing the hero, but I can take care of myself."

It was obvious Lio only tagged along today to protect her. She'd figured that out from the start. He wouldn't have made a career out of saving others if he didn't get something out of it. And honestly, she kind of loved that about him. He was an honorable man, and he'd make some lucky lady very happy one day. Just... not one with kids.

He dragged a hand through his dark locks, tugging at the roots. "You shouldn't go alone. What if—"

"I don't have much choice. I have a daughter, Lio. And I'm all she's got." She shook her head. "I would talk to a million creeps if it meant I could make a difference in her life."

"How does selling massagers make a difference? You have your shop. Isn't that enough?"

She sighed heavily. "I wish it was." She spotted a clothing shop ahead. "Hey, here's our next stop."

Lio frowned as they entered, the scent of fresh cotton thick in the air. "What do you need here?"

"Not me. You do." She pointed to a table up front and center covered in socks. "I'll leave you to it." She turned toward the door.

"Wait. Where are you going?"

She bit her lip. "I have a stop to make up the street. But don't worry, it won't take long. Meet you out front when we're both done?"

Ali didn't wait for him to agree. She just left him standing there with a pair of socks in his hand and a worried look on his face.

She had something very important to drop off, and she didn't need an audience while she was doing it.

Seriously Twisted

Lio

He grabbed five pairs of socks at random and slapped them on the sales counter. "How much?"

The clerk, a bored-looking human teen with a face-full of acne and rumpled brown hair, spit out the total.

Lio dropped some coins on the counter and said, "You can keep the change if you bag them like your ass is on fire."

The kid had the bag in his hand before Lio could blink twice. He sprinted out of the store and was back on the street in record time.

Where was she? There!

Ali's black-bob flashed in the road just before she ducked into a tall building at the end of the intersection. Lio hurried after her, his stomach sinking.

What was she doing? He didn't like her running off on her own, especially after she'd just told him she'd be willing to deal with any creep if it would help Echo. He still couldn't wrap his head around that. What did her daughter need so badly that it would cause Ali to play fast and loose with her safety?

His pace slowed as he drew close and recognized the building for what it was—a shared office space dubbed Horizon Tower. About a dozen businesses were listed on the sign, and not a single one he recognized.

At least the place looked legitimate. Not at all like the kind of place where she'd be in danger. He heaved a sigh as he strolled through the door.

What am I doing? He shouldn't be following her. She'd wanted to meet on the road. But while his inner voice shouted *Stay outside, you fool*, his feet responded with *Too late*.

His boots echoed loudly on the wooden floor. A staircase loomed ahead, and corridors branched off to either side. He had just resolved to turn and leave when the hushed murmur of voices drew him forward as if he was enchanted by a siren's song.

He spotted Ali inside an office, the wide-open door covering the nameplate. She was facing a receptionist, watching as the young brunette stacked coins on the counter.

"You have enough for four sessions, plus the travel fees."

"Just four?" Ali sighed.

"If you'd rather meet here instead—"

"No, let's do four."

"I'll add you to the schedule. Same time each month?"

Ali stuffed an empty coin purse into her jacket; the same coin purse that had been so heavy after leaving the Passionate Parlor he'd been worried a pickpocket might target her. "Actually, I'd like to bump it up to twice a month."

What in the realm? His brow furrowed.

The receptionist's voice rang out loudly. "Sir, please take a seat. I can help you in just a moment."

Great...

Ali turned, spotting him in the hall.

He stammered, "I-I actually—"

"He's with me." Ali spun back to the receptionist. "Same day and time would be best, please."

The receptionist dipped her head and flipped through a book. "We can fit you in biweekly. Your first session can start this week, if that works for you."

"It does. Thank you."

Ali stalked out of the office, shooting him a glare. "What happened to meeting out front?"

"Thought I'd save you from backtracking." Sure, it was technically true, but it was a lame excuse, and he knew it.

Clearly, Ali did too. But she waited until they were out of the building before she spoke, her voice controlled and tinged with a sharp edge. "Look, I know I invited you to Maalik's last night. And I didn't complain when you invited yourself along on my trip today, since I stupidly thought it would be nice to have company for a change. But if you think that means you have permission to butt into every aspect of my life, you're dead wrong."

"What did you expect me to do after you admitted how little you value your safety?"

She rolled her eyes. "The hero act is getting really stale, Lio." She marched off, heading for the mountain pass. "I'm going home."

"Good. Me too." He followed in her wake, burying the urge to growl in frustration as she picked up her pace. By the time they made it to the city's outskirts, she was practically jogging, and he felt even more like a stalker than he had in that office.

Everything about it felt wrong. Ali was perpetually perky, always cracking jokes and putting a positive spin on things. It obviously took a lot to make her angry, but he'd managed to push her over the edge in the space of an afternoon.

He had to fix this. "Ali, wait."

"What now?" She flipped back to face him. "Why did you even come today? Do you get some sick amusement out of following around women who never asked you to?"

"No." Suppose he deserved that. "I did it for Tini."

Ali crossed her arms. "Do you always use your sister as an excuse?"

"Only when it's the truth." He cringed, shaking his head. "She's been asking about our past. Wanting to return to where we were born... which is a terrible idea. I thought maybe she'd lay off asking if we became friends with some of our kind. You don't have to believe me, but it's the truth."

"That's a big change from demanding I keep my daughter on a leash." The ghost of a smile flirted with the edges of her lips. "Remind me again, why were you mad at Echo?"

For following me. He had a good reason to be wary about any nymph taking an interest in him, but that wasn't Echo's problem. The kid didn't know anything about his past. And she hadn't been following him for the reason he'd first assumed. "I was an ass that day. I should've handled it better."

She stared down at the ground, her face pensive. "Hmm."

His fingers fidgeted around the handle of his shopping bag. "I'm sorry, Ali. I shouldn't have followed you into that office. You deserve to have privacy when you want it. Can I at least walk you back without chasing you? Please?"

Her expression softened. "Since you apologized—and finally asked—sure." She resumed walking at a more reasonable pace. The city streets gave way to rocky terrain, and soon they'd left the crowds behind and hiked up a steep incline in silence.

Lio's chest filled with unease. Normally, he'd never complain about walking without the usual mundane chitchat, but there was nothing comfortable about the silence between them. The mystery of what he'd just witnessed was too fresh in his mind—though he couldn't find a way to broach the topic without invading her privacy. He wouldn't make that mistake again after he'd just apologized.

Luckily, Ali took pity on him as the first tunnel on the pass appeared on the horizon. "Suppose you want to know what I was doing there."

Desperately. "Only if you want to tell me."

"Echo's been having issues at school. Her teacher recommended that I take her to a healer in the city. But I've been covering his travel expenses so that he'll visit her at our place instead." She grinned crookedly. "You'll be pleased to note that I *am* taking precautions with her safety and not forcing her to hike to the capital twice a month."

His stomach churned. "Is she... ill?"

"No, it's not that kind of healer. He focuses on mental and emotional well-being."

"Huh. I didn't know there were healers who did that." Maybe he should've taken the seat the receptionist offered him. It sounded like that healer might be exactly what he needed to help Tini with her recurring nightmares.

"I didn't either until Echo's teacher recommended we give it a try." She shrugged. "Just wish it wasn't so expensive."

So that was the crux of her money woes. Her daughter needed help, and Ali found a way to get it for her, no matter the cost. Admiration washed over him, along with a feeling of familiarity he hadn't been expecting.

He'd been put in the same position with his sister. They'd uprooted their lives so she could have a shot at normalcy. It hadn't been easy, or without struggle, but he'd do it all over again if faced with the same decision. They were family, and family meant everything.

Clearly, Ali felt the same. She'd sacrificed so much to guarantee her daughter was safe and healthy.

Goddess, why did I follow her today? It wasn't bad enough that he found Ali distractingly attractive, but here he was, admiring her selfless dedication to her family. If he wasn't careful, she'd have him completely under her spell, without even trying.

"Enough about me." Ali stepped closer. "What's in the bag?"

He sighed, pleased she'd dropped the heavy topic. "What I came shopping for. Socks."

"I'm dying of curiosity." She snagged the bag out of his hand and peeked inside, her eyes widening. "Lio..." Giggles spilled out of the corners of her mouth. "You have a seriously twisted fashion sense with your socks."

Truth be told, he'd barely spared the stupid things a glance. He'd been so worried about chasing after her he'd grabbed everything at random. His gut twisted as she lifted a pair out of the bag, which were blessedly white and plain—he groaned internally—though the ankles were topped with a delicate lace ruffle. He barely stopped himself from blurting out that they were for Tini. The last thing he needed was to get caught using her as an excuse—again.

"Those are for the days when I'm feeling fancy," he deadpanned.

"And these?" She pulled out another pair, which were covered in black-and-white polka-dots and ridiculously fluffy.

"Pfft. They're for cold winter nights, obviously."

She giggled again. "Obviously."

Goddess, she was just so breathtakingly lovely. Her eyes were lit with mirth, her husky laughter wrapping around him, soft and dangerous like the tide. "Here." Her fingers brushed against his as she handed him the bag.

Lio's breath caught as a shiver wracked her frame. "You cold?" He shrugged off his lightweight jacket and wrapped it around her shoulders. He smoothed his hands down her upper arms, lingering longer than he should've.

Her gaze lifted to his. "Don't you need it?"

With her gazing at him like that? Not a chance. His blood was practically scalding just from the sight of her wrapped in his jacket, chill mountain air be damned. "I'll be fine. I run hot."

"Thanks." She slipped her arms into the sleeves and flashed a soft grin. One that he desperately wanted to taste. Then her gaze connected with his again, her dark-lashes fluttering. And when the tip of her tongue darted out, moistening her lips, he suddenly wondered if she craved the same thing.

Friends. The word snagged in his mind, blaring an alarm he couldn't afford to ignore. He needed Ali to be his friend, for Tini's sake. Kissing her when he had no intention of courting her definitely wasn't the way to do it. He forced his feet to move. "Come on. We'd better get going if we want to make it back before school lets out."

"Right." Ali nodded curtly before following. "Let's go."

MUDDLED

Ali

Sighing deeply, Ali slowly spun her mug of cider. Scattered stars winked in the overcast sky as she stared out of Stellar Spirit's window. The nearly empty tavern was much quieter than usual tonight, so close to closing on an evening with inclement weather.

Nora leaned against the bar, resting her chin on her fist. "I ought to be the one sighing like that, not you. I'm going to miss having you and Echo here every day."

Even though she'd been eager to slip into her pajamas and hit the hay, Ali had kept her work clothes on and headed down for a late-night gab-sesh after putting Echo to sleep. They'd been given the okay to move back home from the builder that afternoon. She forced a smile.

"Yeah. Me too." Her chest twinged. She was dying to share all of her problems with her bestie—but she couldn't. It was just as well Nora attributed her glum mood to their impending move.

Maalik's half-filled mug of ale thumped down beside hers. "Not like you won't be stopping in about a dozen times each week."

"True." Nora's eyes narrowed. "Only, that's not what's really bothering you, is it?"

Goddess, why does she have to be so perceptive? Ali shot a sideways glance at Maalik before returning her attention to Nora. "It's nothing."

"Doesn't look like nothing from where I'm standing." The sleeve of Nora's purple dress inched up her wrist as she reached across the bar and squeezed Ali's hand. "I know you don't owe me an explanation, but I'm here if you want to talk. It might help to get whatever's bothering you off your chest."

"It's not that I don't want to tell you, Nor. Trust me, I do. But I made a promise—"

Maalik cut in, "Just tell her already." He tugged at the collar of his checkered button-down before taking a deep pull from his mug. "Go on. I'm tired of watching you mope into your cup."

Ali's eyes widened. "You sure?"

"Not like it stayed a secret for long. I'd rather Nora know what you roped me into than who ended up finding out." Maalik's lips thinned as he pushed his empty mug toward Nora. "This stays between us, mind you." He side-eyed Ali. "I hope you swore your new pet to secrecy while he was following you all over the realm."

"Not gonna lie, I'm completely lost." Nora slid the refilled mug in front of Maalik. "But you know I can keep a secret. It's basically a job requirement in my profession."

Ali was practically vibrating on her stool as Maalik snagged his glass.

"Goddess, Nora. I have so much to tell you! Thank you, Mal."

"Bah." He waved a hand. "Get on with it, then."

Nora grinned. "Yeah, don't keep me in suspense."

"Do you remember the day you finally opened your book?" Ali asked.

Nora had recently acquired a charmed journal that might hold the key to finding her birth family. "You mean, the one that I still haven't worked up the guts to pen a message in?" Nora's nose wrinkled. "Sure, I remember."

Ali leaned in. "Well, everything started that day when Maalik showed us his talent."

"The vibrating mug. I'd nearly forgotten about that." Nora cocked her head. "Didn't you say you could use his gift?"

"I did. And I have." She glanced sideways. "Only Maalik swore me to secrecy when he discovered what I needed his help for." Ali fought the urge to wince, hoping Nora's feelings weren't hurt. She never set out to keep her in the dark. But it had been the only way to get Maalik on board with her plans.

"Ah... the plot thickens." Nora chuckled softly, and an invisible weight lifted from Ali's shoulders. "So what was it?"

She glanced around the tavern, double-checking that the place was empty and silent—which it was, except for the dull shuffles coming from the basement where Tini was conducting inventory. She doubted that Tini would overhear them but decided to keep her description vague and lower her voice, just to be safe.

"You may recall that I have a contract with some of the adult boutiques in Fairvale. I've been supplying them with a particular item for female pleasure."

"Sure, you told me about that befo—oh!" Nora's eyes widened before darting between them. "Ohhhh. Ali, that's genius!"

Her bestie wasn't just perceptive, but quick-witted to boot. "I thought so, too. And let me tell you, the enhancements Maalik and I cooked up have been very popular."

"I bet they are." Nora giggled before her expression turned pensive. "But wait... if it's a success, then why are you so down?"

"It all started with the fire..." She sighed, then spilled everything. Nora held her hand when she shared how she'd discovered Echo had inadvertently started the fire. Maalik couldn't stop laughing when she relayed how she caught Lio being walloped in her room. And they both fell silent as she recounted the events of yesterday's trip to Fairvale.

Nora shook her head. "Wow, you weren't kidding. That's... a lot."

"I know. Now you know why I'm a mess." She twirled her mug on the bar. "I'm just so confused."

Maalik asked, "About which part?"

"About Lio. When we first met, I would've sworn he didn't like me, and after how he treated Echo, I certainly didn't like him. But then my apartment caught fire, and he helped me, even though he didn't have to."

Nora nodded. "That was nice of him."

"I know. And he kept showing up, first at my shop, then yesterday. I was starting to think that maybe he was... into me. And not just the polite version I reserve for first dates. The real me."

Maalik tilted his head. "What do you mean, the real you?"

"You know how it is when you first start courting someone. You've gotta rein in the snark and act like you've got it together." She twisted her lips. "But Lio and I were never on a date, so why bother pretend-ing?"

"And he still kept coming back for more." Nora hummed.

"Yep." She shrugged. "But then he said he just wanted to be friends."

Nora asked, "Is that what you want? You and Lio?"

"No. It would never work. He doesn't like kids." The words slid off her tongue easily enough, but saying them aloud didn't make the dull ache in her chest fade.

"Then maybe it's for the best," Nora replied softly.

"You're probably right." She sighed wistfully. "But I swear, there was a moment on the mountain pass where I was sure he was about to kiss me." And she'd have let him, consequences be damned. Only the kiss she'd been craving had never materialized. "I guess it was all just in my head."

Maalik sipped from his mug. "You got Echo's healer sorted at least. That's good news."

"Yeah, for now. Only I can't help worrying it's just a temporary fix. The healer can help with her emotions, but he's not a nymph." Ali rubbed her temples. "I'd hoped that Echo would take after her father... not me."

"Why would you say that?" Nora asked sternly. "Echo would be lucky to take after you, Ali. You're pretty damn amazing."

She grinned crookedly. "You wouldn't be saying that if you were a nymph."

Nora crossed her arms. "Yes, I would."

"You wouldn't. Trust me." Just look at Lio. He wouldn't have even bothered trying to be her friend if it weren't for his sister.

Nora grabbed Ali's mug and refilled it with cider. "You're always so cryptic about your heritage. Maybe if you explained, we would understand where you're coming from."

"I'll drink to that." Maalik lifted his mug in solidarity, a slightly loopy grin on his face.

Her stomach churned. "Isn't it getting a little late?"

"I don't have anywhere else to be." Nora's head swiveled in Maalik's direction. "How about you, Mal?"

"Nope." His mug thumped on the bar top. "Not a one."

"Fine." Suppose this was overdue. Nora and Maalik were her best friends in the whole realm. They deserved to know more about her past. Maybe it would help them put her feelings into perspective. "But some of this stuff is pretty... cruel. Don't say I didn't warn you."

"Think we can handle it, lass," Maalik said.

I hope so... She couldn't bear it if they heard the sad truth and shunned her for it. Though it wouldn't be the first time it'd happened, and likely wouldn't be the last. "I'm sure you've heard that nymphs discover which element they can control in their teens."

Maalik and Nora both nodded, as she suspected they would. That part was common knowledge.

"And you probably know nothing about the legends associated with each element?"

"That would be correct," Nora replied.

Maalik nodded. "Same here."

She began, "Each of the five elements—"

"Five?" Maalik's brow furrowed, and he stared into his mug like he was afraid he'd downed one too many. "Thought there were only four?"

Nora brightened. "Ooo, I know this! The five elements are fire, water, air, earth, and spirit."

"Ah, spirit. That's the one I was missing," Maalik admitted.

"Most people forget it. And for good reason. It's extremely rare for a nymph to wield spirit magic. But that's not important for this discussion." Ali frowned. "Do either of you know what the second rarest element is for nymphs?"

Nora tapped her chin. "No. But if I had to guess... Is it fire?"

Ali grinned. "Good guess." Her grin faded. "According to legend, the talent to control fire was a gift from the underworld, reserved for the dregs of nymph culture. They were all killers and thieves—or if they weren't yet, then they would be one day. For centuries, anyone who wielded fire was treated warily as soon as their talent surfaced. They were grudgingly tolerated in some communities. Completely shunned in others."

Nora gaped. "My goddess! That's horrid, Ali. Please tell me that practice is ancient history in today's day and age."

Ali smiled sadly. "Wish I could. But my experience says otherwise." She shrugged, her heart clenching.

Maalik wrapped an arm around her shoulders and squeezed. "Idiots, the lot of them! Tell me where to find the bastards and I'll drag them all into your shop and show them exactly what a fire nymph can do."

Her eyes watered. "Relax, Mal. It was a long time ago. No dragging necessary." Still, her heart warmed all the same, having him stick up for her so fervently.

"Were you really shunned when you were younger?" Nora asked, her voice wobbly.

Ali nodded and lowered her gaze. "I watched as so many kids in my village were celebrated when they learned what they could summon. The elders rallied around them, teaching them how to use their magic. But me? All anyone wanted me to do was suppress it. It's one reason why I left. It was better living with humans than being surrounded by nymphs who suddenly couldn't stand to be around me."

Nora grabbed her hand again. "I'm so sorry. That sounds awful."

"What was the other reason?" Maalik hiccupped. "You just said that was *one* reason why you left."

She twisted her lips. "Yeah… That's a bit harder to explain, and just as awful. Have either of you heard anything about birth rates among nymphs?"

They both shook their heads.

"So this is just an estimate, but I would guess that female nymphs outnumber the males by about ten to one."

"Really?" Nora blinked repeatedly. "I had no idea."

"Most folks don't. But you'd figure it out pretty quickly if you ever visited a nymph village. It's not unusual for males to have multiple partners and a lot of children."

Maalik chuckled. "Too bad I wasn't born a nymph."

"Yep. You would've had tons of ladies begging for a peek in your trousers." She tipped her glass in his direction.

Nora frowned. "And I'm willing to bet none of the guys wanted to give you the time of day because of that silly superstition."

"Pretty much." There'd been no future for her there. No chance of ever finding love when the men had scores of women who weren't blessed with a power from the underworld vying for their attention.

"I don't get it… Why are there so few men?" Maalik asked.

She explained, "Legend says it's a curse that started when nymphs began mingling with other races. You see, the only way for a mother to give herself a chance of birthing a male is by choosing a nymph to be the father. And even with a nymph father, male babies aren't guaranteed. But if the father is human, elf, or any other species, the baby is always born female."

Maalik squinted. "Don't tell me you wanted to make sure you had a girl?"

"Not at all." She sighed. "To be blunt, Echo wasn't exactly... planned. Of course, now that she's here, I wouldn't change how she came to be for anything."

"Of course," Nora said.

"Honestly, when I found out I was pregnant, the fact that Echo's father was human did come as a relief. But not because I knew she'd be a girl."

"Then why?" Maalik asked.

"Because nymph halflings often take after their non-nymph parent when it comes to their talent." She flashed a rueful smile. "I hoped to spare Echo the hardships I went through. But look how that turned out. She's spun from the same thread as me. And now I'm supposed to do what? Take her back to a community that will look down on her so that she can get her fire magic under control?" Ali shook her head. "I—"

A door slammed, and they all froze.

Please don't let that be Echo. She'd been so careless, sharing her past with her daughter asleep upstairs. But the voice that rang out, while just as hurt and confused as she suspected her daughter's would be, didn't belong to Echo.

"Echo manifested her power already?" Tini shuffled away from the basement stairwell, her eyes glistening. "And she's only ten?"

Oh no. How much of that conversation did she hear? If Tini had been listening in on the whole thing, then she'd just been privy to all Ali's muddled feelings about Lio. Doubtful she was planning to keep that information to herself.

Nora cleared her throat. "Tini, Ali was speaking to us in confidence. That conversation wasn't meant for your ears."

"I'm sorry." Tini wrung her hands, her light blue dress swishing as she crossed the room and stopped in front of Ali's stool. "I know

I shouldn't have listened in, but when I heard you talking about the five elements nymphs can summon as I came upstairs, I couldn't help myself."

Ali exhaled, relief hitting her hard and fast. At least she'd missed the part about Lio, thank the goddess. "It's all right. No harm done."

Tini bit her lip. "I-I still don't know what my talent is. It's practically unheard of at my age, isn't it? Do you think that means"—she swallowed—"I know my dad was a nymph. At least I thought he was... But what if he wasn't? If what you said about halflings is true, then that could explain it."

Maalik and Nora shot each other confused looks. But Ali couldn't tear her eyes off Tini. She seemed so... lost.

"It's possible," Ali began. "But honestly, I really don't know. Maybe you should talk to your brother about it."

Tini shook her head, making her dark-brown curls bounce. "I can't. He shuts me down whenever I ask anything about our past."

Ali's stomach twinged as she recalled what Lio had mentioned yesterday. That returning to their home would be a terrible idea. "Maybe he has a good reason for that."

"I just don't understand why he won't tell me." Tini's lower lip wobbled. "It's awful being kept in the dark. I just want to know why. Is that really too much to ask?"

The twinge in her belly turned into a stabbing blow. She'd been doing the same thing to Echo. Keeping her in the dark. Was Echo just as desperate to know more about their heritage?

Tini pulled in a sharp breath and plastered a smile on her face that seemed forced. "You know what? It's not your problem." She ducked behind the bar and pulled out a yellow raincoat. "Did you need me for anything else, Nora?"

Nora stepped toward Tini. "No. But Tini, please don't—"

"I have to go." Tini marched toward the door and buttoned up her coat. "The rain just tapered off. I'd hate to get stuck in a downpour."

Ali watched her leave, dread sinking deep into her bones. *Why did I have to go and open my big mouth?* Forget being friends, Lio was liable to murder her when he discovered what she'd let slip in front of his baby sister.

Foolish Ideas

Lio

"Hey big horn, you busy?" Lio asked as he strolled into the smithy.

Davos glanced up from his spot behind the sales counter and shot him a grin. "Naw, just killing time before I close up."

"You in the mood for a drink? I was thinking about grabbing one at Stellar Spirits. You should come with me." Tini wasn't working today, which was fine by him. He needed Davos's advice, and didn't need her listening in.

"I'll pass. You'll have to wet your whistle without me."

He wasn't surprised. Davos never accepted his invitations to go out, but that didn't stop him from asking. One day, he'd get over his fears, and Lio planned to be there for his old friend the day that happened. "Still hiding your hide, I see." He pulled a flask out of his jacket pocket. "Good thing I came prepared."

Davos plucked the metal container embossed with an intricate etching of a massive oak out of his hands and studied it with a nostalgic smile before twisting off the lid. The flask had been a gift from Davos—one of the first they'd exchanged, long ago. "What's the occasion?" Davos took a sip, only to hack a cough after he'd swallowed. "Whoo boy, what is *that*?"

He shrugged. "I'm not sure. Johan gave me the bottle."

Davos handed it back. "What's bugging you so bad that you need to fry off your taste buds?"

Lio tipped the flask into his mouth, trying to swallow the sharp, bitter liquor without tasting it. Of course, it didn't work, and he ended up coughing harder than Davos. His stomach warmed as it settled and gave him the courage to spit out the truth.

"It's Tini." He replaced the lid. "She's not doing well, and I don't know how to help her."

"She sick or something?" Davos asked, the front of his flannel pulling taut against his barrel chest as he leaned on the sales counter.

He shook his head. "Not physically. More like sick of me."

"Took her long enough." Davos snorted at his stupid joke. "Isn't that what you've been waiting for? What happened to yearning to be on your own?"

"I still do." He'd been thrust into a role he hadn't signed up for, when he was far too young to shoulder it. The only thing that stopped Lio from resenting his baby sister was the knowledge that one day he'd be free from the responsibility of raising her. "But I don't want her to hate me."

"Pretty sure that's expected at her age." Davos chuckled. "And it's not like you've got sunshine blasting out of your eyeballs. Maybe ease up on the moodiness when you're with her."

"It's not that." He frowned. "She's been having these awful nightmares for years. And she's got it in her head that the only thing that will help is returning to Paradise Plains."

"So take her," Davos replied simply.

"You know I can't do that."

"Why not?"

"It will only make her more upset to learn what happened, that's why."

Davos crossed his arms. "Maybe. But maybe not. The mind does strange things when your life gets turned upside down without warning. I'm willing to bet it was worse for her, on account of how young she was."

His chest burned with a pressure he couldn't shake. "Tini doesn't even remember what happened. She was too young. I can't expose her to all that pain."

Davos cocked his head, making his horns tilt sideways. "But she could be right. Going back might help her. You won't find out unless you take her."

"I can't. I just wish I knew how to help her *here*." He pursed his lips. "She's also been pretty upset that her talent hasn't manifested. I keep telling her she's just a late bloomer."

"There were a few of those back at the Plains. She'd see that if you agreed to take her."

He barely resisted rolling his eyes. Was all Davos's advice going to circle back to the one thing he refused to do? "Did you know Ali's been having a healer visit Echo?"

"Yep. She told me."

"Maybe I should hire him. I bet he could help Tini."

Davos grunted. "You better hurry if that's your plan. Ali says he only works with kids. Tini won't be a kid for much longer."

Don't remind me. He'd always been so eager for that day to come, but now that it was finally approaching, he couldn't stomach the thought of sending her off on her own while she was still struggling with those nightmares.

The situation had come to a head last night. She'd burst into the cottage, drenched in rain, and barely spoke two words to him before stomping off to bed. Then, in the middle of the night, her screams woke him. He'd burst into her room, planning to comfort her like he always did, but instead of sinking into his embrace, she'd shooed him away. He had to assume that his refusal to agree to the trip caused her to push him away. They'd been fine otherwise.

Davos reached for the flask again, and Lio handed it over without complaint. "You know, if you're willing to bring a healer into the mix, I know someone who'll help Tini way more than that expensive bloke Ali's been using."

"Really?" He snagged the flask after Davos downed a swallow. "Who?" He lifted the flask to his lips and took another burning sip.

"Hearthmother Nelida."

It was a miracle he didn't spew the foul brew all over the counter. "Really, Dav? You trying to make me choke?"

Davos shrugged. "You know she's the best woman for the job. Admit it."

Lio ground his teeth. "Except for the fact that she's back in Paradise Plains."

"Hey, do you want my advice, or are you just hoping I'll nod along to whatever foolish ideas you've dreamed up?"

Lio narrowed his eyes.

"I'm serious, Stelios." Clearly, he was. Davos never dropped the nicknames unless he really wanted to get a point across. "Take Tini to see Nelida. She'll set her right."

He pocketed the flask. "Some help you are."

"Think about it, water boy," Davos called to his retreating back.

"In your dreams, bull brain."

"More like bullseye," Davos yelled out. "If I hadn't just hit the mark dead on, you wouldn't be running away."

The front door slammed shut, cutting off Davos's laughter.

Was Davos right? Should he take Tini back? Or was he right to stand his ground and shut the idea down—for good?

Grim Indeed

Ali

A high-pitched shriek intruded on the quiet in her apartment, making the hair on the back of her neck stand on end. Ali burst out of her bedroom, panic clawing at her chest.

"Echo!" She raced toward the living room, her heart thudding violently. *Goddess, please let her be okay.*

She'd left Echo sitting on the couch with the healer, Arlan, only a few moments ago. He'd sworn it was best. That Echo would feel more comfortable sharing her feelings without her mother hovering over her shoulder, listening in. But as the shrieking turned into a groan of pain, she suddenly regretted giving in so easily.

Luckily, the apartment wasn't large. Within a few steps, she skidded to a stop on the carpet, her pulse skipping a beat.

"Echo? What happened?"

The groan sounded again—and thank the goddess—it didn't belong to her daughter. But that didn't make matters much better, because as soon as Echo spotted her, she burst into tears.

"I-I b-burned him!" she wailed.

Ali's stomach sank. "Oh, baby." She wrapped her arms around her daughter's shuddering frame, and Echo clung to her tightly.

The healer cradled his hands against his chest, hissing in discomfort, before stretching out his visibly pink palms—a shade that stood out starkly against his pale, freckled skin. "Echo," he forced out, his forehead creased, teeth clenched, "don't blame yourself for this. It was my mistake to push you." He unleashed a chuckle that sounded more like whining than laughter had any right to. "It's not as bad as it looks. I'll be fine."

Ali hoped he was right. His hands looked pretty painful from where she kneeled on the couch, with her teary-eyed daughter shaking in her arms.

Arlan rose from his seat, holding his hands awkwardly in front of his white tunic. Sweat beaded on his brow and dotted his receding hairline. "Ms. Mikelli, could I have a word with you in private?"

She shot him an incredulous stare. "Now?"

"I'm afraid I must insist."

Ali held Echo at arm's length. "Will you be all right if I talk to Arlan in the kitchen? I need to bandage his hands and hear what he has to say. But if you need me to stay with you, I can wait."

Echo scrubbed her wet cheeks with the back of her fist. "No, I'm okay." Her lip wobbled. "I'm really sorry, Arlan."

He stepped forward, his hand outstretched as if he planned to comfort Echo with his touch, before he halted in place with a wince. "No apology needed. This was my fault, Echo. Remember that, okay?"

She nodded blankly before tucking her knees against her chest and wrapping her arms around them.

Ali hated seeing her make herself small almost as much as she hated knowing that Echo had harmed someone with her magic. She'd known this was a possibility, but seeing it happen... *Goddess, what am I going to do?*

She led Arlan into the kitchen and gestured to a wooden seat at the tiny table for two. "I'll grab the burn ointment and bandages." In her profession, she was no stranger to the occasional burn, and her medicine cabinet was well stocked to prove it.

"Ms. Mikelli," Arlan began.

"It's Ali." She sank into the seat across from him, dropping the supplies on the table. "Your hands, please." She breathed out a sigh as he placed them palm up on the tabletop. Upon closer inspection, the burns weren't too bad. Not even blistered.

"Thank you." He winced as she slathered burn ointment on him. "I'd like you to know I meant what I said to Echo. This wasn't her fault. She was reluctant to share during our session, and I could sense she was becoming emotional, but I urged her to continue. I've used the same technique a hundred times before, with dozens of children. Usually the exercise is cathartic, but with Echo—"

"You got burned." She wrapped his first palm in a clean bandage. "Were you holding hands when Echo's emotions overwhelmed her?"

He nodded. "It's part of my process, so long as the children are receptive to it."

"I'm so sorry." She moved onto the second hand. "For what it's worth, I've been burned much worse than this before. You ought to be fine in a few days."

He smiled politely. "I'm sure I will." He took in a measured breath. "Unfortunately, this experience has shown me I'm not the right healer for Echo. It would be a disservice to you both if I continued seeing her after today."

"Arlan, please—"

"I have a recommendation if you're open to it." She sensed from his firm tone that his decision had been made, and she'd have no hope of swaying him.

"What is it?"

"I'd like you to visit a community about two day's journey from Everpass, called Paradise Plains. There's a hearthmother—"

"Let me stop you right there. I have no interest in bringing Echo to a hearthmother." She'd been to see one before in her youth. The experience had been strange. Nothing she wanted to subject her daughter to.

He hissed as she wrapped the second hand, perhaps a bit too tightly. "Your concerns are valid, Ali. I understand hearthmother methods can be unorthodox. But I truly believe this is the only thing that will help your daughter. If you change your mind and would like a reference, please contact my office."

She blew out a defeated sigh. "Okay."

"In the meantime, I'll have my secretary return any funds you've prepaid. Now, if you don't mind, I'd like to break the news to Echo myself and reassure her I'm well."

"I would appreciate that. I'll clean up and join you."

As Arlan walked out of the kitchen, Ali rose, collecting the supplies in her trembling hands. The accident could have been so much worse.

Echo's powers were clearly out of control. If her emotions had overcome her at school instead of with Arlan...

She shoved the awful thought out of her mind at the same time she shoved the supplies back into the cabinet. Maybe he was right. She'd been avoiding the very idea of seeking other nymphs because of her history, but she couldn't deny that the hearthmother in her village *had* helped her control her power back when it first emerged.

Taking Echo back there was completely out of the question. The thought of her hearing those awful legends and being subjected to disdain from people who still believed them made her dizzy and flush. But maybe in a different village—one where no one knew her or Echo—things might be different.

No matter what, she had to do something. There'd be no more burying her head in the sand and hoping against all hope that things would work out for the best. *I just pray I don't destroy the rest of Echo's childhood in the process.*

Sweat trickled down Ali's neck as she stood in her backyard the next day. The morning was unseasonably hot, making her yearn for autumn's return. She'd always loved that season best, when long days spent in her workshop weren't quite so sweltering.

"I don't know how you work out here, Dav," she grumbled as she stoked the fire in the smithy's forge with her magic, her fingers tingling. "Doesn't the sun beating down on you drive you crazy?" Sure, her workshop could get stuffy, but at least there was shade. She cut off the flames, turning to face him.

"Doesn't bother me. A benefit of having a hide instead of skin." He swatted the air with his hand. "These damn bugs, I could live without."

Ali chuckled as the cloud of gnats hovering around his head dispersed. "Can't win 'em all, I guess." She sighed as the statement brought back the memory of her own woes.

"You look like your favorite sword just snapped." Davos leaned against his anvil. "If something's got *you* down, it must be grim indeed."

"Remember the healer I told you about?"

"Sure."

"He quit on me yesterday, after Echo burned him during their session." Her heart clenched. She still could barely believe that had happened.

"The bloke's all right, I hope? And Echo?"

"Yeah, it wasn't too bad of a burn. And he was great with her afterward, making sure she knew he didn't blame her. But goddess, it could've been so much worse."

Davos crossed the yard and rested a huge hand on her shoulder. "I'm glad they're both all right."

"I don't know if I'd go that far. I didn't even send her to school today since we're both worried about it happening again. She's upstairs reading." She bit her lip. "I don't know what to do. I was so certain that healer was the answer. And now..."

"Now you find another," Davos replied. "I even happen to know one who could help."

"You do?"

He nodded. "Before I moved to Everpass, I apprenticed in a town where a skilled healer lived."

"I don't know, Dav... Echo isn't injured or sick. This isn't something a typical healer can fix. If that were the case, I'd just get Nora to work her magic."

"You think I don't know that? Trust me, Nelida knows her stuff. Folk from all over would come to see her for maladies of the spirit."

Her skin prickled at the last word. "And where exactly will I find her?"

"Paradise Plains."

Her eyes narrowed. "Are you in cahoots with Arlan?"

Davos cocked his head sideways. "Who?"

Ali set her hands on her hips. "The healer who abandoned us. He recommended the same thing. That we journey to see a hearthmother in Paradise Plains."

"Funny. Almost seems like you ought to listen, then, doesn't it?" Davos chuckled. "But let me guess, you don't want to."

Was she so easy to read? "Yeah, well, I lived in a nymph village before. It wasn't exactly a picnic."

Davos shrugged. "Hey, I was there for years during my apprenticeship. I know the way of life out on the plains isn't for most. But I'm not telling you to stay. You just have to visit long enough for Echo to get a handle on her magic."

"They'll ruin it for her." She shuddered as unwanted memories assailed her. "Magic is supposed to be a blessing, but I've never met a nymph who didn't make me feel like wielding fire was a curse."

"You think Echo's going to think it's a blessing if she keeps burning people and starting fires?"

She shook her head, her heart sinking.

"Listen, I know you had it rough back home," Davos continued.

That was an understatement. She'd shared a few details with Davos over the years. Not as much as she had with Nora and Maalik, but clearly it had been enough for him to piece together how bad her life had been back then.

"You know, not all nymph villages are the same. Have you ever even stepped foot in another after you left?"

"No." She'd never been brave enough—or possibly stupid enough—to chance it. Not after spending so long walking on eggshells in her childhood village.

"If you don't believe me, I can prove it."

She cocked a brow. "How?"

"You said you'd never met a nymph who didn't make you feel like your magic was a curse, but that's not entirely true, is it?"

Her brow furrowed. "Yes, it—"

"I know damn well it's not. If Lio thought you were some evil villain from the underworld, would he have stuck around and helped you in your shop?"

She froze, suddenly overcome by the truth of his assessment. Lio had never judged her for summoning fire. She'd even thought he'd seemed a bit impressed when he'd hung around her shop last week. "Okay, fine. Lio's an anomaly. But you can't use that as proof that the folk in Paradise Plains will react the same."

Davos chuckled. "Sure, I can. Where do you think I met him?"

"Lio and Tini are from Paradise Plains?"

"Yep. I think you'll be pleasantly surprised if you stop being so hardheaded and follow the advice you've been given."

Ali chewed on her lower lip as she considered his words. He'd been the second person to suggest this hearthmother could be the answer to her prayers. Didn't she owe it to Echo to try?

"All right. Maybe I will." Resolve coursed through her, and she grinned. "Thanks for the advice, Dav."

"One more thing," Davos added as she turned for her back door.

She swiveled back to face him. "What is it?"

"You can't just wander into the village without an invitation."

Her stomach wobbled. "You're right." Her childhood village had been the same. They'd been wary of outsiders and reluctant to trust anyone new. Then again... She brightened. "Arlan said he'd send me with a reference when he made the recommendation. That ought to get us an in."

Davos grinned, his bovine lips curving to reveal a row of flat teeth. "Sure you wouldn't prefer a traveling companion who's been there before?"

"Really?" she asked incredulously. "You want to come with us?"

"Not me." Davos snorted. "I have too many custom orders due. But I was just chatting with Lio about his sister. Seems Tini could benefit from a visit to Nelida as well."

Her heart fluttered. "Oh... that's a strange coincidence. When are they going?"

"That's the problem. I don't think Lio is too keen to take her."

She shot him a glare. "And you want me to convince him."

He shrugged. "I already tried, but he ignored me. You, on the other hand..."

"What's that supposed to mean?"

"Don't give me that face. You could charm coins out of a dragon's hoard, and you know it."

"Eh, when you're right, you're right." She grinned. "Guess I have a stop to make before opening the shop. Do you mind if I let Echo know you're around in case she needs something?"

"When do I ever say no?" Davos chuckled. "Let her know she's welcome to keep me company if she gets tired of her book."

"Don't be surprised when she races down here as soon as I tell her." Echo liked books nearly as much as she did, but she never missed a chance to bug Davos on the not-so-rare occasions that Ali asked him to watch her.

"Looking forward to it," Davos called over his shoulder as he plunged a half-finished sword into his forge. "Good luck with Lio."

"Thanks, Dav. I'm gonna need it."

SUGAR

Lio

"Be right there," Lio shouted, slinging a towel around his hips.

He'd been soaking in the tub after a grueling overnight shift where they'd been called to put out not one, but two small fires. And just as he'd begun to relax, the hot water soothing his aching muscles, incessant pounding rattled his door.

It had to be Tini. She'd offered to hit the market after discovering they were out of eggs and a few other staples they'd needed to whip up breakfast. No doubt she'd forgotten her key—again. Who else but his sister would be rude enough to keep banging even after he'd replied?

"Keep your shirt on. I'm coming," he hollered. His feet left wet spots on the carpet on his way to the door. As he pulled it open, he grumbled, "You'd better have my sugar—"

"Sorry to disappoint." Ali barged in, eyeing his bare chest as she passed him. "If I'd known you had a sweet tooth, I would've come prepared."

He froze in place as shock reverberated through him, along with a good deal of embarrassment. "I—"

"Don't worry. I have no plans to take my shirt off, either." She waved at his torso. "Although you might consider taking your own advice."

"You interrupted my bath." Scowling, he shut the door. "What are you doing here?"

"I need a favor." She plopped onto the sofa, smirking. "But I'm sure you want to get dressed. I can wait."

"Oh, can you?" Funny, he'd have thought otherwise from how relentlessly she'd pounded on his door.

Was he destined to always put his foot in his mouth around her? At least she had a good sense of humor about the situation. It would've been far worse to answer the door and be greeted with a shriek.

"Mm-hmm. Though waiting is not one of my strong suits." Her gaze stayed trained on his chest, and he took small solace in that fact. It was only fair if she was a little off-kilter as well. "Think you could get moving on that?"

He had half a mind to refuse. Clearly, she wasn't inclined to continue the conversation with him half-naked and dripping. Maybe she'd forget the whole thing and leave him to continue his bath in peace. But curiosity got the better of him before long.

"Fine. Stay there. I'll be right back." He stalked off to his bedroom and hastily threw on a pair of blue slacks and a white shirt. His hand stilled as he reached for his sock drawer, and he abandoned it without selecting a pair. Then he marched barefoot back into the main room.

He leaned against the wall and crossed his arms. "All right. What do you need?" *Too bad it wasn't something I could've taken care of while in the towel. Or, better yet, out of it.* He shook the wayward thought out of his head.

Ali's hands twisted in her lap before she smoothed them down her black trousers. "You remember how nice I was, letting you tag along on my trip to the capital?"

He narrowed his eyes. "Uh huh."

"Fantastic. So I'm sure you won't have any problem returning the favor." She grinned, her long-sleeved tunic pulling taut against her chest as she draped an arm across the back of the sofa.

Clever. What better way to convince him than the subtle pressure of a supposed debt? "You need to go to Fairvale again?"

"Not exactly. But I could use a travel buddy." She lifted a brow. "Are you in?"

"Depends." He pushed off the wall and sank into an armchair across from her. "Where are you headed?"

"Paradise Plains," she said cheerily.

"Too bad." He stood, his stomach roiling. "I'm out."

"What? But Dav said—"

He groaned. "Of course he put you up to this."

She stood as well, planting her hands on her hips. "Only because we both need to go."

"What do you need in Paradise Plains?"

"Echo needs to see the hearthmother." She sighed heavily, her gaze dropping to the floor. "It's our last hope. The healer I hired gave up trying to help her."

A pang hit him square in the heart. But he couldn't let the traitorous organ sway him. "I'm sorry to hear that. It's a pleasant enough journey this time of year. I can draw you a map if you'd like."

"You're kidding, right? Why won't you come with us? Tini needs to see the hearthmother, too. Don't bother denying it. She told me as much herself."

He frowned. "When did you talk to Tini?"

Ali's hands fell at her sides, and she swayed from one foot to the other. "The other day at Stellar Spirits. She overheard me talking to Nora and Maalik—"

He cut her off, "Talking about what?"

"Awfully presumptuous of you to demand a recap of a private conversation between me and my friends."

Apparently, the glare he aimed her way was enough to keep her talking.

She pursed her lips. "If you must know, I was telling them about my past. More specifically, about the challenges of growing up as a nymph."

"What?" His voice hardened. "Why would you bring that up in front of my sister?"

Ali jabbed his chest with her forefinger. "Hey, I said she *overheard*. I didn't sit her down for story time."

Sure, it was probably unintentional, but it didn't stop Lio from feeling like steam was about to burst out of his ears.

"Besides, it's a good thing she heard me. You can't keep your sister in the dark forever, Lio."

"Who says I can't?" His nostrils flared. "Trust me, no good will come out of Tini going back."

"Are you sure about that?"

He barked, "Yes."

She backed up a step. "Really? Because it sounded to me like your sister was pretty... lost. She's aching for a connection to her past, one that you refuse to give her."

Lio palmed the back of his neck. "Yeah, well, she'll get over it." The statement flew off his tongue, full of certainty. But deep down, he couldn't help wondering if Ali was right.

Was he doing Tini a disservice by sheltering her from the past?

Ali shook her head sadly. "I hope you're right. Or you might wake up one day and discover she's gone."

"Do you think I don't know that?" He set his jaw in a grim line. "Hell, do you think I'd deny her a visit to a hearthmother if I thought it'd help?"

She tilted her head. "I don't know. You seem *really* against it."

"Maybe because we tried it already—and it didn't work." He sank back into his chair. "The last time Tini visited a hearthmother it did not go well." He closed his eyes, the echo of her childish screams so ingrained in his memory he could still hear them. "I can't put her through that again. I won't."

Ali squeezed his shoulder. "Lio, I'm—"

A key rattled in the lock. Lio tensed, his gaze shooting to the front door. A heartbeat later, Tini strode in, balancing a bag in one hand and her keys in the other. "Hi, Ali." She smiled warmly, seemingly not fazed at all at finding them in such close proximity.

Ali lifted her hand off Lio's shoulder and waved. "Good morning."

"Are you staying for breakfast?" Tini asked.

"Actually, I just popped over to ask Lio something." Ali flashed a crooked grin that was barely half as bright as her usual. "Now that I have my answer, I'd better head into work."

Tini dropped the bag onto the kitchen countertop. "I'll go with you."

Ali's nose wrinkled. "Hm? Do you need something at Our Glass?"

"To Paradise Plains." Tini gestured to the window overlooking the front porch. The same one that was cracked open, letting in the spring breeze. "I heard what you asked." She winced. "Sorry I keep sneaking up on you, Ali. Promise I won't make a habit of it."

Lio's heart sank. Tini couldn't be serious? Could she?

Ali muttered, "It's fine," then her gaze shot to his. Whatever she found there made her expression darken and her shoulders slump.

"I'm honestly not sure what Lio's talking about," Tini continued. "I was so young when I left Paradise Plains, I don't have a clear memory of those years. But I'm ready to go now. I want to meet the hearth-mother you mentioned. I'm tired of not knowing what element I can summon. Maybe she can help."

Ali glanced at him again. Then she smiled sadly and said, "Listen, Tini. Normally, I'd be the first to say, 'the more the merrier,' but—"

Ali was about to tell Tini to stay home, and Lio knew he was the reason. Tini would end up feeling even worse after being rejected by the very person he'd hoped she'd befriend. He couldn't let that happen.

"We'll both go," he blurted.

Ali and Tini spoke in unison. "Really?"

"Yeah." He rose from his seat, scowling. "I know when the tide's turned against me. But don't say I didn't warn you when things get weird."

Tini squealed. "I can't believe this! Thank you, Lio. Thank you!"

He dug into the groceries, pulling out the sugar. "You'll need to take time off from work. A week ought to do it."

"I can't wait!" Tini bounced in place, then darted for her bedroom door. "I'm going to start packing right away."

He turned to Ali. "Same goes for you. This won't be a quick there and back trip, like it is to Fairvale. You prepared for that?"

Ali grinned. "Won't be a problem. I'll close up the shop for a week." Her smile fell. "How about you? Can the brigade spare you?"

"You're lucky Johan owes me a favor." He grabbed a mug from the cupboard. "We'll leave in two days. That'll give us enough time to gather supplies."

"Perfect." Ali hovered beside him. "Thank you, Lio. I'm really glad you changed your mind." She winked. "And that you finally got your sugar."

He rolled his eyes as he dumped a generous portion of the powdery sweetener into his tea. Something told him he'd need to stock up if he was actually going through with this. He'd just signed up for a week in the wilderness with the three females who got under his skin more than anyone else in the realm. *What the hell was I thinking?*

No Kidding

Ali

Ali eased open Stellar Spirit's door the next day, her stomach fluttering. "Oh good. Just who I needed to talk to."

Paige glanced up, her eyes widening. "You don't mean me, do you?"

"I do, actually. That's why I scheduled my lunch break when I knew you'd be torturing Nora."

The country witch had been giving Nora magic lessons for the last few months, which had quickly earned Paige a permanent place in their friend group. Today, the pair sat at a back table in the tavern, beside an open window, while Maalik watched from his favorite stool, a half-eaten sandwich clutched in his hands.

Nora huffed, using the apron she'd tied around the waist of her red dress to swipe sweat from her brow. "It really is torture. Who knew learning lightning magic would be the thing that breaks me?"

Paige grinned. "You're doing great. I see a huge difference from last week."

"Oh really?" Ali plunked onto a bench. "Can I see?" She never got tired of watching her bestie conquer a new talent. *If only nymphs could be blessed with more than a single element...*

"Go on, Nora. You got this," Paige encouraged.

Nora dipped her hand into a glass of clear liquid, letting a small pool collect in her open palm. "Okay, but don't laugh if I fail miserably. Again." She blew out a breath, then her brows pinched with concentration. Humming filled the air.

At first, nothing happened. But then the air just above Nora's palm shimmered, and a tiny spark appeared, seemingly from nowhere.

A slow smile spread across Ali's face. "Nor, you're doing it!"

As suddenly as it had appeared, the spark vanished. Nora frowned, shaking the moisture from her hand. "That's not what I was picturing. At all."

"It's a start." Paige handed Nora a hand towel. "Just wait. You'll master lightning in no time."

"Yeah, if no time is months from now." Nora sighed. "I wish it hadn't taken me so long to discover I'm a witch. It feels like I'll never catch up."

Paige patted Nora's shoulder. "You will eventually. Luckily, with enough study, most magic is simple to master, especially if you have a natural affinity for it."

Since Nora had mastered light magic so quickly, it wasn't too big of a jump to assume she could learn to control lightning as well. Seemed it was just taking her a bit longer.

Paige glanced at Ali. "How long did it take you to learn to control fire? Only a few years, I'd wager?"

She winced. "Actually, it was more like a day."

"Seriously?" Nora tossed down the towel, her mouth agape.

Ali twisted her lips. "It's a bit different for nymphs. In fact, that's kind of what I'm here to talk about."

Nora's brow wrinkled. "What's going on?"

"It's Echo. I think I finally found someone who can help her. But it's going to require travel. I'm leaving tomorrow, and I'll be gone for at least five days, maybe as long as a week." She glanced at Paige. "Would you mind running book club in my place?"

Paige pressed a splayed palm against the collar of her pink and white polka-dotted sundress. "Are you sure you want me? Not Nora or Maalik? They've been members longer."

She had a feeling Paige's hesitancy had more to do with her lack of confidence than genuine reluctance. Even after months of repeated visits, many of Everpass's residents still eyed her warily.

Ali had always found it a little strange that humans were so fearful of witches and not the other races who could control magic. But at least with the races who were only blessed with one talent, you always knew what you were going to get. Witches could be infinitely more powerful. They'd even played a major role in the last great war to darken their realm. But she'd certainly never let that bother her.

"Yes, I want you. You're the biggest reader in the bunch—besides me, of course." Ali grinned. "Besides, Nora has to keep an eye out for customers. And Maalik joined at the same time as you, plus he's far too crotchety to run things."

"Don't think I didn't hear that," Maalik interjected as he brushed a crumb off his tailored slacks.

"So will you do it?" She hated to ask, but there wasn't much choice. Echo would always be the top priority in her life.

A tentative smile curved Paige's lips. "Okay."

"Great! Just do me a favor and make sure Nora doesn't leave without blushing at least once." She wiggled her brows. "If you need a few firefighter innuendos, I can leave you a list."

Paige giggled. "Think I'll manage." She sighed. "Besides, planning the discussion questions will be a nice distraction."

"From what?" Maalik asked.

Paige lowered her gaze. "From waiting to hear from Emil. Can you believe he hasn't reached out since the dance? Not even once."

Ali's heart clenched. "I'm sorry, Paige."

"Not as sorry as I am." Nora patted Paige's hand. "Ali told me what happened. My brother's an ass."

Paige twisted her lips. "Yeah, no kidding."

Ali had hoped Seth and Paige would've patched things up by now. It was bound to become awkward if they didn't, considering how important they both were to Nora.

Paige sighed again. "At least my fictional men won't disappoint me. Are you okay with me choosing next month's read?" Her face lit up.

"Sure. I trust you." Which was even more true after she'd finished Paige's last selection. She'd blown through it in less than three days, the engaging plot enough to keep her turning the pages, even though her mental image of the hero was suspiciously similar to a certain fire chief.

"What about your shop?" Nora asked. "Will your assistant keep it open while you're gone?"

She shook her head. "He's too new to run things for that long. I'm going to close it down for a week and post a sign in the window. Lots of shopkeepers on my street do it when they need time off."

Nora added, "I've done the same."

"I honestly didn't think I'd be able to afford to take time off anytime soon, but I lucked into a bit of a windfall." She could thank Arlan for that. She was planning to use the coin he'd returned for Echo's canceled sessions to finance the trip.

Maalik cleared his throat. "Where you headed?"

"Paradise Plains. There's a hearthmother in a nymph village who came highly recommended." She dragged a hand through her short locks. "I just hope the experience isn't too much for Echo."

"I've always wanted to meet a hearthmother. They're said to be the most skilled with spirit magic in all the realm," Paige mused. "Have you met one before?"

Ali nodded. "Visiting a hearthmother is like a rite of passage when you're a nymph."

"Then why do you seem so wary about taking Echo to see her?" Nora asked.

"Hearthmothers are what make it possible to master your element in a day. They perform a ritual that just makes everything click. But... it's a strange experience. I'd always hoped I could spare Echo from it."

"How strange?" Paige leaned forward, her eyes filled with curiosity.

"Well—" Ali's mouth slammed shut as the back door flew open.

Seth burst in wearing a huge smile. "Nor, I have fantastic news! I couldn't wait to tell you."

Paige's chair legs scraped loudly on the tile. "I need to head out."

Nora's brow wrinkled. "Paige, don't go. I was just about to whip up lunch for us."

Seth froze in place, his smile fading.

"You'll have to eat without me. I've suddenly lost my appetite." Paige brushed past Seth and slipped out the back door without a backward glance.

Seth cast a sidelong look at the door. "She's clearly insane."

Nora gasped. "Seth!" Her gaze darted to the open back window.

No way Paige hadn't heard that insult. Ali's stomach churned.

"Come on, Nor. Anyone who'd turn down your cooking *must* be crazy." He dropped onto the stool beside Maalik's with a crooked grin. "You can count me in. I'm famished."

Nora crossed her arms. "Why am I not surprised?" She sighed, heading for the kitchenette. "You're lucky I love you. If you weren't my brother, I'd kick you out on your ass for chasing my friend away."

Maalik tipped his mug in Seth's direction. "So, what's the news?"

Seth's grin returned, brighter than ever. "I just put in an offer for the perfect farmhouse. I won't find out if I get it for a while, but I have a really good feeling about this one."

"That is fantastic news!" Nora brightened.

Ali added, "I'll be ready with congratulations when I get back from my trip."

Seth cocked his head. "What trip?"

"Ali's heading off on a holiday jaunt to Paradise Plains," Nora said. She snorted. "A holiday... right."

"Why not? Just cause you're heading there for an important reason doesn't mean you shouldn't treat it like a holiday." Maalik's mug thumped on the bar top.

Nora hummed. "He's right. I don't know anyone who deserves a break more than you, Ali."

Ali pursed her lips. "You know what? That's not terrible advice..." She grinned and stood, her spirits lifting. "Well, I'd better get back to work. I'll be sure to think of you all fondly when I'm lounging around on my holiday." She winked.

"Rub it in, why don't ya?" Maalik grumbled, a tiny smile tugging at the corners of his lips.

Nora handed her a paper to-go box. "Have a great time, Ali. I'll see you next week."

Seth added, "Stay out of mischief, if you can manage it," with a wink of his own. "Or don't. More fun that way."

She waved, knowing she'd miss her friends more than anything. But at least they'd given her a new perspective.

Who says this trip can't be fun? Sure, visiting the hearthmother was bound to be draining. But they still had days of travel through the countryside to look forward to. The least she could do for Echo was to make the rest of the journey an adventure worth remembering. *Paradise Plains, here I come!*

TROUBLE

Lio

The sun beat down, bright and hot, on the morning their journey began. Lio hauled his and Tini's supplies onto the porch, frowning as a bead of sweat rolled down his forehead.

"Something wrong?" Tini rocked on the porch chair, her head cocked.

"Just wondering why I let you talk me into this." He swiped the droplet away with the back of his fist. "Sure you don't want to postpone until the weather's nicer?"

"Yeah… I don't think so. If I let you put it off, you'll have me waiting until I'm ninety." She chuckled. "Besides, it's a beautiful day. I have no clue why you're complaining."

He scowled. "Oh, I don't know. Might be the fact that I'm destined to end up carrying most of our supplies." He nudged her stuffed backpack with the toe of his boot. "Couldn't you have packed lighter?"

Tini wrinkled her nose. "Just because you have no appreciation for fashion doesn't mean the rest of us have to suffer."

"He appreciates fashion," a familiar voice interjected. "You must not have seen your brother's extensive sock collection."

His shoulders stiffened, and he breathed in, long and slow, before swiveling to face the newcomers.

"Good morning, Ali." Tini grinned. "You too, Echo. Are you excited for our trip?"

Echo's head bobbed, setting her pigtails bouncing. "I'm glad you're coming, Tini! I like fashion, too. Will you let me see the outfits you packed when we stop for the night?"

Tini hopped to her feet. "I'll do you one better than that. You can try some of them on. We can have our own fashion show." She slung an arm around Echo's shoulders. "How does that sound?"

Echo squealed. "So fun! Yay, I can't wait."

Lio got caught up for a moment, basking in the glow of Ali's smile. She was positively luminous as she watched Tini and Echo giggling together on the porch. Unlike the girls, who'd opted for summery dresses, Ali was dressed much like him, in simple traveling garb, the pants loaded with pockets. But one thing was suspiciously absent...

"Where's your supplies?" He crossed his arms, hoping he wouldn't be forced to share his tent with two more bodies. It would be tight already with him and Tini wedged inside.

Ali stepped aside, revealing a narrow, hovering cart that had been hidden behind her. "I borrowed the shop's supply wagon. Figured we'd make better time if we weren't loaded down with bags. There's room for your bags, too, and it's imbued with enough kinetic magic to get there and back."

"Clever plan." He grunted as he hauled Tini's bag off the porch and tossed it inside. "Thanks."

Ali grabbed his forearm before he could return for the rest. "No. Thank you, Lio." She lowered her voice. "I know you didn't want to do this. But I'm so glad you changed your mind."

His arm tingled from the heat of her touch. He lifted his gaze from her fingers and met her eyes, his breath catching as he spotted the sincerity shining back at him. And gratitude. Nothing about that look screamed desire, but that didn't stop his lips from tingling and his body from swaying closer. *Goddess, why is she so ridiculously tempting?*

He shook off her touch. "Don't mention it," he stated gruffly.

"Too late," Ali sing-songed. "I already did."

They made good time throughout the morning, and before Lio knew it, the sun was high overhead. They chose a shady spot beneath a willow tree to break for lunch. He'd been planning to munch on a fruit and nut bar, but when Ali spread out a picnic blanket and doled out an impressive spread of crusty bread, garlicky bean dip, and a rainbow of cut up vegetables, he decided to save his bar for later.

"Finish your veggies, Echo," Ali said sternly.

Echo crammed a carrot into her mouth, crunching noisily. After swallowing, she hopped up on her knees and pointed to a field of wildflowers just ahead. "Can I go pick a bouquet? Pleeaasse?"

Ali grinned crookedly. "Sure—after you finish your veggies."

Echo scooped her remaining vegetables into her hand and stuffed them all into her mouth. "Fere. Oow cab I gof?" she somehow managed to utter around them.

Tini giggled. "You want me to come with you?"

Echo's head bobbed excitedly. She thrust out a hand, and Tini took it. Then they skipped off together, heading for the field.

"Your sister is amazing." Ali sighed. "I was worried they wouldn't have much to talk about, considering their age gap. But boy, was I wrong."

"I know what you mean. I never would've guessed they'd be thick as thieves this fast."

Echo and Tini had spent the entire hike chatting together, the subjects ranging from serious to silly and everything in between.

"Echo's been having a rough time lately. It's so nice to see her having fun again."

A dull pang settled in Lio's heart. "Tini has been having a rough go, too. Guess they have that in common."

"Suppose they understand each other in a way no one else can. Must feel nice to finally discover a connection like that." Ali nudged his side with her elbow.

He snagged a snap pea, chewing thoughtfully. He couldn't deny that Ali was right. Tini was clearly enjoying herself as much as Echo. There was a new lightness in her spirit, almost as if she'd found something in Echo that she'd been craving for ages. Something that, try as he might, he just couldn't provide for her.

"Hey, you all right?" Ali asked.

He buried his morose thoughts. "Yeah, I'm—"

"Lio!" Tini shouted. "Come quick! Echo's stuck!"

Ali bolted to her feet and sprinted across the field, leaving Lio to race after her. His mind swam with worry as his feet pounded the dirt.

Was Echo okay?

What could she have gotten stuck in?

What would they do if she was seriously injured out here in the middle of nowhere with no access to a healer?

But as he skidded to a halt beside Ali, he shoved all the worries aside. He was trained for this. The brigade didn't just put out fires, they handled their share of rescues as well. He'd just have to rely on his training to save her from whatever trouble she'd gotten herself mixed up in.

"Where is she?" Ali screeched. "Echo? Are you all right?"

"I'm okay, Mom," she replied, though they still couldn't see her. Lio's gaze zeroed in on the likeliest hiding spot—an enormous pricker bush half-hidden behind the knee-high wildflowers.

Tini chewed on her lip and pointed at the bush, confirming his suspicions. "I told her not to go in there. I should've grabbed her before she climbed in."

"Good goddess! Baby, are you hurt?" Ali called into the bush.

"Only when I try to back up," Echo said.

"Hold on. I'm coming to get you." Ali bent at the waist, her gaze hard, jaw set.

"No, you don't." Lio snagged Ali's waist and lifted her before she could drop to her knees. "Stay right where you are, Echo. Backing up will only make it worse."

Ali wiggled in his grasp. "I have to get her out of there!"

"Let me handle this. I've dealt with this bush before."

Ali's scowl turned into a quizzical head tilt. "You have?"

"Yep. Usually it's livestock that get stuck, not little girls." He dropped Ali behind him, ignoring how perfect she felt in his arms. *Time and a place, Stelios.* He turned to Tini. "Run back to the supply cart and bring me my pack."

"On it." Tini sprinted off.

"Don't worry." He flashed Ali the reassuring grin he reserved for terrified parents. "I'll have her out of there in no time." Then he dropped to his knees and inspected the prickers, planning the most efficient way to slice through them.

Echo's voice warbled. "You sure you can get me out, Lio?"

"Don't worry, Trouble. You'll be free before you know it."

Tini's footsteps smacked the ground. "Here." She wheezed, tossing him his pack.

"Thanks." He dug inside and pulled out a large hunting knife. "Echo, I'm going to cut the branches that are keeping you from backing up. I need you to stay very still. Can you do that for me?"

"Okay."

He drew a deep breath and got to work. The first branch snapped easily. Then the next, and the next.

Ali paced behind him, wringing her hands. "How much longer?"

"Almost done." He sawed through one more branch and tossed it aside. "All right. I think that ought to do it. When I say go, I want you to try backing out again, Echo. Very slowly. If anything starts to hurt, I need you to stop and tell me. Got it?"

"I can do that."

"All right. Go." His heart thudded heavily, the moments passing like hours. But before long, he spotted her legs wriggling out. She shimmied like a worm, crawling backward until her head popped out.

"Echo! Thank the goddess!" Ali scooped her up, raining kisses on her hair.

"Jeez, Mom. I'm fine," Echo insisted.

"What in the realm would possess you to crawl in there?" Ali asked as she released Echo, her gaze traveling up and down her body, searching for injuries, no doubt.

Echo held out her hands, revealing a tiny black kitten cupped in her palms. "Look. I heard her meowing. She was stuck, too."

"Well, guess you're both lucky Lio was here to save you." Ali nudged Echo's shoulder. "Go on. Tell him thank you."

"I don't know if I wanna." Echo scowled. "He called me trouble."

Lio's stomach clenched.

Tini giggled, breaking the tension. "Don't be upset, Echo. Lio only gives nicknames to people he likes the most. You should hear all the dumb names he calls his best friend."

Ali laughed. "She's right. I've heard him and Dav at it. You'd think they don't even know each other's names from how many goofy things they call each other."

Echo's brows pinched together. "Really? Then what does he call you?" she asked Tini.

Tini rolled her eyes. "Runt. It's silly, isn't it?"

"Guess I can be trouble if you're a runt." Echo giggled.

"I'll help you think up a good nickname for him." Tini grinned mischievously. "Or you can use mine if you want."

Echo bounced on her toes. "Ooo, what is it?"

Tini leaned in, her voice hushed and eyes alight, as if she were sharing forbidden knowledge. "Big Butt."

Echo burst into a giggle fit. "Big Butt. That's hilarious!"

Tini said, "I know. Fits him perfectly, doesn't it?"

Lio dragged a hand down his face.

"Hey, can I hold the kitten?" Tini asked as she scanned the little ball of fluff in Echo's arms. "Aww, look, I think she's a girl."

Echo nodded and passed her over. "She's purring like crazy. That means she likes us, right, Mom?" Then she glanced up at Ali, batting her eyelashes.

"Oh no. I know that look. You're not keeping her." Ali crossed her arms. "We spend too much time at work and school to take care of a pet."

Tini frowned. "You sound like Lio." She narrowed her eyes in his direction. "I always wanted a kitten, too, but Big Butt would never let me have one."

"Watch it, Runt." Lio stuffed his knife into his pack. "And you know we can't keep her either. Same reason."

Echo grabbed Ali's sleeve. "Can we at least take her with us while we're hiking? She's all alone. Someone needs to look after her."

"I don't know..." Ali started.

"I bet someone in Paradise Plains will want her," Tini added.

Lio knew he should shut it down. Tini and Echo were cut from the same cloth. Give them a foothold, and they'd build a fortress before anyone even realized what was happening. But as he gazed into their hopeful faces, he just couldn't bear to crush their dreams.

"Let them keep her—for now," he advised. "There were always plenty of cats on the plains. Shouldn't be hard to find her a new owner, I reckon."

Echo squealed. "Can we, Mom? Lio says it's okay."

Ali flashed a lopsided grin. "I guess it's only fair not to separate you so soon, after you risked your life to save her."

Echo nodded sagely. "I did. You all saw it."

Tini chuckled and handed the kitten back to Echo. "Come on. I'll help you think up a name for her, too." They skipped off together again, heading for the picnic blanket.

Lio and Ali trailed behind them. "Sorry. I'm sure you'd rather I'd back you up about the kitten, instead of giving in." He grimaced. "I'm not usually such a pushover."

"It's all right. I kind of like knowing there's a soft, gooey center under that hard shell of yours." She grinned. "And thank you for helping Echo. I know you don't want to hear it, but I'm really glad you came."

His cheeks warmed. "It was nothing I haven't done for dozens of lambs over the years."

"Sure." Ali squeezed his forearm. "Don't worry. I'll hold off on swooning at your feet, my humble knight." She lifted a brow, smirking.

He let out a rare chuckle. "That's all I ask."

Ali jogged ahead and started cleaning up the remains of their lunch. Lio hung back with a sigh, his gaze drifting to where his sister stood with Echo, cooing and petting the kitten. He could hardly believe she'd gotten herself stuck in that bush just to save that tiny ball of fluff. *I had it right. Trouble with a capital T.*

Tini's words returned to plague him. Was he actually starting to *like* Echo? He'd sworn for so long that he'd never make the mistake of shackling his life to another child he had no business raising.

Maybe she's not the one in trouble after all. I am...

STALEMATE

Ali

Some holiday. Ali shook her head as she attempted to set up her new tent, dragging a flexible metal pole out of the canvas. She'd gotten it wrong the first time and had to start over. And she wasn't faring much better on her second attempt either.

At least Echo was having fun. Her laughter filled the clearing as Cinder, the kitten, waged war on a long blade of grass that Tini wielded like a sword.

"Need some help with that?"

Ali flinched, then peeked over her shoulder. Lio stood behind her, bathed in the last rays of the dying sun. "Desperately. I'm positive an imp designed this. Feels like I'm solving the realm's trickiest riddle."

"Did it come with instructions?" he asked, kneeling beside her.

She grabbed the sheet of parchment and handed it over. "Yep. But I'm still lost."

He glanced at the sheet, then squinted at the tent. "I think I see where you went wrong." He handed back the paper, their fingers brushing.

Ali fought to hide the shiver that ran through her. "I'm glad you do. Echo and I would probably end up sleeping under the stars if I had to figure this out on my own."

"I've done that before. It's not too bad, so long as it doesn't rain." He moved deftly, his strong hands making quick work of the maddening puzzle. "Help me feed this pole through."

She followed his instructions while mulling over his words. Lio had always been stingy when talking about his past. Should she push for more, or would he clam up immediately?

"Did you enjoy that moonlight slumber alone... or with a sweetheart?"

The corners of his lips ticked up. "How did you guess?"

She chuckled and lowered her voice. "I might've snuck out to a few fields in my day." She glanced at him as he drew closer, but his gaze was glued to the tent. "Funny, I didn't peg you for a rebellious teen."

He kneeled beside her while securing the pole to the ground. "I had my moments, before..." he trailed off, frowning.

"Before what?" she asked softly.

"I think that should do it." He stood and smoothed a hand over the tent's side.

Yep, clammed up right on cue. She swallowed her disappointment and flashed a grateful smile. "Thank you. My hero."

He stepped closer, and her breath caught. "I wish you'd stop calling me that." His hand drifted up between them, and he tucked a lock of her hair behind her ear. "I'm not a hero."

She scoffed. "Okay, Chief. If you say so." She waited for him to drop his hand. To step back. Instead, he trailed a warm touch down her neck, setting off tingling embers on her skin.

Ali watched him, not daring to move a muscle. He stared back, his gaze darting between her eyes—and her mouth.

Just put me out of my misery and kiss me already! She had half a mind to do it herself. It would be so easy to lift onto her toes and finally find out if his lips were half as soft as she'd pictured in her head. But something—an instinct she couldn't quite grasp hold of while caught in the spell of Lio's hypnotic gaze—held her back.

"Mom, the tent looks great! Can I go in now?"

There's the something. She backed away, blowing out a sigh as she realized the tent had been blocking her and Lio's frustrating stalemate from Echo's view. "Sure, baby. You can go in." She rounded the tent and slid down the zipper.

Echo popped up from her spot and grabbed Tini's hand. Then she hauled her toward the tent, all smiles. "Come on, Tini. We can play fashion show now! Cinder can be our audience."

"All right, I'm coming. Let me just grab my bag." Tini chuckled. "Here, take Cinder inside." She handed the kitten to Echo.

Lio strode forward, his gaze on the ground. "I'll start the fire."

"I can help with that." Ali strolled to the firepit that Lio had already loaded with downed branches they'd collected throughout the day.

"Suppose you'll get it going quicker than I will." Lio turned for the cart. "I'll work on dinner then."

Ali called on her talent, releasing twin streams of flame from her hands. The wood crackled and hissed, lighting easily.

"Wow. I hope my talent is fire," Tini exclaimed.

She cut off the flames and turned with a rueful grin. "Sure you don't want to wish for something else?"

Tini had heard what she'd said in the tavern. She had to know how much easier her life would be if she were blessed with a different element. Still, she shook her head. "Nope. That was way better than watching Lio get everything all wet."

Lio strode up behind Tini and tousled the top of her head. "I ought to soak you for that."

Tini shrieked and darted away. "Oh no you don't!" She giggled as she ducked into the tent, lugging her stuffed bag inside.

Ali took a tentative step toward Lio. "So what are we cooking? I'm not half as good as Nora, but I can do more than just burn stuff."

"Good to know." Lio placed a bag on the ground beside the fire. "I brought—"

"Mooom! We need your help!" Echo yelled.

"Go ahead." Lio jerked his head toward the tent. "I'll get the food started."

"You sure?"

He nodded. "Yeah. I'm all set."

She slipped into the tent, chuckling at the mess. "Wow, you really didn't waste any time, did you?" Clothes were strewn everywhere, covering most of the floor. Cinder pawed at a fluffy sweater, circling it to create a makeshift nest next to a lantern glowing brightly with light magic.

Echo waved her forward, the sleeve of her borrowed blouse flapping off the edge of her fingers. "Get in here, Mom. Tini needs your help with her hair."

"You do?" Her gaze shot to Tini, who sat cross-legged among the sea of cloth.

Tini nodded shyly. "Echo mentioned you had a trick for straightening yours. I've always wondered what my hair would look like straight." She gathered her curly brown locks in one hand. "Would you mind—"

"Of course, I don't mind." Ali nudged a pair of trousers aside and plopped down behind Tini. "Can I use your brush? And I'll need a few hair ties."

Tini handed the items over. "Sure."

"First step is to section it." She divided Tini's hair into four sections, tying three into quick, messy buns. "Let me know if I'm hurting you."

"You're not," Tini replied.

"Now, the trick is to apply plenty of heat." She placed the brush between her hands and called on her talent again, more carefully this time. The bristles heated under her touch, but she cut off the flow of magic before they burst into flames. Then she dragged the brush through Tini's hair, beginning with the bottom section she'd left loose.

"It's working?" Tini asked.

"Yep. I helped Davos imbue metal brushes that work the same way. I'll bring you one when we're back in Everpass. Just be careful to keep the bristles away from your scalp; they can get really hot."

Echo grinned. "I like it already. You look so pretty, Tini."

"Thank you." Tini's voice choked up, and she swiped a thumb beneath her eye.

Ali's strokes slowed. "Are you all right?"

"Yeah. This is just... really nice." She sighed. "It's always just been me and Lio, and he's not exactly into this kind of thing."

Ali's chest ached. She could certainly relate. In her youth, she'd always worn her hair in braids, often much more intricate than the pigtails Echo favored. Her childhood village was full of women who were experts at plaiting hair. But once she'd struck out on her own, she couldn't replicate the style. Yeah, she did a passable job on her daughter, but braiding her own hair? Not a chance. It had always ended up looking like a hot mess and left her yearning for the community she'd left behind.

So she'd shorn off her long locks and started using her magic to straighten the rest. And surprisingly enough, she loved it. It was one of the first times in her life she'd found a use for her talent that she could be proud of. Since then, the short straight bob had become her signature look.

But now didn't seem like the time for a stroll down memory lane. And though she was dying to ask why Tini and Lio were all alone, it wasn't her place to pry. So she just said, "It is nice, isn't it?"

Luckily, Echo had no problem snooping. "What about your mom? Why doesn't she help you with your hair?"

Tini shrugged. "My parents died when I was really little. I barely even remember them."

"I'm sorry." Ali's heart clenched as she let down the next section of Tini's hair. "That had to be really tough on you."

"Yeah..." Tini's fingers tangled in the hem of her dress. "But at least I have Lio. He tells me stories about our parents all the time, since he remembers them way better than I do. He even had a portrait made, so I'll never forget what they looked like."

Ali's eyes stung as she recalled the painting hanging over the mantel in their living room.

"Can I see it?" Echo asked. "When we get back home?"

Tini chuckled. "Sure. You'll both have to come over for dinner one night. I bet Lio would like that, too." She reached up, fingering the straight ends on one side of her head. "I'm glad he's making new friends."

"Me too." Echo glanced up at Ali, a poorly fitted floppy hat shadowing her eyes. "Mom, you get to be friends with Lio, and I can keep being friends with Tini. Deal?"

Ali flashed a bright smile and lifted a brow. "Hey, why do I get the grumpy one?"

Echo giggled. "Because he likes you. He thinks I'm trouble, remember?"

Her stomach clenched. *Leave it to Echo to remind me of the sad truth.* She couldn't let herself forget that. No matter how selfless Lio had been, taking care of his sister like she was his own child, that didn't change the fact that he wanted nothing to do with *her* kid.

She put on a show of sighing heavily. "All right. Suppose I can stand in the line of fire for this one. But you owe me. Remember that the next time I beg you to eat your vegetables."

Echo giggled again, then pouted her lips. "Ugh. Fine."

Ali set the brush down. "You're all done. Did you pack a mirror?"

Tini nodded and dug into her bag. Then a luminous smile crossed her face as she stared at her reflection. "It's lovely. Thank you, Ali."

"Ooo, do me." Echo leaned forward eagerly.

Tini spun the mirror around. Echo tilted her head this way and that, making the hat flop all over. "I. Look. Amaaazz-ing!"

Ali and Tini's chuckles rang out in the tent.

Echo stopped primping in the mirror and threw her arms around Tini's waist, squeezing her tightly. "Thanks for playing fashion show with me, Tini. You're the best!"

Ali couldn't deny... this was nice. Really nice. Tini fit into their lives like a lost puzzle piece. Pity that her brother's edges were slightly askew.

Lio's voice intruded on the peaceful moment. "Um... I might need a little help out here."

Echo nudged Ali's leg. "Go on. He's yours, remember?"

She rose with a chuckle. "Yeah, yeah. I'm going." The stars glowed brightly overhead as she stepped into the clearing. "What seems to be the problem? Oh…" The fire had guttered down to embers, the skewers of meat hanging above it still raw and dripping with juices.

Lio palmed the back of his neck. "I left to gather more wood and came back to this. Think you can save them?"

"Sure." She strode closer, raising her hands. Fire blazed from her palms, setting the logs alight and the meat sizzling. "You're welcome to call me your hero. I don't mind at all."

He let out a rare chuckle. "Suppose you earned it, hero." He yelled over his shoulder, "Girls, time to eat."

As they gathered around the fire, eating and laughing under a blanket of stars, it finally felt like the holiday she'd been imagining. But before long, Echo's increasing yawns became too difficult to ignore.

"All right. Off to bed with you." She started to rise from her spot, but Echo grabbed Tini's hand.

"Will you tuck me into bed tonight?" Echo asked.

Tini glanced her way, seeking permission with her gaze.

Ali nodded. "Good night, sweetheart. I'll join you shortly."

"Night, Mom." Echo planted a wet kiss on her cheek. "Night… Big Butt." Echo darted off, giggling riotously, with Tini following closely behind her.

Ali's heart raced. She stared into the fire, taking comfort in the familiar movements of the dancing flames.

She'd assumed Lio would head to bed as soon as the girls did. Did he want to talk? Was that why he was still there, staring at the fire pensively?

Then again, he was a man of few words. Maybe he was waiting for her to say something. *Dammit, say something, Ali.*

Tini ducked out of their tent and headed for the one she was sharing with Lio, waving as she passed.

Still, Ali sat there, suspiciously tongue-tied.

Lio shifted on the log he'd been using as a makeshift bench. "It's going to be another long day tomorrow."

"Right." She tugged her knitted shawl around her shoulders.

"Guess I better put out the fire and head to bed. You should probably do the same."

She gulped. "Yeah. I will." She stood. "Good night, Lio."

"Night," he replied. Then he stepped up to the fire pit, lifting his hands. Twin streams of water shot out, extinguishing the fire swiftly.

Ali plodded toward her tent, burying a sigh. It was just as well he'd sent her to bed. She had to stop imagining a future with him that could never happen. She'd never been surer of it than when she watched his talent snuff out her own. *Who am I kidding? We're just like fire and water. We might spark and steam, but we were never meant to mix.*

Harsh Realities

Lio

"Are we there yet?" Echo whined as they crested a small rise.

"Almost," Lio answered. "If we keep hiking at this pace, we're only about an hour out."

Tini groaned. "An hour? Are you sure? Feels like we've been walking forever."

He scanned the girls, spotting droopy shoulders and heavy footsteps. He'd been hoping to reach Paradise Plains by nightfall, but ending a hair too short wasn't so bad. If he'd been on his own, he'd have pushed harder, yet that didn't seem wise with Tini and Echo flagging.

He pulled Ali aside. "I think we should find a spot to camp for the night. If I'm remembering it right, there'll be a stream over there." He pointed to a grove of trees, which stood out starkly among the rolling grass hills of the plains.

"Agreed. Let's go." Ali started off without another word. And no grin either.

The stream was right where he recalled. As the sun sank slowly into the trees, he pitched the tents. Ali started a fire and got to work on dinner while the girls played with Cinder. Then together they scarfed down a quick meal of crackers, jerky, and apples by the fire, and the girls headed off to their tents, leaving him and Ali alone.

She'd been strangely quiet throughout the day, her smiles dimmer than usual. He didn't like it. Not one bit. He was starting to wonder if he'd done something wrong.

Goddess, why did I touch her? That had to be it. He hadn't meant to make her uncomfortable, but clearly, he had.

He wasn't sure what had possessed him at that moment. It was like his fingers had a mind of their own; the stupid digits had been determined to discover if her hair was as soft as it looked. Her skin, too. And of course it was. Now that he knew it for a fact it didn't bring him any relief. He was dying to touch her again, but he curled his hands into fists to deny himself from giving in to the urge.

"You tired?" she asked softly.

He shrugged. "Not really." The sun had barely sunk below the horizon. Yeah, his legs and feet were a tad sore from walking all day, but he had a demanding job, just like Ali did. It would take a lot more than a long hike to send him to his bed so early.

"Me neither." She sighed.

"Seems like something's bothering you today." He gulped heavily. "Can I ask what it is?"

He braced himself, preparing for her to chew him out. She'd demand he keep his hands to himself. Tell him they'd never be anything more than friends.

"I'm nervous about tomorrow. Visiting a nymph village. I didn't exactly have the best experience at my last one."

Relief washed over him, along with a jolt of surprise. "You didn't?"

She shook her head. "Nope."

Silence fell over them, lasting so long he was certain she would leave it at that. But then she exhaled and said, "I have a feeling my upbringing was a lot different from yours. I come from a village far from here, a few weeks' travel at the least. It's on the outskirts of Seahaven, near Sunken Cove."

"Seahaven. That is far." He'd never been there, but he'd seen it on a map. You couldn't even reach it on foot, not entirely. There was one stretch of water that had to be crossed by boat.

"Yep. Was a time when I didn't care where I ended up, so long as it was far away from there."

He picked up a stick and busied himself rearranging the logs in the fire. "Must've really been bad if that was the case."

"You could say that." She tilted her head. "Can I ask you something?"

"Shoot."

"Are there harems in Paradise Plains?"

"Some." It was bound to happen, considering how hard it was for nymphs to have sons. No one batted an eye if a man on the plains decided he wanted more than one partner. The women, least of all. It was one thing he disliked most about how things worked back home.

"Why don't you have one?"

He almost choked on his own tongue. Then he set down the stick and faced Ali, lifting a brow. "I can barely handle the three girls with me now, and none of you are demanding I give you babies. What would I do with a damned harem?"

Ali winced. "Sorry. Sore subject?"

"Something like that."

Her hands twisted in her lap. "I'm only asking because... my father had a harem."

"He did?"

"Yep. My mother was just one in a long line of women who slept with him on the off chance that she might have a son. Sad to say that he didn't care to bond with me—or any of the rest of his many offspring."

Anger roiled in his gut. "That's a damn shame. For what it's worth, I'm sorry."

"Yeah. Me too."

"What about your mother?"

"She wasn't very thrilled when the son she was hoping for turned out to be a girl." She grinned ruefully. "I could always tell she was disappointed in me while she was still around."

"What happened to her?" he asked.

"She kept trying for a boy. She'd leave me with neighbors when it was her turn with my old man. But she never ended up getting pregnant again, no matter how hard she tried. Then she got sick and died when I was nine."

"I'm sorry to hear that." He certainly knew what it was like to lose a parent. "What about your father's kids? Did you get on with them?"

"Some of them were nice to me. One of their mothers even took me in after my mom passed. But things weren't so great after I discovered I could summon fire, just after my sixteenth nameday." She stared into the fire, her gaze heavy with remembered sorrow. "My village followed the old ways. They took all the ancient legends to heart."

"Oh…" He'd heard all the old tales. Everyone in his village had. But he'd never once imagined that they were real. "I didn't realize people still believed in those."

She brightened slightly. "They don't follow the old legends in Paradise Plains?"

"Nope."

"Davos hinted as much, but I wasn't sure if I could believe him." Her shoulders slumped. "I'm glad to hear that. The folks back home wanted nothing to do with me after I discovered my talent."

"No one on the plains will think you're cursed. There are a handful of fire nymphs living there. There was even a fire summoner elder when I left." He shrugged. "No one treats them any differently."

Her mouth dropped open. "You're serious?"

He nodded.

"Good goddess. That's so different from where I come from." She rubbed her palms down her legs. "My life would've probably turned out way differently if I'd grown up without that stupid superstition hanging over my head."

"Do you wish it had?"

Her gaze turned pensive. "Maybe." But after another moment, she shook her head. "No, I take that back. Because then I wouldn't have Echo."

"I'm going to guess you didn't join a harem to have her." His stomach turned at the mere thought.

She scoffed. "Definitely not. Though I didn't do much better choosing a partner, when all was said and done."

"I'm sorry to hear that." *Though not as sorry as I should be.* She'd just admitted a huge regret, but he couldn't help feeling a little relieved that she wasn't secretly holding a torch for Echo's dad.

She explained, "I left my village when I turned eighteen and found work at the fish market in Seahaven. At first, I just kept to myself, and it was surprisingly... nice. No one there knew me. And there was no one judging me for something I had no choice about." She wrinkled her nose. "Then I met Echo's dad. He was a sailor, and our time together was passionate and exciting—until I discovered I was pregnant. He didn't stick around long after that."

Anger swelled in his chest again. "So he was a fool."

"Pretty much." Ali's head bowed. "It's funny, I thought I would save Echo the pain I went through by never courting a nymph. There's not much chance of a human ever collecting a harem, you know? But her father just ended up running away the first chance he got. Now she's even worse off than I was. At least my old man was there, even if he wanted nothing to do with me."

He wasn't sure what to say to that. Luckily, she saved him the trouble by changing the subject.

"Remember when I told you I created that new model just to help earn enough coin to help Echo?"

"Yeah."

She stared into the fire. "That wasn't the whole truth. I like knowing that something I created might save another woman from making the same mistakes I did. Maybe if I'd had all my books and a massager back then, I wouldn't have spent so long with a man that I knew was all wrong for me."

That was certainly understandable given what that scoundrel put her through. He was impressed she'd found a way to channel her pain into something that could help others.

Ali had lived a hard life. She'd been abandoned by the people who should've loved her the most. Perhaps that was why she took nothing too seriously, breezing through life with smiles and jokes by the dozen.

She must be using humor to keep people from probing into the harsh realities she'd escaped from.

But she'd shared the truth with him. Suddenly he found himself eager to do the same. There weren't many people in his life that he trusted with the sad facts of his past. Maybe she could be one of them...

"My dad didn't have a harem."

"No?"

"Don't get me wrong, there were plenty of nymphs with harems on the plains, but not him. He loved my mother too much to want anyone else."

"Is that why you got so steamed when I asked why you don't have one?"

"Not exactly..."

Laying Bare

Ali

Ali perched on the edge of a large rock ringing an old firepit. She could hardly believe Lio was sharing his past with her, or that she'd spilled so many details about hers. Still, it felt good to let it all out. And knowing that she—and more importantly, Echo—wouldn't be subjected to the disdain she'd grown up around, calmed a lot of her fears for tomorrow.

But now, curiosity prickled her spine. She hadn't expected Lio to react so strongly when she'd asked him about harems. There had to be a story behind it.

His chest rose and fell as he sat beside her, the firelight reflecting off his pinched features. "I bet you've been wondering why it's just me and Tini who moved to Everpass."

"Tini talked about it with us a little yesterday. I'm sorry about your parents."

Lio stiffened. "Did she tell you how it happened?"

"No. Just that she was so young, she barely remembers them."

"That's true. Tini had just turned five, and I was seventeen on the night we lost our parents."

"You were both so young." She could certainly relate. Losing her mother at nine had been devastating. No one should have to say goodbye to their parents so soon.

"They died in a fire," he choked out, barely above a whisper.

She grabbed his hand and squeezed, her mind whirling with questions she refused to ask.

How did it start? Were either of them there when it happened? She found it hard to believe that Lio wouldn't have done all he could to save them, had he been there, unless... Had his talent not surfaced yet?

But as much as she was dying to discover the answers, he clearly needed a moment to collect himself, and she was willing to wait.

After a long pause, he drew a shaky breath, then said, "Remember that sweetheart you asked about the other day? The one I'd sneak out to meet?"

She nodded, her stomach churning.

"It wasn't just one. I had a few. And on the night of the fire, I was with one of them." His eyes pinched closed. "It was like a nightmare. First, I smelled the smoke. Then I spotted the flames. We were far enough off that we couldn't be sure what was burning, but I knew..." His fingers clenched around hers so tight she could scarcely stand it.

"We ran back so fast. No one else from the village had gotten there yet, but by then the fire was everywhere."

Ali lifted her free hand to her lips, her eyes filling with tears.

"I went in after them. My parents were upstairs and Tini was on the ground floor, so I went for her first. I managed to put out enough flames to get to her. I carried her out, and by then, lots of folks had arrived. I left her with a healer and tried to go back in... but the elders wouldn't allow it. The fire had spread so far and so fast that the top floor was completely engulfed. And I... couldn't save them."

"I can't even imagine... I'm so sorry, Lio." How awful it must've been, to witness that. He'd tried so hard to save his family, only for it to end in tragedy.

"They must have been fast asleep when it happened. It's the only explanation that makes any sense. My father could summon water. And my mother summoned air. They could've put out the flames if they'd realized what was happening." He sighed. "I always wondered what would've happened if I'd been there that night. Maybe I'd have been able to get to them all in time," he admitted gruffly, his voice thick with pain.

"Or maybe you'd have been sleeping, too." She squeezed his hand again. "Did you ever find out what started it?"

"It was a lightning strike. A random fluke of nature that could've happened to anyone. I just wish it hadn't been them."

She smiled softly. "Well, I'm glad you made it out. And that you saved Tini."

He scoffed. "Leave it to you to point out all the positives."

She wrinkled her nose. "Would you rather I curse you for being a normal teen, doing typical things that everyone else does at that age?"

"Not when you put it like that."

"The way I see it, that fire was no one's fault, and you certainly couldn't have predicted it. Sure, you weren't where you were supposed to be, but if you had been, there's no telling if it would've made things better, or worse. And you did everything you could once you realized what was happening. Without you, Tini would be gone, too. You saved her, Lio."

"I should've saved them all..." His jaw tensed.

Suddenly, his refusal to think of himself as a hero began to make a lot more sense. No wonder he'd dedicated his life to saving people and fighting fires. He was determined to make up for the one mistake he just couldn't forget.

"Anyway." He exhaled heavily. "I told you all that so I could explain why your question rubbed me the wrong way."

She nodded, allowing the topic change, even though she had a lot more that she wanted to say. One day, she'd get Lio to see how wrong he was. She'd never met anyone half as heroic, and even if it took her a lifetime, she'd make him see that.

"After they passed, I started taking care of Tini. I had to grow up really fast. No part of me was ready to be her dad, but I wasn't willing to let anyone else raise her. I was all she had left."

"I know what you mean. I wasn't much older when I had Echo." She'd been nineteen when she discovered she was pregnant. "It's not easy being a parent so young."

"It was hard, but that wasn't the only thing I was dealing with back then. I started to realize how much my parents had been sheltering me from. While they were alive, they always kept us on a short leash. They'd refused to let me court anyone while I was still finishing school. I can't even say how many times I tried to talk them out of that rule."

"Thus the sneaking out," she added.

"Yeah... But it didn't take me long to figure out why they'd been so strict. Women started throwing themselves at me. I was barely grown, and suddenly I had women older than my mother chasing after me."

Her eyes widened. "Seriously?"

"That wasn't even the worst of it. Because when I turned them down, they'd try shoving their daughters at me." He stared into the flames blankly. "Sometimes it was little girls scarcely older than Echo."

She swayed slightly as a dawning realization washed over her. *Good goddess. That's why he was so adamant about Echo not following him the first day we met.* All this time, she'd been so certain he was just being a grumpy jerk. That he hated kids—or at the least, that he wasn't a fan of hers. But now... this explained so much about how he reacted that day, and why.

"Before long, the elders started in, lecturing me about birthrates and my duty to the future of nymph-kind." He shuddered. "All this while I was learning how to take care of Tini. I felt like I was being corralled into a future I'd never signed up for."

"That sounds horrid." She'd always hated the way harems worked, but she'd never thought about it from the male perspective. The burden they were under to provide the women of their villages with sons must be so intense. She wasn't surprised so many of them caved under the pressure.

"I didn't make it another year on the plains before we packed up and left. I knew I had to give Tini my full focus. There was no way I could handle raising a bunch more kids. And I knew I could never be one of those men who ignored their children. If I ever have a kid of my own, I'd want us to have the same close relationship I had with my dad."

Her heart warmed. She really wished her own father had felt the same way...

He sighed. "We've been bouncing around from one village to another ever since."

"Sounds like your experience with nymph villages was pretty bad, too."

"I don't know if I'd go that far. The years I had with my parents were wonderful. It was just the end that soured the place for me." He pressed his lips into a thin line. "I just hope I did right by Tini, leaving home. I can't help wondering if she'd be better off if we'd stayed."

"You've got the parenting part down pat. I'm always worried I'm doing the wrong thing, too."

He lifted a brow. "I don't know if I believe that. You're always so positive."

She grinned wryly. "Yeah, well, parenthood makes worriers out of us all."

"I know that's right. And I know I've made plenty of mistakes."

She twisted her lips. "Same here. I still can't believe I let things get so bad with Echo before I made this trip. I didn't tell you before, but that healer who skipped out on us? She burned him during one of their sessions. He's okay now, but I don't know if Echo will ever forgive herself for hurting him."

"I'm sorry." He let out a humorless chuckle. "If it makes you feel better, I've been making a big mistake with Tini that I didn't notice until recently."

"Yeah? What's that?"

"I've spent years chasing off any guy who even seemed remotely interested in her."

She interjected, "Keeping your parents' spirit alive. I like it."

He huffed out a faint snort. "Yep, only I finally caught on at the spring dance that Tini only wanted to dance with one person. And it sure wasn't a guy..."

Ali hid her smile behind her hand. "Oh."

"Want to take a guess at how many sleepovers they've had since we moved to Everpass?"

She chuckled. "On the scale of screwups, that's not too bad. Lots of teens find their first sweetheart at that age. And it's not like they're going to end up with any surprise kids."

He scowled. "Yeah. But I still spent the whole dance feeling like a clueless fool."

"Surely not the whole dance... I spotted you dancing with Tini towards the end, and you both looked like you were having a good time. Did you say anything about her choice of dance partners?"

"Naw. I didn't want to ruin her night. And like you said, she's almost grown. I figure I ought to get used to the thought of her courting soon." He sighed. "It's exactly what I've been waiting for all these years."

Ali's brow wrinkled. "What do you mean?"

"I had to give up a lot to raise her. I kept telling myself that once she was grown, I'd do all the things I missed. And now, the time is almost here. I suspect after this trip, once she gets her talent sorted, she'll be ready to strike out on her own. Then I can have my freedom back."

Her chest ached. She'd likely feel the same if she'd been in his shoes. Hell, she often wished she could have a little taste of what it'd be like to be on her own. No one to worry about. The freedom to come and go as she pleased.

But every time the urge struck her, all it took was one hug from her baby to wash it away like it'd never existed. She might not have planned to become a mom so young, but now that she was, she wouldn't change it for anything. This conversation had shown her that she and Lio had an awful lot in common. Terrible childhood tragedies. Single parenthood. Worries and mistakes by the dozen. But on this, they couldn't have been more different.

"You know..." Lio shifted, dragging his gaze off the fire. She felt his eyes on her profile, the weight of his gaze lingering like a soft touch. "That wasn't the only mistake I made at that dance."

She turned to face him, meeting his gaze. "It wasn't?"

He shook his head. "I wish I'd dared to ask you to dance."

Shock speared her. She'd caught him staring once or twice, but she had no idea he wanted to dance—with her. "I'm not surprised you didn't. I was on a date. You would've had to cut in. Make a scene. That doesn't seem like your style."

He leaned back, breaking eye contact. "Yeah, well, guess I missed my chance."

A sudden idea struck her. She popped to her feet and held out a hand. "Then let's dance now."

"Now?" He stared at her hand incredulously. "There's no music."

She cocked a hip. "What are you talking about? I think the crickets are doing a bang-up job." She grinned. "Come on, Lio. Don't you want to fix your mistake? Or were you just trying to butter me up when you said you wanted to dance with me?"

His gaze shot skyward. But a heartbeat later, his calloused palm slid against hers. "All right. You win." He stood, sliding his free hand down to her waist. "I still think this is ridiculous."

"Duly noted." She looped a hand loosely around his neck, her fingers tingling. Then she smiled up at him as he began to softly sway. "But I have to disagree. There's something magical about dancing under the stars, wouldn't you say?"

He grunted noncommittally.

"And isn't this better than cutting in?" she asked with a chuckle. "Though I bet that would've been fun to watch. I doubt Seth would've been too happy to lose his partner."

Lio cleared his throat. "Is that what you are? Partners?"

She shook her head slowly. "We decided we were better off staying friends."

"Sorry to hear that." His grip tightened slightly on her waist.

"I'm not." She leaned a little closer and lowered her voice. "I caught him sneaking peeks at someone else about a dozen times that night."

"So he's as dumb as he is big."

She swatted his chest. "Lio! That's my best friend's brother you're insulting."

"I stand by my assessment. You have to be ten kinds of stupid to look at anyone else when you're dancing with the prettiest girl in the room."

Good goddess. He needed to stop saying things like that and staring at her like he actually meant it. "You can stop laying on the compliments so thick. It's already been decided that we have to be friends."

His brow furrowed. "Decided?"

She nodded. "The girls told me as much last night in the tent. And we'll be popping by for a dinner date when we get back to town. Tini invited us, and Echo couldn't accept fast enough."

His expression shuttered, and all the warmth that had been brewing between them drifted away on the spring breeze. "I look forward to it," he said, but she sensed his heart wasn't in it. He stepped back and dropped her hand. "Thanks for the dance. And for listening earlier. Think I'm gonna turn in. You want me to leave the fire going?"

She wrapped her arms around her middle and stepped toward her tent. "No thanks. Put it out. I'm heading to bed, too." She made it halfway there before she turned back. "Hey, Lio?"

He spun to face her as the fire guttered out behind him. "Yeah?"

A million words burned on the tip of her tongue. She nearly confessed that she'd spent half the dance peeking at him, too. That if he had tried to cut in, she'd have accepted. And that her thoughts had been consumed with him since the night of the fire—whenever she wasn't worried about Echo.

But the thought of Echo made her choke all the words down. She couldn't ignore that Lio had clammed up the moment she mentioned her daughter. No matter how many compliments he gave her, no matter how desperately she longed to kiss him—just once—she couldn't forget that.

"Good night," she said softly. Then she ducked inside her tent, feeling more like she'd just said goodbye.

"Mooomm, wake up!"

Ali groaned and pulled the blanket over her head. "Go back to sleep, Echo."

"I can't. I'm too excited! Can we pack up and start walking now?"

With a sigh, she abandoned her futile attempts to catch a little more shut-eye. "It's barely dawn." The tent was still washed in shadows, with only a dim glow seeping in from outside. *Guess letting her go to bed so early last night wasn't the smartest plan in the realm.*

"I know, but I can't sleep." Echo pouted. "Let's wake up Tini and Lio—"

"No, let them sleep. Just because you're silly enough to wake me up at first light doesn't mean we have to force them to join in." She threw off her blankets. "Come on. Let's wash up in the stream and get started on breakfast—quietly. They'll get up when they're ready."

"Okay," Echo whispered.

Ali grabbed their toiletries and the lantern, then they strolled down to the stream. She selected a spot that was out of sight of the tents, and said, "All right. This will do. Quickly now. And stay where I can see you."

The chill morning air and even colder stream made washing less than pleasant, but Ali gritted her teeth and got it over with.

Echo waded in until she was waist-deep and splashed around happily until her teeth chattered. By the time Ali coaxed her out, it was bright enough that they had no need for the lantern any longer.

As she helped Echo dry off and get dressed in a blue and white striped frock, Ali's heart raced. After her talk with Lio, she'd felt a tad lighter. But a much heavier weight still pressed on her shoulders. She'd decided it was time to change that last night while lying in the tent, unable to sleep.

"Echo, remember when you asked me about our family?" she asked softly.

"Yeah. You wouldn't tell me until I'm older."

"I did. But I see now that wasn't fair to you. I'd like to tell you now, if you still want to hear it."

"Even though it's sad?" Echo asked.

She nodded. "Think you can handle being a little sad today?"

It would likely be one of the hardest things she had to do, but it had to be done. Now, before they reached the nymph village, and Echo started to see firsthand some of the peculiarities she'd hidden from her for so long.

"Course I can." Echo unraveled the towel from her head and tossed it on the ground.

Ali picked it up and folded it. "Why don't we sit down, and you can ask me anything you want to know while I braid your hair?"

"Okay." Echo perched on a boulder beside the water. "Do we have family I haven't met yet?"

Ali sat beside her and began carefully parting Echo's damp locks. "You have a lot of half-aunts and half-uncles, but they all live far away, in the village I grew up in."

"Why half?" Echo's nose wrinkled.

"My father had a lot of kids with different mothers. And my mother only had me."

Echo's head twitched as if she wanted to cock it, but then she remembered to stay still. "That's kinda weird."

"Sure, to you and me, since we're not used to it. But big families with lots of half-siblings aren't weird at all to nymphs. I wanted you to know because we might see more families like that where we're headed."

"What about my grandma and grandpa? Do they live far away, too?"

A pang in her heart flickered, then faded as she twisted the first hair tie. "No, sweetie. They both passed away before you were born. My mother got sick when I was a little younger than you. And my father passed in his sleep just after I found out I was having you." She'd heard the news when a nymph from her hometown stopped by the fish market. Her father had been much older than her mother, so it wasn't a huge surprise, and even less of a loss, considering how he'd treated her.

Echo bit her lip. "I'm sorry, Momma. That is sad."

"Thank you, baby."

"What were they like?" Echo glanced in Ali's direction, her eyes brimming with curiosity.

She smiled sadly. "I could lie and tell you they were wonderful, but the truth is my parents were"—she searched her thoughts, trying to come up with the perfect description that would make sense to a ten-year-old—"more like a curse that never lifted."

Echo stifled a giggle. "Really?" Her eyes widened, then her expression morphed into one of concern. "I mean, sorry. That's sad. Why were they like that?"

She sighed. "I'm pretty certain my mother wished I had been born a boy. And my father just ignored me."

Her brow furrowed. "Because he had so many other kids?"

"No, he didn't pay them much mind either."

Echo's eyes narrowed. "That's silly. Why did he even bother having them if he didn't want them?"

"It's a little hard to explain..." Ali took a deep breath and did her best to explain the intricacies of nymph birth dynamics. Echo peppered her with questions by the dozen, and she answered them all honestly. By the time they were through, she'd finished braiding Echo's hair, and the scent of hotcakes drifted down from the campsite.

Echo fell silent, her forehead etched with worry. "So that's why your mom wished you were a boy... Were you sad I wasn't a boy?"

She wrapped an arm around her shoulders. "Never. I love you just the way you are. Always have, and I always will."

"I love you too, Mama." Echo drew a shaky breath. "What about my dad? Is he dead, too? Is that why you never want to talk about him?"

Ali's heart clenched. She'd been dreading this question more than all the rest, and frankly, she was a little surprised it took Echo so long to ask. "Honestly, baby? I don't know. I haven't seen your father in a very long time." Didn't stop her from being plagued with his ghost. Every so often she'd see a man who looked so much like him she'd stop short, her heart lodged in her throat. And she always compared other men to him, without meaning to. "He left before you were born."

"Where did he go?"

"He was a sailor, so somewhere on the sea, I'd wager. But I don't know for sure."

"He didn't tell you where he was going?" Echo's voice warbled.

Ali's chest ached. "I think he was a lot like my dad. He wasn't very interested in being a father." It was difficult to admit it. She'd left her home behind, made a conscious effort not to court nymphs, and still ended up with a man who was so similar to her own father it was alarming. "I'm sorry I didn't do a good job picking him. And I'm sorry it took me so long to tell you. I just didn't want you to be hurt like I was growing up."

Echo's lips wobbled. "If he didn't want me, then I don't want him either."

Goddess, this was a terrible idea. The hurt she'd been so desperate to avoid heaping on her daughter was etched onto her face. She tugged her close, wrapping her in a warm embrace. "I need you to know that I've always wanted you, baby. You've been such a blessing in my life."

"You mean it?" Echo whispered, her words barely audible as she burrowed against Ali's chest.

"It's the goddess's truth. Do you know why I named you Echo?" she asked softly, even though she already knew the answer.

Echo peered up at her, her eyes glossy. "No."

"When your father left, I was all alone. My life was so quiet, and I hated it. But then the goddess gave me you, and you chased the silence away. That's why I named you Echo, because I knew I'd never tire of hearing your sweet voice. I'll always want to hear it, again and again and again."

Her lips curved into a soft smile. "I like that story."

"Me too, baby. Do you want to know anything else?"

Echo shook her head, then her lips pursed. "Wait, just one more question. What was his name? My dad?"

"Joffin Tood."

Echo's eyes widened with horror. "Tood? Are you serious?"

Ali grinned crookedly. "I was never crazy about that surname either."

"No kidding. I'm glad he's gone now." Echo wiggled out of her arms. "I can't believe I was almost a Tood." She shuddered. "Mikelli is much better."

"I think so too." She squeezed Echo's hand.

Echo squeezed back, then popped to her feet. "Can we go eat now? I smell breakfast."

"Sure, but if you have more questions, I want you to ask me later, okay?"

"Okay, I will." Echo threw her arms around Ali's waist as soon as she stood. "Thank you for telling me everything, Mama. I hope it didn't make you too sad."

Ali sighed as she hugged her back, feeling much lighter now that everything was out in the open. "As long as you're happy, I'm happy."

"I'm *really* happy I'm not a Tood." Echo giggled. "The kids would call me Echo the toad." She gasped. "Or Echo toots. Gross." She spun around, then froze. "Lio. What are you doing? How long have you been standing there?" Her voice rose in pitch until she was practically shrieking.

Lio strode forward, his arms loaded with a towel and toiletries. "Just got here. Did you need something?"

Ali's eyes narrowed. She sensed from how carefully nonchalant he was acting that he might have heard a lot more of their conversation than he was letting on.

Echo toed at the ground with her boot. "No."

"Breakfast is ready. You better head up before Tini gobbles it all up," Lio replied over his shoulder as he continued toward the stream.

Echo grabbed Ali's hand. "Come on, Mom. I'm starving!"

Ali spared Lio a last glance before collecting their things and following Echo back to the campsite. There'd be time to confront him about snooping later. For now, she was planning to cling to the fragile sense of relief she'd earned by laying her past bare.

Too bad the feeling won't last. They'd reach Paradise Plains before the morning was through, and then she'd have a new reason to worry. She forced the thought aside. *This is going to be fun, remember? A holiday.* If she just kept thinking positively, maybe it would actually come true...

THE WOOL BASKET

Lio

His gut churned with each step he took toward Paradise Plains. They'd packed camp swiftly after breakfast and gotten an early start on their hike. But as they grew closer to his old home, unease coiled tightly around him, as though something vital had slipped his mind.

It didn't help that he'd been out of sorts since talking to Ali. He'd tossed and turned all night, playing the conversation back in his head. And of course, that dance...

When he started this trip, he never imagined he'd cap off his night with a dance under the stars. He didn't have a whimsical bone in his body, but Ali had a way of making him forget that. He'd even started to wonder if he had it all wrong. Maybe he didn't need to wait until he was free before he started enjoying life.

Goddess, she'd felt so perfect in his arms. And when she'd confirmed Seth wasn't her partner, he'd been so tempted to show her how much he wanted a chance at the position.

But then she'd mentioned the girls growing closer, and he'd been struck with so many conflicting emotions. He'd backed off, needing time to think. Not that it had done him much good. He couldn't stop wrestling with himself; his heart daring him to be reckless, and his head warning him of disaster.

"Echo, don't run so far ahead," Ali shouted. Then she hiked her pants higher on her waist as she hurried to catch her.

He'd happened upon them that morning by the stream and overheard a bit of their conversation. It seemed Ali hadn't been content just to share her past with him but had filled in Echo as well. He couldn't help being impressed by her honesty.

Clarity struck him. *That's what's missing!* "Hey, Tini. Walk with me for a moment?" It was beyond time he took a page out of Ali's book. His sister deserved the truth, no matter how hard it would be for him to relive it.

Tini slowed her pace, and soon they lingered behind Ali and Echo, who were hopefully out of earshot, though not out of sight. "Did you need to talk about something?" she asked.

He nodded, his chest burning. "I wanted to check in with you before we arrived. See if you have any questions about what you're walking into."

Tini grinned. "Took you long enough to ask."

He dragged a hand through his hair. "Yeah, well, better late than never."

"I think I have a good idea of what to expect on account of the book I bought. But something I overheard Ali say has me wondering..." Tini chewed on her lower lip, then leaned closer, lowering her voice. "Are they going to be okay? Because if one person says anything awful about Ali and Echo summoning fire, I won't be afraid to tell them how stupid they are."

You and me both. His heart warmed. At least he'd done one thing right. He couldn't be prouder that Tini was willing to stick up for someone who was being belittled for something entirely out of their control. "You don't have to worry about that. The folk in Paradise Plains aren't superstitious about fire summoners, like the nymphs in Ali's old village."

She lifted a brow. "She told you about that, too?"

He nodded.

Tini grinned and bonked his upper arm with her shoulder. "You like her, don't you?"

"I finally give you permission to ask me anything, and that's what you want to know?"

She clicked her tongue. "Fine, don't answer. I can already tell you do."

He pinched the bridge of his nose as the first sign they were nearing the village reached his ears, the bleating of sheep carrying on the spring breeze. "Listen, just stay close to me when we get there. And don't be worried if things seem... odd. Especially when we meet with the hearthmother."

"That's the second time you've mentioned that. What's so strange about hearthmothers?"

"It's hard to describe..."

She dipped her head. "Can you try?"

He sighed. "They're incredibly secretive. Did the book you bought say anything about their rituals?"

"Not much." She pursed her lips. "What happened when you tried taking me to them before we left?"

"I can't really say. They wouldn't let me in. I had to barge in and carry you out of there when you wouldn't stop screaming." He'd hoped the hearthmother could help Tini with her nightmares, but all he'd ended up accomplishing was terrifying her.

"Weird. I don't remember that at all. How old was I?"

"Five. But I doubt you'd remember even if you'd been older. It's always that way with spirit magic. I can't recall anything that happened during my ritual, only that I left it with the innate knowledge of how to control my element."

"So I'm going to forget everything again?" She frowned. "And that's normal?"

"Pretty much. But this time, I'll be there. They wouldn't let me in with you last time on account of my age. They mentioned some nonsense about young minds being too susceptible to the spirits." His jaw clenched before he forced himself to relax. "I just know our parents were there for me when I discovered my talent, and I'm older now than they were back then."

"Good to know. Speaking of our parents..." She drew in a trembling breath. "This is really tough to ask, but is it possible that our dad isn't my real father?"

Lio gaped at her, stunned. "Absolutely not. What would make you ask that?"

She shrugged. "Isn't it true that children who are only half-nymph don't always manifest a talent? I thought maybe since mine is nowhere to be seen, it could be the case."

He shook his head. "No. You're a late bloomer, Tini. Simple as that."

"Are you sure?"

"Positive. I know you don't remember them much, but Mom and Dad were in love. It was kind of disgusting how much, in fact." He chuckled. "Can't tell you how many times I yelled at them to get a room over the years."

What his parents had was rare. He knew that now. Not many couples continued to be smitten with each other the way they had been. He had no reason to believe that Tini's fears had any merit.

"Okay, I believe you." She sighed. "Are you ever going to tell me what really happened to them?"

His heart stalled. "You already know what happened. They died in a fire."

Her voice softened. "Yeah. But there's something else, isn't there?"

Lio swallowed thickly. He had thought he was ready for this. He'd even told Ali last night, and she hadn't berated him for his senseless mistake. But facing his sister and telling her he was the reason their parents were dead was just too painful to stomach.

Up ahead, Echo squealed. She whipped around, waving frantically. "Tini, I can see the village! We're almost there. Come look!"

Tini clasped his shoulder. "I hope you feel comfortable enough to tell me the whole truth one day, Lio." Then she jogged ahead, leaving him standing there, reeling.

Paradise Plains was exactly how he remembered it. Unlike Everpass, Fairvale, and every other place he'd lived in since leaving, the village wasn't filled with stationary homes. Instead, wheeled caravans dotted the plains. Some were incredibly small one-room wagons that were worthless for anything but a dry place to sleep. Others—like his parents had been—were two-story behemoths that sat on the edges of the community, giving families a modicum of privacy.

And of course, there were the sheep. The fluffy critters covered the rolling green plains in all directions, their wool in varied hues of white, brown, and black. They were still pretty far off from the central caravan circle, where they'd find the elders and hearthmother Nelida, but sheep already had them surrounded.

"Wow," Echo exclaimed. "I've never seen so many sheep in one place!"

Lio nodded. "Paradise Plains is the wool basket of the realm. And the best place to find fresh mutton."

Tini's nose wrinkled. "Aw, do they really eat them? But they're so cute!" She waved at the closest sheep in their path, its tan fleece shaggy, mouth busy chewing a wad of grass. And no sooner had she finished waving than the beast unleashed a pile of dark, pellet-shaped droppings on the grass.

"Still think they're cute?" he teased.

She shoved his shoulder.

Echo giggled. "I still think they're cute." Her eyes narrowed. "Why do all the houses have wheels?"

He explained, "All those sheep need plenty to eat. The caravans follow them across the plains, so they never run out of grass."

"Cool!" Echo sprinted ahead a few paces.

Ali shouted, "Echo, watch where you're stepping!"

"I'll keep an eye on her." Tini jogged ahead, catching Echo swiftly, and leaving Lio and Ali to linger a few paces behind.

Ali sighed wearily before turning to him. "How did you know where to find them if they're constantly moving?"

"I lived here for seventeen years. Memorized the route." It had always been the same, as long as he could remember. Hell, just standing there with bleating beasts on every side, inhaling the pleasant aroma of fresh grass—and the not so pleasant whiffs of sheep dung—had him feeling like a teen again.

"Where will we find the hearthmother?" Ali asked.

He pointed ahead. "See that tight circle of tents?" Though the village's chief business was sheep herding, that didn't mean the community only contained shepherds. The shopkeepers and craftspeople always erected massive, open-air tents at each stop. And the hearthmother and elders set up their tents among them.

"I see them," she said.

"One of those belongs to her." He squinted. "I'm betting it's the colorful one on the far side." The tent in question bore stripes of orange and purple, unlike most of the others, which were far plainer, no doubt crafted from wool that no one had bothered to dye.

Ali strode forward. "Then that's where we need to go."

He grabbed her elbow. "Not so fast. No way we can just barge in there straight away. We'll need to greet the elders first."

She grumbled, "I was hoping you wouldn't say that."

Lio released her before the urge to slip his hand into hers became too hard to bear. "Don't fret. They're a pleasant sort, from what I remember. I'm sure you'll fit right in."

"And you'll stick out like a sore thumb." She smirked. "I have to admit, this is not at all what I was expecting."

"Your village was a lot different?"

"Loads different. There were trees everywhere. And hardly any sheep. Plenty of mushrooms, though."

He cocked a brow. "Mushrooms, huh?"

She nodded. "If this is the wool basket, that was the fungal garden. It was cool and humid most of the year, allowing dozens of varieties to flourish."

"Interesting…" Was that why fire summoners continued to be so distrusted there? A community based in a thick forest that relied on the land to make their living would surely fear fire more than most.

He forced the thought aside as they drew closer to the tents. As he'd expected, their arrival had not gone unnoticed. They'd already passed a few shepherds, who were content to let them pass with a wave, but now that they were closer, dozens of people had stopped what they were doing to turn and stare.

Yet so far, they'd spoken to no one. But when a gray-haired woman and a bald, stocky man, both wearing long tan robes over their plain hand-spun clothes, ducked out of one of the largest tents and headed their way, he knew that was about to change.

"Hullo," the man began. "Welcome, visitors. What business brings you to—"

"Stelios?" the old woman interrupted. "Is that you?"

A jolt of embarrassment struck him. This woman clearly knew him, but though he racked his brain, he couldn't place her. He strode forward, his hand outstretched. "I go by Lio now. I'm sorry, I don't recall your name."

The elder's bright blue eyes sparkled as she slipped her wrinkled hand into his and shook. "I'm not surprised. It's been a decade since you left Paradise Plains, hasn't it?"

"Thirteen years," he corrected.

"I'm Elder Lorna." She dropped his hand and waved at the man beside her. "And this is Elder Dramen."

Lio introduced his companions swiftly, wondering why the name Lorna sounded so familiar. He got his answer when she smiled widely at Tini and lingered on her handshake longer than the others.

"Katini. My goddess, look at you! All grown." Lorna patted the back of Tini's hand fondly. "You were so small when I saw you last."

Tini slipped her hand free. "I'm afraid I don't recall much from back then."

Lorna flicked her long gray braid over one shoulder. "No, I don't imagine you would. I'm your great-aunt. Well, great-*half*-aunt, on your mother's side. And I'm so pleased to see you."

Of course... She'd been one of his mother's best friends. Memories flooded back, all featuring Lorna much younger, her hair a rich brown. *Fantastic. I completely forgot about her. How many more distant relatives are about to pop out and surprise me?*

Lorna's gaze flicked back to him. "May I ask what brings you back?"

Lio cleared his throat. "We've come to see hearthmother Nelida. Tini and Echo both need her expertise."

Dramen smoothed the lapels of his robe. "I'm sure that can be arranged. What should I tell her to prepare for?"

Lio said, "They need guidance with their talent."

"Ah, I see." Dramen glanced at Echo. "What element do you summon, dear?"

Ali stiffened, her whole body going taut. Luckily, no one but him seemed to notice. He hated seeing her on edge. And knowing that the old legends he grew up eagerly listening to had caused her distress.

Echo replied, "Fire."

"You've been blessed with a rare gift indeed." Dramen smiled broadly. "Nelida will be delighted to hear that."

Ali blinked repeatedly, and her shoulders slumped. Lio's speeding pulse settled.

Then Dramen turned to Tini, and his pulse kicked right back into high gear. "And you, my dear? What else can I tell Nelida to expect?"

Tini shrugged. "I'm not sure... My talent hasn't emerged yet."

Dramen's brow furrowed. "Hmm. A late bloomer." He looked her up and down. "How old are you?"

"Almost eighteen," Tini answered.

"Quite late, I see." He frowned, then nodded at Lio. "You were right to bring her. I'll speak to Nelida. She'll get you young ladies sorted."

"Thank you so much." Ali smiled warmly.

"Of course." Lorna clapped her hands. "In the meantime, please allow me to show you around."

"That would be lovely," Ali said.

Lorna tapped her chin. "You'll need to spend the night, I wager, so we'll see about finding lodgings. Come, there are a few vacant caravans just past the marketplace." They fell in step beside her, while Dramen peeled off, likely to inform Nelida about their impending visit.

"I'm certain once word spreads you're here, Lio, there will be plenty of family who'd love to catch up." Lorna chuckled. "Not everyday one of our wayward flock returns home."

"I'm sure they have better things to do than catch up with me," Lio grumbled.

"Don't be silly." The delicious scent of roast mutton drifted in the air as Lorna led them past a square dotted with enormous wooden tables, with dozens of nymphs seated, munching happily. "It's always a pleasure to spend time with family. Wouldn't you agree, Katini?"

Tini fiddled with the ends of her hair. "I suppose."

"And of course everyone will be dying to learn what you've made of yourselves." Lorna inclined her head.

Tini smiled proudly. "Lio was just promoted to brigade fire chief in Everpass."

"How wonderful! A fitting profession for your talent." Lorna gazed at Tini. "And what about you?"

"I work in a tavern." Tini lowered her face.

Lio braced himself. If Lorna said 'tavern wench' even once, his tenuous calm would crack like thin ice over deep water.

"Ah... I understand that can be a rather pleasant occupation." Lorna chuckled. "In fact, I suspect it's not very far removed from what I do."

Tini's eyes widened. "How do you figure?"

Lorna grinned. "You have to be willing to speak with all manner of people, both familiar and new. And be a kind ear when folks wish to air their troubles. If not for the drinks, it'd be practically identical."

Suddenly, a curvaceous woman with long red curls rushed toward them, her ankle-length brown skirt whipping around her legs. "Oh my goddess. Stelios Callas! I don't believe it. What are you doing here?" Her arms banded around him, lingering for ages as if she couldn't bear to release him, no matter that he stayed stiff as a board throughout the embrace.

He groaned internally, wishing he could forget her name just like he'd forgotten Lorna's. *No such luck.* "Hello, Gildi. Just brought my sister to see Nelida. You remember Tini?"

Tini sidled up beside them, pointedly glaring at the manicured hands Gildi still hadn't removed from his upper arms. "Nice to meet you again." She reached out in welcome. "How do you know Lio?"

"We're old friends." Gildi shook Tini's hand perfunctorily and finally took the hint, dropping the other hand when he stepped back.

She chuckled lightly. "Was a time when your brother and I were *very* close."

Sure, they'd shared a romp or two, but that was ancient history. And Gildi was clearly insane if she thought she could snag him on her hook by insinuating as much in front of his baby sister. "Yes, well. It was nice to run into you, but—"

She spoke over him, "You must stop by my place later tonight. I'll cook for you, and we can chat about old times."

A warm touch slid over his arm, and Lio flinched. But as he glared down at his arm, the dainty fingers he spotted didn't belong to the grabby hand he'd been expecting.

Ali pitched her voice sweetly and batted her lashes as she gazed up at his face. "Lio, aren't you going to introduce us to your old friend?"

He swallowed heavily. "Gildi, this is Ali and Echo."

Ali turned her attention to Gildi. "Lio and I are friends, too. *Very close.*" She flashed a saccharine smile. "So are we *all* invited over for dinner?"

Gildi's mouth gaped open before she snapped it closed. "Oh, I'm afraid I only have enough for two. What do you say, Lio?"

His jaw clenched. *The gall on her. No wonder I had to leave.* Not even an hour into the visit, and he'd already been propositioned. And he didn't hold out much hope that Gildi would be the last.

Elder Lorna cut in smoothly, "Not to worry, Gildi. There's plenty to go around in the square. Why don't you save your ingredients for another time, hm?"

"I-I—" Gildi started.

Lorna brushed past her without a backward glance. "Come along, visitors. There's someone just ahead I'd like Echo to meet."

Lio blew out a sigh as they left Gildi in their dust. Ali had saved him. But why?

Surely she hadn't been jealous. Had she? Not when she'd made it clear about a dozen times that she only saw him as a friend.

Goddess, why do matters of the heart have to be so infuriatingly confusing?

Echo's delighted squeal drew him from his thoughts. She tugged Ali's hand, dislodging Ali's arm from the crook of his elbow, then pointed excitedly toward a forge—and the nymph summoning fire in front of it. "Look, Mom! He's using his magic to make metal just like you use yours to make glass."

And of course, the idiot lifted his head, revealing the ruggedly handsome face of a man he recognized. Wen was five years older than him, but because there were far more girls in the village, they'd spent plenty of time running in the same circles, despite the age gap.

"Lio? I didn't expect to see you today." Wen dropped the horseshoe he'd been heating into a bucket, making the water within sizzle and hiss. His gaze flicked away from Lio, his smile widening as he gazed at Echo and Ali, standing just beside him, holding hands. "And you brought a fire summoner with you? What a pleasant surprise!"

Lorna handled the introductions. Lio silently seethed when Wen took Ali's hand. Then when Lorna moved onto Echo, and Wen crouched down to eye level and she smiled at him like she'd just found a new best friend, Lio wanted to rage.

How had he forgotten about Wen? He'd just spent the entire journey with Ali, growing more infatuated with her each day, only to deliver her to a man who was far better suited for her.

Wen hadn't scowled once. Or told Ali to keep her daughter away from him. He even summoned fire and was an artisan, just like her.

Brilliant plan, Stelios. You just lost her for good.

WOWED

Ali

Her awed gaze refused to stop bouncing between the small outdoor forge and the male nymph who'd just been openly summoning fire at it. Never in her wildest dreams did she think she'd find this—a community that not only didn't look down on fire summoners but allowed them to work their magic among them in peace.

Out of nowhere, a gaggle of elderly ladies appeared, each of them talking over the other, and all of them eager to greet Tini and Lio.

Ali stepped back, giving them space. *What do we do now?* Suppose she and Echo could wander a little on their own. She'd spotted at least a dozen tents on their brisk walk through the marketplace she'd have loved to explore; some selling clothes woven from dyed wool, others displaying soaps, food, and even a few mysterious curiosities she didn't recognize.

At least the people seemed friendly enough. They'd earned their share of curious stares, but most greeted them with a nod or a smile if they were caught staring. And the elders had certainly been welcoming, along with Wen.

She shot the handsome blacksmith an awkward smile. *Jeez, there must be something in the water out on the plains.* His brown skin glistened under the sun, dark-brown eyes sparkling nearly as brightly. And of course, he was built as you'd expect a blacksmith to be, with huge biceps straining at the sleeves of his long-sleeved white tunic.

Wen chuckled as he dragged a hand through his short, curly black hair. "Looks like word got out to Lio's aunties and cousins he's back. This could take a while. How would you two like a tour of my shop while they catch up?"

Echo clasped her hands under her chin. "Can we, Mom? Pleeease?"

A pang lodged in Ali's heart. She disliked the idea of encouraging her daughter to follow a strange man they'd just met, but it's not like he'd invited them into his home. The workshop and showroom were just ahead, within eyesight of where Lio and Tini had been waylaid. And the tent stood wide open, allowing anyone wandering by to see what was happening inside.

And how much of that first spark of distrust stemmed from her past, and the old scars that still hadn't fully healed? It was time she began moving forward without allowing those lingering wounds to dictate her decisions.

"I suppose it won't hurt." She smiled. "Thank you for the offer."

"Of course. It's always nice to meet a fellow artisan. Did I hear your daughter right when she said you craft glass?"

"You did. I own Our Glass in Everpass."

Wen smiled as he led them inside the spacious tent. "Do you really? Pretty sure I have one of your lamps around here somewhere. My mother stopped in on holiday a few years back." Wen let out an embarrassed chuckle. "You know how mothers can be. It's like the realm will end if she doesn't return home with the perfect souvenir for me."

Actually, I don't. "What a chore, accepting all those free things," she replied lightly as she checked out his pieces. She hadn't been expecting them to be so well made, but nearly everything within rivaled the craftsmanship of Dav's pieces back home.

Wen's delighted laughter wrapped around her. "You're funny, Ali. Good thing I love to laugh."

"Me too," Echo added. "You know any jokes, Wen?"

"Hmm." He turned to her daughter, gifting her a pensive stare. "I could've sworn I knew a dozen. But the moment you asked, they all flew away. Isn't that always the way?"

Echo nodded sagely. "That happens to me, too."

"You know what?" Wen grinned. "I bet my son Tamas will know a few. Should I call him over?"

Ali waved a hand. "You don't have to go to any trouble—"

"It's no trouble at all. He's my assistant." Wen raised his voice. "Where are you hiding, Tamas?"

A teen that she pegged at about sixteen, who looked like a miniature version of Wen, only with striking green eyes, popped out from behind a display case full of weapons a heartbeat later. "You need something, Dad?"

Wen smiled fondly and slung an arm around his son's shoulders. "Yep. I want to introduce you to Echo. She's visiting Paradise Plains and asked to hear some jokes. Think you can oblige?"

"Happy to." Tamas unleashed a smile that mirrored his father's. "Come on, Echo. I just helped my dad make a dagger. You wanna see it? I'll tell some jokes when we're done checking it out."

Echo's face lit up. "Okay. I like daggers. Is it for throwing?"

"No throwing," Ali insisted.

"Fine." Echo pouted. "Parents can be so lame," she muttered as they strode off.

Tamas replied, "Tell me about it."

Wen chuckled. "Fun age, huh?"

"More like exhausting." Ali sighed. "Is Tamas your only child?" She steeled herself, ready to hear a number in the double digits. There was no way a nymph as handsome as Wen didn't have dozens of women begging him to give them sons.

"No, I have two more. Tamas is my oldest and the only child from my late wife. My second wife blessed me with twin daughters before she traipsed off to goddess knows where." He cringed. "Sorry, I have a bad habit of oversharing."

She shook her head. "It's all right. I don't mind. I'm sorry about your wives. That must've been hard."

He shrugged. "You could say so. But we all have our burdens to bear. Mind if I ask why you're here in Paradise Plains, Ali? Well, besides the obvious."

She lifted a brow. "Don't tell me I'm missing something obvious…"

Wen chuckled. "It's paradise, of course."

"Right." She laughed softly. "Bet you use that one a lot."

"Not as often as you might think. So what brings you here?" He leaned back against a glass display case filled with small metal trinkets.

"My daughter needs help to control her talent. She's half-human, so I wasn't even sure if she'd develop magic at all, but no such luck."

"You say that like being gifted a talent is a bad thing."

"Where I grew up, summoning fire was more like a curse."

Wen stood up straight. "Wait, your daughter summons fire?"

She nodded.

"Then you've truly been blessed. None of my kids inherited my talent."

"Really?"

He leaned closer and lowered his voice. "Truth be told, I think it bothers Tamas some. He wants to follow in my footsteps and take over the shop one day. I keep telling him summoning water can be just as useful in metalwork, but you know how kids can get."

"Sure." Their conversation was surprisingly... nice. She had a lot in common with Wen—even former partners who'd abandoned them—and it was pretty obvious he loved his kids. "Maybe he's worried you'll have another kid who can summon fire, and he'll be ousted."

He snorted. "Fat chance of that. I'm not planning on having more anytime soon. Unless I met the right woman and got hitched."

"Well, best of luck finding wife number three."

"Thanks." He chuckled. "Third time's the charm, isn't that what they say?"

She bit her lip. "Mm-hmm." *Goddess, is he flirting?* She forced her lips together. *Am I flirting back?* "You know, I'm a little surprised you'd go to the trouble of marrying."

"Can I tell you a secret?" His eyes twinkled as he leaned even closer. "My mother would have my head if I didn't."

Ali laughed. "Moms always know best." She should probably be turned off that Wen was a self-admitted momma's boy, but she wasn't. The unshakable bond with his kin said a lot about what kind of man he was.

Echo's laughter burst through the air, lighting Ali up from the inside out.

"Sounds like they're getting along great." Wen leaned back again. "You know, we've been missing a glassblower in Paradise since the last fellow retired. Just thought you should know, in case you're ever looking for a change of scenery."

That's something to think about... "I'll keep that in mind." She glanced back at the entrance, but one of the display stands had blocked her view. "You mind if I check on my friends? I just want to see if they're still tied up."

"Not at all." He smiled warmly and stayed put as she backtracked through the shop.

Within a few steps, she spotted them. Tini was still occupied by the women Wen had dubbed their family, her smile pinched as a pale, statuesque brunette talked her ear off, and a woman who'd stacked her salt and pepper hair into an enormous bun nodded along. Lorna appeared to be in an animated conversation with another, her brow creased as she listened intently.

A few steps away, Lio had attracted a new circle of admirers. Four gorgeous women crowded around him, vying for his attention. And from the way they giggled at his scowls and jumped at every chance to touch him, she had a sneaking suspicion none of them were related.

Her stomach clenched. Who could compete with that? Yeah, Lio seemed pretty upset at the thought of having a harem the other day, but he'd also been very clear about craving freedom. He wanted a chance to experience everything he missed when he became a stand-in father so young. Pretty sure the picture in his head didn't include someone like her.

Wen's soft tenor came from somewhere behind her, making Ali jump. "They're still chatting away, aren't they?"

"Yep." She strode back slowly. "Looks like you're stuck with us for a little while longer. Unless you're busy?"

"Nothing I can't delay until later." Another giggle resounded, mixing with Tamas's chuckles. "Besides, I'd hate to break up the laugh fest."

Her heart swelled. "I'm glad they're having fun. It's been a tough couple of months."

"Been there. It's always a challenge when your kids first discover their talent."

"So I'm learning."

"How about you?" he asked.

She crossed her arms. "What about me?"

"Can't let the kids have all the fun. I think I may have just the thing to do the trick for a fire summoner, like yourself. You in?" Wen smiled again, his expression open, earnest. If she didn't have another man's surly visage burned into her brain, she could easily see herself being completely charmed. As it was, she only felt a calm comfort in his presence, and a lingering curiosity to discover what he wanted to show her.

"All right. I'm in." She grinned. "Where are we going?"

"Not far." He crossed the showroom and threw open a tent flap, leading her to the open-air space just outside. "Though we do need to visit the workshop for this."

She whistled as she surveyed his gear. "Nice setup you have here."

"I do the best I can with the limitations that come with living in paradise."

"Oh? And what are those?"

He patted the small tool rack. "Gotta make sure all my favorite tools are mobile. There's a forge at each of our main campsites, but you get used to working with a special tool, and it almost becomes an extension of your arm, you know?"

She grinned. "I do. A few of my favorites they're likely going to need to pry out of my cold dead hands."

He grinned back. "I already have it in my will that clampetta here"—he lifted a pair of oversized metal pliers—"is being buried with me."

"Smart plan." She cocked her head. "Do you name all your tools?"

He shook his head. "Just the special ones. I'm not completely crazy."

That was just ridiculous enough to make a cackle spill out of her chest.

He carefully placed the pliers down—and *winked* at them. "I'll be back for you later, clampetta."

"Don't make me regret following you, Wen."

"Trust me. You're gonna love this." He led her to the far corner of his workshop and stopped in front of a huge object covered with a tarp. "Ready to be wowed, Ali?"

"Sure."

He tossed off the tarp with a flourish, and she squinted, unimpressed with the blocky piece of metal covered in strange holes, which seemingly had no rhyme or reason.

"Please don't hate me for this... but what is it?"

He chuckled. "Good to know you're so concerned with staying in my good graces."

She made sure he saw it when she rolled her eyes.

Wen only laughed louder. "I know it doesn't look like much... yet. But do me a favor?"

She pursed her lips. "What?"

He pointed to a small hole in the bottom. "Funnel a stream of fire right through here."

Ali gulped, her stomach fluttering and her face feeling flushed. A part of her expected nymphs to jump out screaming 'shame' the moment she raised her hands.

No. It's different here. No one will judge you. With the self-reassurance ringing in her ears, Ali took a deep breath and summoned.

"Perfect!" Wen's smile ignited at the same moment her magic funneled through his creation, completely transforming it.

"Goddess..." Her eyes watered around the edges as the plain hunk of nothing turned into a fire-breathing dragon, each of the tiny holes becoming a small part of its body. Scales, claws, wings, even the flames flowing from her hands became part of the living work of art he'd crafted; the stream flowed into the perfect spot, making it appear as if the dragon were spitting fire from its mouth. "It's gorgeous, Wen."

"Told you. Wow, am I right?"

She glanced at him, soaking up the warmth of his smile. She couldn't help feeling a kinship with Wen. He'd made her feel welcome almost instantly with his sunny personality and fantastic sense of humor. He was clearly just as passionate about his craft as she was and insanely creative, too. "Wow is right. I can't wait to tell Davos about this."

Though she wasn't sure it was possible, Wen's face lit up even more. "Davos... is he a minotaur?"

"Yep, he is. He's my neighbor back in Everpass. Owns the village smithy."

"I'm glad to hear the old bloke landed on his feet. We apprenticed together for a time."

"Really..." She cut off her magic and turned to him with a smirk. "Bet things got pretty wild during an apprenticeship in paradise. Do you have any stories to share about your good old buddy?" She wiggled her brows, hoping to score big. It would amuse her to no end if she had something to hang over Dav's head when she got back to town. Maybe she could even use the right tidbit to encourage him to unshackle himself from the smithy for a change.

Wen grinned. "You want stories? Grab a seat. I've got a million."

Ali hopped onto a stool. "Wen, have I told you yet how happy I am that we met?"

"Oh my goddess, you're kidding! I can't believe he did that!" Ali roared with laughter, positively delighted that Wen had given her all the ammunition she'd need to embarrass Davos to no end when she made it back home.

"Who did what?" Lio strode into the workshop, his typical scowl firmly in place.

Wen grinned. "I was just telling Ali about the time Davos sneezed mid-hammer swing and the sparks set an elder's beard on fire."

She giggled again, her belly aching. Wen had made her laugh more with his bevy of bumbling apprentice stories than she had in ages, even throwing in a few that made him the butt of the joke, not just Davos.

Lio nodded curtly, not even cracking a smile. "Sorry we got ambushed for so long."

"It's all right. Wen was nice enough to keep me company," she said.

"You ready to move on?" Lio asked gruffly. "Where's Echo?"

Wen hopped off his stool. "I'll track her down. Tamas is probably showing her every single item he's helped me forge." He flicked the tent flap up and slipped into the showroom.

Ali jumped off her stool as well. "Did you have a pleasant time catching up with your relatives?"

"Pleasant? No. More like dreadful." Lio shuddered. "I barely got a chance to say hello before a bunch of harpies cut in and started pawing at me."

"Sorry." Her stomach wobbled. *At least he's honest. And clearly not into the attention as much as I'd imagined he would be.*

He stepped closer, his voice dropping an octave, the tone so low and intimate it made her blood sizzle. "Too bad you didn't stick around and save me again."

"I'll make it up to you the next time the harpies descend." She trailed her gaze around the workshop. "Maybe I should ask Wen for a sword."

"I'd prefer it if his sword never came anywhere near you." The corner of his lips ticked up, and for some strange reason, that tiny shadow of a smile lit her up far more than any of Wen's wide, welcoming grins.

Good goddess, is he... jealous? "Noted," she replied, too flustered to think up another quip. Not when he was staring at her so intensely, and standing so close his woodsy cologne overpowered the rusty tang of metal lingering in the air.

"Found them." The tent flap fluttering signaled Wen's return.

Ali backed up a pace and turned just in time to notice something she hadn't seen Wen wearing yet. A frown.

She asked, "They weren't up to no good, I hope?"

His smile returned. "No, not at all. But they insisted on having a moment to finish their game. If they don't show up soon, I'll lure them out with the promise of sweets."

"Ah, bribery. Always a good tool to keep in your back pocket." She chuckled lightly.

Wen tapped his temple. "Great minds think alike." Then he glanced at Lio. "Been ages since we caught up. How's life been treating you?"

Lio shrugged. "I'm doing all right. Landed a job with the brigade in Everpass."

"Dangerous job. Can't imagine your wife likes you running into burning buildings…" Wen's gaze flicked between them.

She could see what the leading statement and suspicious glances added up to. Wen was clearly trying to gauge how involved they were. She held her breath, waiting to see how Lio reacted.

Lio crossed his arms. "Someone has to do it."

A perfect reply if you want to reveal nothing. Ali choked down the urge to snicker. "Don't be modest, Lio." She patted his shoulder and held Wen's gaze. "You're looking at the most eligible bachelor on the brigade. I'm amazed he doesn't have to chase off the ladies of Everpass with his ladder."

Lio's scowl deepened.

Wen chuckled. "Why am I not surprised? You were always popular in Paradise, too, if memory serves."

He still is. Ali's stomach clenched.

"Mom! Guess what?" Echo burst out of the tent, all smiles. "Tamas taught me a new game. It was so much fun!"

Tamas followed behind her. "If you have time before you leave, you should stop by for another game. I'm always up to play."

"Can we, Mom?" Echo bounced on her toes. "Please?"

"We'll see, sweetie. For now, we have to go. Tini and Elder Lorna are waiting for us." She smiled at Tamas. "Thanks for keeping Echo company."

He grinned shyly. "It was no trouble. I had fun."

"Me too! See you later, Tamas." Echo waved and bounded forward on springy steps.

"Careful, Echo! There are sharp things everywhere." She sighed wearily. "I better follow her. Nice meeting you both." She hurried off, breathing another sigh when Echo emerged from the workshop unscathed, and soon they met back up with the rest of their party.

"I hope you had a nice chat with our talented blacksmith." Lorna smiled at Echo. "I wanted you to see some of the marvelous things folk with fire talent can accomplish when they put their skills to good use."

Echo nodded furiously. "It was great!" She threw her arms out wide. "I love Paradise Plains so far!" Her nose wrinkled. "Bet no one makes fun of anyone just for being a nymph here."

Ali's chest ached. She was pleased Echo had found somewhere she felt like she could fit in. Wen's words boomed in her ears. "*We've been missing a glassblower in Paradise.*"

Would relocating to Paradise Plains permanently be the best move for her daughter? It would mean giving up the business she loved, but surely that wouldn't be too bad, so long as she could keep practicing her craft in a different location.

She shoved the question aside, knowing now wasn't the right time to debate all the pros and cons. "Where to next?"

Lorna waved them forward. "Let's head to where you'll be staying. I bet you're dying for a chance to drop off your things and wash up."

Ali glanced at the supply cart, a bemused smile crossing her face when she spotted Cinder asleep atop it, curled up in the same sweater she'd made a bed out of in the tent on their first night camping. *That reminds me...* "Elder Lorna, do you know anyone who's looking for a pet cat?"

Echo gasped. "Mooom! No."

She crossed her arms and shot her daughter a stern look. "Echo... we talked about this."

Echo pouted, her gaze dropping to the grass.

Lorna chuckled. "I'll ask around."

"Rats." Tini scooped Cinder off the cart, cuddling her tightly. She cooed sadly, "You're going to make some lucky shepherd so happy. Aren't you, pretty girl?"

Cinder meowed, and the sound cut straight through Ali's core. She'd been worried about this. The girls were already smitten. It would be a shame to tear them apart, but—

"Forget that, Lorna. Don't ask around," Lio stated gruffly.

"What?" Tini's eyes lit up. "Wait, are you serious? Can we keep her?"

Lio scowled at the little ball of fur curled up in his sister's arms. "Yeah. We can keep her."

Echo clapped her hands. "Yay!" She converged on Tini and petted Cinder softly. "I'll come visit you all the time, Cinder. Tini's gonna be your momma."

Tini smiled. "Thank you, Lio. Best brother ever!"

Lio's gaze flicked forward. "Right."

Ali blinked, more than a little stunned. She'd been so sure he had no desire to ever own a pet. But perhaps there were more layers hidden within Lio she hadn't uncovered just yet.

"Ah, here we are." Lorna stopped in front of a wooden, two-story caravan parked on the edge of the marketplace. "There ought to be enough room for all of you inside. Unless you'd rather have your own space?"

"This'll do," Lio announced before she had a chance to mull over the offer. "We're only staying long enough to visit Nelida."

"Of course. But just know, if you decide to extend your stay, you'd all be very welcome for as long as you'd like." Lorna strode to the door, but before she could grasp the handle, a voice called out from behind them, making everyone turn.

"Hullo again, travelers!" Dramen hustled forward, his robe whipping in the spring breeze. "I'm glad I caught you. I have good news! Nelida will meet you this evening. Feel free to head over after dinner." He pointed to a large tent—the same one with purple and orange stripes that Lio had pointed out to her earlier. "That's her tent, just over there. Best of luck with the ritual, girls. I'm certain Nelida's guidance will offer precisely what you need."

It was exactly what they'd come for, but that didn't stop Ali's stomach from churning like mad. Tonight, her daughter would finally get a handle on her magic.

Goddess, please, let nothing go wrong...

DESTINY

Lio

Tini groaned, her eyes lighting up with delight. "I take back everything I said. This mutton stew is to die for."

Ali chuckled from her spot across the wide wooden table in the village square. "I know what you mean. I'm tempted to ask for seconds."

The twilight sky slowly darkened as they enjoyed their dinner. They'd taken a little time to settle into the caravan after Lorna left. He'd insisted on sleeping on the top floor, even after Echo begged to be the one who got the giant loft bed. Surely it didn't win him any points with her, but he was pleased Ali backed his decision. He just didn't feel safe with any of the girls up there, considering what had happened to his parents.

Hell, what am I thinking? He tried to shove his worries about Echo's feelings out of his mind. *Not your place, Stelios.* He'd told himself the same thing at least a dozen times, but for some reason, the words didn't ring true any longer.

It was this place. Being surrounded by so many smiling children and proud parents made him yearn for things he'd never imagined he would. Seeing all the blissful families in the village reminded him of his childhood. Would he ever again know the quiet joy of unconditional love surrounding him? Did he even deserve it after what he allowed to happen to his parents?

Something hit his foot under the table. He glanced up, catching Ali staring at him with a lifted brow.

Lio forced a small smile and dug into his bowl.

Her eyes narrowed, but she said nothing. Probably wise. He wouldn't have breathed a word about what was bothering him with the girls listening.

He looked away, spotting another sight that set a different string of thoughts unfurling. There were a few men holding court, blushing ladies tittering behind their hands as they sought to catch their attention. That's what he'd be in store for if he finally got the freedom he'd always craved.

And yet, the idea of that life suddenly didn't hold the same draw it always had. He'd gotten a taste of it today, when Ali was off being wooed by Wen. He wasn't ashamed to admit that he hated every moment.

He'd found himself comparing every woman who'd approached him to Ali—and, big surprise—they all came up short. None of them had her expressive eyes. Or her quick wit. And their hands on his arm didn't set off a cascade of tingles, like Ali's did. He'd just wanted to shake them off and find her. All he could think about was whether that blasted blacksmith had charmed her into doing something horrid, like giving away the kiss he'd longed for and been too much of a fool to claim.

Echo's spoon scraped the bottom of her bowl. "I'm done. When can we go see the hearthmother?"

Ali patted her daughter's back. "The realm doesn't revolve around you, silly. Let's wait for everyone to be finished, hmm?"

Echo pouted and crossed her arms. "Fine."

"I'm almost done, Echo. Don't worry," Tini said.

Ali asked, "Not going for seconds?" Her voice trembled slightly, and he wondered if she was purposely stalling.

"Nope. I'm stuffed." Tini scooped another bite onto her spoon. "Just one more taste. It's so good!"

"It's not *that* good," Echo stated matter-of-factly. "Haven't you ever eaten one of Nora's desserts?" She licked her lips, her eyes going hazy.

"You have a good point." Tini set the bowl aside. "Do we need to bring these somewhere?"

Lio stood and collected the bowls. "I'll take care of it. Meet you out front?"

"Okay," Echo popped up, grabbing Tini's hand. "Come on, Tini! I promised Cinder I'd bring her back something yummy." She lifted a folded napkin off the table.

Tini chuckled and glanced at Ali. "Mind if we pop back to the caravan quickly? I'll keep an eye on her."

"Go ahead. And thank you, Tini," Ali replied. She stood as well, stacking their empty mugs.

He deposited the bowls with the dirty dishes, and Ali dropped off the cups.

"I'm sorry Echo keeps stealing Tini away. If you need some alone time with her, just let me know. I'll find something to keep Echo busy."

Like another visit to Wen? No thanks. "It's fine. If Tini needs a break, I'm sure she'll let you know. I doubt she will, though. When she was small, she always used to tell me she wanted a sister. This is probably like a dream come true."

As they ambled out of the square, Ali softly asked, "Did you ever consider giving her a niece or nephew as a playmate?"

He shook his head. "Can't say that I did. She was enough to handle on her own." Of course, it didn't help that he'd never courted anyone seriously over the years, either.

"I can understand that. What about after she's all grown up? Do you want a family of your own one day?"

If she'd asked him that question just a few days ago, he'd have had an answer at the ready. But now... "I don't know. Maybe."

That minor concession to the plans he'd held onto for so long released a torrent of powerful feelings he didn't have the time to examine. He wasn't entirely certain what to make of them all, especially the one that stood out strongest from the bunch—deep, stomach-churning fear.

Ali's hand landed on his forearm. She squeezed gently, dragging him back to the present. "Hey, are you all right?"

"Yeah. Just worried about the ritual." That must have been what the fear was all about. Wasn't it?

She leaned in. "I am too. Can you remember anything that happened during yours?"

"Not really. I remember showing up with my parents and being given something to drink. The rest?" He lifted a fist to his head, then made his fingers shoot out. "Poof. Like a dream."

"Same." She shuddered. "Is it weird that I'm more scared of being the one watching a ritual instead of the one who gets to forget?"

"Not weird at all. I feel the same."

She nudged his arm with her shoulder, smirking. "Look at us, talking about our feelings like a couple of court poets."

"Will wonders never cease?" He shot her a crooked grin.

Her gaze caught on his mouth, and she bit her lip.

I really need to start smiling more often. If every flick of his lips earned him a hungry glance from Ali, he'd never keep a straight face again.

"We're back," Tini announced loudly.

He spun on his heel, spotting her waving from a good distance away. No doubt she'd clued into the tension lingering between them and spoken up before Echo noticed anything awry. He ought to be thankful, but he couldn't help feeling a little sore that yet another opportunity to kiss Ali had passed him by.

"You sure you're ready?" Ali asked as they approached. "If you need more time—"

"Let's go!" Echo bounded off at a skip.

Tini chuckled. "I'm ready too. We both are." Then she raced off, shouting for Echo to slow down.

Lio's heart raced along with them, but he knew he had to keep his composure. Not just for the girls, but for Ali. "It'll be all right. We survived it. They will too."

"You're right." Ali exhaled deeply. "Let's get this over with."

It took them no time at all to reach the hearthmother's striped tent. Unlike the rest of the marketplace, her tent swept the ground on all sides, blocking the interior from view. The girls stopped at the entrance, their curious gazes trained on the tiny crack that appeared each time the flap blew in the spring breeze.

"Come in, travelers," a weathered voice called from within. "I've been waiting for you."

Lio swallowed thickly as he pulled back the tent flap. He waved the girls forward, entering last.

"Katini. My how you've grown!" Nelida sat cross-legged on a floor cushion, an impressive feat of flexibility, given her advanced age. She'd seemed ancient to him during his ritual, and that had been nearly fifteen years ago. It was a miracle she was still alive at all, and yet, she appeared to be just as sprightly as she'd been back then, with a keen intelligence shining in her kindly hazel eyes. "Come, come," she waved a bony, liver-spotted arm energetically. "Please, have a seat in the circle. Girls closest to me."

Echo was the first to plop down on one of the brightly colored cushions that had been arranged in a tight circle on the floor. "I'm Echo. Nice to meet you, hearthmother. I like your dress."

"Why, thank you, dear." Nelida glanced down at her multicolored floral frock before clasping Echo's proffered hand in both of hers. "And I'm very pleased to meet you, Echo. You must call me Nelida."

"Okay." Echo grinned.

By the time they'd finished their handshake, everyone was seated. Lio's thighs ached slightly, but he managed to tuck his legs into a crossed position without knocking over the pot of tea in the middle of the circle.

"So, Elder Dramen tells me you're both seeking help with your talent. Is that correct?"

Tini said, "Yes, hearthmoth—Nelida."

Echo nodded, her twin braids bouncing.

"Wonderful. You've come to the right place." She grabbed the teapot. "Let's get you girls the guidance you need." A heady mix of fragrant spices he couldn't place drifted through the air as she poured dark liquid into two worn mugs.

Echo took a small sip as soon as she had the mug in her hands.

Tini stared into the cup, her eyes narrowed. "What happens after we drink this?"

Nelida smiled. "The spirits will come to guide you, of course." Tini shuddered, and Nelida patted her knee. "Don't fret, child. I'll be with you, as will your brother. You're safe."

"Yeah, don't worry, Tini." Echo licked her lips. "It tastes pretty good." She tipped the cup back, draining it in a few swallows. "Can I have some more?"

Nelida chuckled. "'Fraid not, dear one. That brew is very special, and the ingredients are exceedingly rare. We must save the rest for others seeking guidance."

Tini tentatively lifted the cup to her lips. She sipped slowly, then said, "Hmm. Not bad." Soon her cup joined Echo's empty mug beside the teapot.

"What now?" Ali asked softly.

"Now we wait." Nelida tilted her head. "The spirits come as they please. Some are overeager, jumping to help. Others move slow as molasses. But they always come."

Time ticked slowly. Lio's stomach churned as first Echo's, then Tini's lashes grew heavy, their heads tipping forward.

"Are they supposed to nod off like that?" he whispered.

"Yes." Nelida smiled. "It is the way. The spirits only visit those who linger on the edge of sleep. Unless you're a hearthmother, of course." She chuckled. "The spirits are not content to let us rest."

That must be why he couldn't remember any of it...

"Ah," Nelida focused on a spot over his shoulder. "Here comes one now."

He glanced behind him, seeing... nothing. No movement. No shadowy form creeping closer. But a chill swept over him all the same.

Nelida threw out her arms in welcome. "Come, brave spirit. We beseech you. Share your knowledge with your kin."

Ali stiffened. "Kin?"

"Yes, kin. It's always a spirit from your bloodline that imparts knowledge on their descendants." Nelida squinted. "I see a woman with ebony hair, eyes of obsidian, skin dark as the starless sky."

"Mother?" Ali whispered.

Lio's heart stalled. After everything that awful woman put Ali through, she was probably the last person Ali wanted visiting her daughter.

"No. That doesn't feel right... This spirit is strong. I sense centuries of knowledge in her. And heat." Nelida grasped the collar of her dress and wafted air toward her face. "She burns with it."

Ali's mouth fell open.

Lio tensed. There must have been a fire summoner far back in Ali's lineage.

"She knows you." Nelida's gaze shot to Ali, then focused on a point over her shoulder. "She visited you before, dear one. Long ago."

"She did?" Ali pressed a hand to her heart.

"Yes." Nelida's eyes watered. "I can *feel* it. She is awed by you, Alsira Mikelli. By all that you have done with your gift. And now, she's come to share her knowledge with your daughter. Yes. Eager, this one is. *Very* eager."

Lio gaped, tongue-tied and utterly daunted. How had Nelida known Ali's full name? Hell, how could she see presences that weren't there? Was it all just a trick? Or was there actually a spirit sharing the tent with them?

Nelida's gaze trailed slowly, tracking the invisible specter as it closed in on Echo. "Thank you, brave spirit. This child needs you."

Ali's voice warbled. "What's happening?"

"She comes. Just wait." Suddenly, Nelida gasped. "She is with her now." She fanned her face frantically. "So strong. So *hot*." Her eyes pinched shut, and she grimaced.

Echo's loose limbs stiffened. And though her head hung heavy, her chin resting against her chest, both of her arms slowly rose.

"What's happening?" Ali muttered.

Lio grasped her hand, squeezing tightly.

Nelida's eyes flew open. "Yes! She speaks." Her face was red and blotchy. Sweat dripped down her temples, despite the chill in the air that had only deepened since she announced the spirit's arrival. "And young Echo listens."

Echo's arms halted their movement, stopping as they reached shoulder height. Her hands slowly spun, turning until her cupped palms faced up. Then the air warmed without warning, the chill banished in an instant.

Lio's eyes widened, and he squeezed Ali's hand tighter.

Twin streams of flame erupted from Echo's palms, shooting skyward and stopping just shy of the domed tent ceiling. Ali gasped.

Lio stared in awe as a heartbeat passed. Then another. The heat only grew, the air in the tent so stifling his mouth became parched, and a drop of sweat rolled down his back. Then the flames disappeared, and the heat went with them. Everything happened so fast he could almost believe he'd imagined it.

Echo's hands dropped back into her lap, and she remained still, her head lolling on her shoulders and her chest rising and falling as if she were peacefully asleep.

"It is done." Nelida smiled. "Thank you, kind spirit. Go in peace."

"That's it?" Ali asked.

"Yes. Your daughter will have no trouble controlling her magic from now on." Nelida glanced at Echo. "We must let her rest. It's weary work, soaking up centuries of knowledge."

The chill slowly receded, leaving behind the fragrant spring air.

"She is gone," Nelida announced. "Now we wait for another."

Lio's stomach churned, his gaze falling on his sister. "Will the spirits still show up if her talent hasn't surfaced?"

"The spirits always come." Nelida squinted at Tini. "And she is ready. I can feel it. A deep well of magic pools within her. The spirits will dig down and set it free."

He shuddered, uncomfortable with the imagery.

Ali squeezed his hand. "Can you sense what her talent is?"

Nelida shook her head. "Not yet. Soon."

They waited in silence. Lio held tight to Ali's hand, drawing strength from her steady support.

What would Tini's talent be? Nymphs never knew what element they'd be blessed with. Often they ended up with the same gift as one of their parents, but that wasn't always the case. As long moments passed in silence, he pictured Tini with each one, imagining careers she might choose that would benefit from her mastery of that element.

Earth and water summoners often became farmers and shepherds. Wind summoners were a boon to sailors, and fantastic weavers—like his mother had been.

And those were only a few of the practical things. If Tini had a desire to try her hand at music, wind would be best. He'd known a few nymphs who could play a dozen instruments at once, using gusts of wind to pluck strings and blow through brass.

Fire would come in handy if she wished to become an artisan. Water if she wanted to follow in his footsteps and join the brigade. The opportunities were truly endless, and he passed a good deal of time imagining each.

But at some point, he began to tire of his thoughts. He glanced back at the tent flap, spotting darkness when the breeze lifted the edge.

How long had they waited? It felt like ages.

A prickle of anxiety teased his spine. What if Tini's worst fears were genuine? He'd been so certain she was worried for nothing. No part of him had believed his mother would disrespect his father and welcome another man into her bed.

But as time continued to pass with nothing to show for it, that tiny seed of fear grew.

No. It's not true. Nelida had sensed magic within her. He had to be patient. The spirits would come.

Just as the thought filled his mind, Nelida stiffened. The air stirred, a new, deeper chill blowing through the tent.

Lio exhaled, his eyes widening as his breath clouded before him.

"Oh..." Nelida's brow pinched. "This is most unusual."

"What is?" he asked, panic worming across his spine.

Ali tightened her grip, grounding him in the moment.

"There are two." Nelida squinted. "Goddess." She gazed at him, her eyes watery. "It's your parents, Lio. They *both* came."

His heart pounded so fiercely he was sure Ali could hear it. "Wh-what?" He glanced around frantically, but just like last time, he saw nothing.

"They're... pleased. Yes." Nelida closed her eyes. "I feel warmth. And love. So much love for you both."

"I don't believe it. Are they really here?" If it were true, it answered the question of his sister's parentage, once and for all. Perhaps that was why they'd come. They'd sensed the doubt lingering in Tini's heart—and his own—and sought to banish it.

Nelida nodded, her eyes still closed. "Yes. It's them. I knew them well on this plane. I would not mistake them on the next." Her eyes slid open. "So strange. Why two? There's never two... Unless..." Her hazel eyes popped wide. "Oh, Katini." A tear slid down her cheek. "I've waited so long for this. For *you*."

Lio's stomach dropped. "What are you talking about?" Something about this felt... wrong. Why weren't Tini's hands lifting? Why was Nelida *crying*?

Without warning, Tini's head shot up. Her eyes fluttered open, her gaze immediately snagging on a point in the air above his head. "Hello?" Her voice was hoarse, her breath clouding before her. "Mom? Dad? Is that you?"

"Good goddess!" Lio exclaimed. "What's happening?"

"Shh." Nelida waved a hand frantically. "They speak, and she listens."

He clung tight to Ali's hand, his pulse careening through his veins like a riptide. He watched as Tini's head tilted. Her brows etched with concentration, her gaze flicking from one point to another just beside it.

"Yes, I understand," Tini said.

Understand what?

She giggled. "I will." She paused, then nodded. "I know." Suddenly her attention shifted, her gaze landing directly on his. Tini stared into his eyes with a furrowed brow.

Lio leaned forward, his stomach in knots. *Why is she staring at me?* The question tickled the tip of his tongue, but he held it in. Nelida had just shushed him, after all. He wasn't meant to interrupt this, right?

Then Tini's gaze flicked back up. "I can do that." Another long pause. "I love you too. So much."

Goddess, is this really happening? He blinked furiously, absolutely stunned.

The cold receded. And unlike with Echo, Tini didn't fall back asleep. She remained awake and alert, a serene smile on her face.

"They're gone. It is done," Nelida announced.

"What's done?" he barked. "What the hell just happened?"

Tini blinked three times, then her gaze connected with his. "Lio. Did you see that? Mom and Dad were here!"

Nelida patted her knee. "He didn't see them, child. But you did."

"Huh?" Tini's brow wrinkled. "I don't understand..."

"You're a spirit summoner, Katini." Nelida swiped a tear off her cheek. "The first to be born in Paradise Plains in nearly a century."

"You're kidding," Lio choked out.

"I would never joke about such things." Nelida pursed her lips. "This is her destiny. Think back, and you'll see the signs were always there. Spirit summoners discover their talent at the same age as all nymphs, but the spirit realm always touches them."

His blood ran cold. "What signs?"

"Vivid dreams that feel real," Nelida began.

He met Tini's gaze. "Your nightmares."

Nelida continued, "An instinctive ability to bring peace to troubled souls."

An offhand remark Nora made days ago snagged in his mind. *"All the customers love her... She has an uncanny knack for easing their worries."*

"Deep empathy for all creatures, living and dead," Nelida finished.

That fits too. Tini had always insisted on honoring their parents on the anniversary of their death. And she was always the first to lend a hand to someone in need. Hell, she'd even felt bad for the stupid sheep when she heard they were bound to become dinner.

Nelida turned to Tini. "You, my dear, are destined for this. One day, you will take my place. Hearthmother Katini."

Tini lifted a shaky hand to her lips. "A hearthmother? Me?" She shook her head. "No, I-I can't be..."

Nelida chuckled. "I know just how you feel, dear one. I was once in your shoes. Take a moment to let it all sink in. Then you can ask me anything you'd like."

Lio slumped, his mind reeling. How? Why? What did this mean for Tini? For her future? Had all those limitless options just been snatched away, leaving her with a single inescapable path that he'd never imagined?

We shouldn't have come here. I knew something would go wrong. Goddess, help me. Why the hell didn't I listen to my gut?

Lio gently placed Echo in bed beneath the dim lights inside their borrowed caravan. He'd offered to carry her back when she didn't rouse. The offer had been practically the only thing he'd uttered in the last hour.

He'd listened in stunned silence as Nelida spoke to Tini, outlining the apprenticeship she wished her to take. She'd droned on about Tini's destiny and how much good she could do if she accepted her role as hearthmother.

Tini had listened raptly, asking questions by the dozen, while Lio sat there seething. He felt like he was watching history repeat itself, except instead of the elders lecturing him about his duty to father children, the hearthmother was pressuring his sister to take on a role she'd only just begun to consider.

Anger boiled inside him, but he refused to let it loose. Not here. And certainly not now.

With a sigh, he pulled the blankets over Echo's shoulders. It wasn't so long ago he'd done the same for his sister. She'd begged him to tuck her in every night, well into her teens. If only he could go back then, when things were simpler. But that was a foolish dream that would never be realized.

He strode outside, finding Ali and Tini seated on a pair of lawn chairs beneath the stars, their voices hushed. It had been so late when they emerged from Nelida's tent that the entire village was sleeping, only the soft bleating of sheep and chirping of crickets keeping them company.

"I can't even imagine what's going through your mind right now," Ali said. "Fire magic is rare, but spirit... that's on a whole different level. Are you sure you're all right?"

Tini nodded, flashing another of those serene smiles she'd worn in the moments after his parents had appeared to her. "Oddly enough... I am. It's strange, but something about this just feels... right. It's like I've spent my whole life staring through a dirty pane of glass, and Nelida wiped it clean."

Lio's stomach clenched.

"So are you planning to stay?" Ali asked.

"Absolutely not," Lio insisted.

Tini glared at him. "Why not?"

"You listened when she blathered on and on about your destiny. Your expectations. But you have those back home as well." He drew a deep breath through his nose, fighting to keep his voice level. "You have a job that's expecting you back. And all your friends."

Tini's shoulders slumped. "You're right. It wouldn't be fair to them if I disappeared without a word."

Lio crouched in front of her and grabbed her hands. "Listen, Tini. I know the decision ultimately lies with you. But I want you to promise me you'll think long and hard about what you want to do. Just because Nelida says this is your destiny doesn't make it so. It's your life. No one should pressure you to do anything you don't want to do."

Tini chuckled humorlessly. "Funny thing to tell me after you demand I return home."

"Point taken." He sighed heavily. "I just want to make sure you have some time to think. And the chance to do it where no one will be in your ear, seeking to sway you."

Ali added, "Listen to your brother, Tini. This is a huge decision. Not something you want to rush into."

Tini nodded solemnly. "You're both right. I'll think on it. Carefully." She squeezed Lio's hands, then stood. "If you don't mind, I'm gonna turn in."

"Good night, Tini," Ali said.

"Good night," Tini called over her shoulder as she strode through the door.

Lio sank into the seat she'd just vacated and rubbed his temples. "Thanks for backing me up."

"Of course," Ali said softly. She didn't speak again until the bumps and rustles of Tini moving within the caravan died down. "Do you want to talk about tonight?"

He shook his head. "No." He couldn't be certain he wouldn't start to rage if he gave voice to all the bottled-up thoughts clattering around his head. "I need some time to think."

"Sure." Ali stood. "If you change your mind, you know where to find me. Good night, Lio."

His chest ached as she slipped inside the door. Then he sat all alone in that chair, staring off into nothing, trying desperately to make his thoughts fade away to nothing, and failing miserably.

He just couldn't wrap his head around it. There hadn't been a spirit summoner born in the better part of a century. Why did it have to be her?

He ought to be excited. If she accepted, Tini would have a place to go and an entire village that would take care of her. But he couldn't seem to shake off the bone-deep dread that plagued him.

Are all the people closest to me destined to leave me, one way or another?

He flinched. Where had that thought come from?

A timid voice rang out. "Lio?"

He glanced up, spotting Echo in the doorway. "Hey. Everything all right?"

She nodded, one arm clutching Cinder, a fist lifted to rub her eyes. "I woke up and saw you out the window, sitting here all alone. Why do you look so sad?"

"It's a long story." His head drooped. "And nothing you need to worry about. Go back to bed, Trouble."

She shot him a scowl. But instead of ducking back into the doorway, she padded closer, her bare feet sinking into the grass. "Here, you take her." She placed the kitten on his lap and smiled shyly. "Cinder doesn't want you to be alone."

Lio frowned down at the little ball of fluff as she promptly curled up, making herself comfortable.

"You'll take care of her, won't you?" Echo asked, the final word stretched around a yawn.

His heart clenched as Cinder began to purr softly. "Yeah, I will. Promise."

"Good night." Then Echo darted back inside without turning back. If she had, she would've surely noticed the soft smile that briefly flashed across his face.

At Odds

Ali

The next morning Ali rolled out of bed, careful not to disturb the others. It had been a long night, and they deserved the rest. They'd planned to begin the trek home today, and though she was tempted to stay longer, it was probably wise that they stuck to their original plan. While Echo would likely enjoy another chance to play with Tamas, Tini—and especially Lio—needed some space from this place.

She wasn't sure what to make of his reaction. For a man who claimed to want freedom, he certainly seemed distressed when Tini was presented with an opportunity that would provide him with it. But there wasn't much she could do to help if he insisted on keeping everything bottled up inside. Maybe with a little time and distance, he'd be willing to talk.

After dressing for the day in traveling clothes and quietly packing her and Echo's things, the others still hadn't roused. So she slipped out of the caravan, determined to bring back some tea and breakfast.

Early morning in Paradise was peaceful in a way she'd not experienced anywhere else. Dewy grass stretched out in all directions, and birds sang sweetly on her walk to the square. Plenty of folk milled around, but none appeared to be in a hurry, as they so often were back home.

The tables in the square were already half full. Giggling children ate side by side with their friends while the parents mingled, chatting and sipping from steaming cups. Savory aromas wafted from enormous platters set up buffet-style. Ali grabbed two plates and joined the food line, smiling politely at the older couple ahead of her.

"Fancy seeing you here."

She turned around with a grin. "Good morning, Wen. How are you?"

"Fantastic as always." He met her grin with one of his own. "Heard you folks visited Nelida last night. Is Lio's sister really a spirit summoner?"

Suppose it's not so different after all. Gossip traveled just as fast here as it did back in Everpass. "Yep." She took a step forward as the line moved.

"Sorry, I shouldn't have pried. It's just all anyone can talk about this morning." He chuckled good-naturedly. "You know how small towns are."

"It was a bit of a shock. And the experience was exhausting."

"Always is." Wen shuddered. "Being visited by my dead relatives kinda gave me the creeps, if I'm being totally honest."

She paused beside a platter loaded with crispy bacon and heaped a generous portion onto the first plate.

"Big appetite today?" Wen asked.

She shook her head. "I'm bringing it back to the caravan for everyone to share. They were still snoozing when I left."

"Smart. Breakfast in bed always guarantees a good start to the day. Need some help to carry it back?"

"Thanks, that would be great." She'd been prepared to make more than one trip, but with Wen's help, she likely wouldn't have to.

She made her way through the line, taking a bit of everything. When they reached the end, Wen filled a pitcher with tea, and they strolled slowly back toward the caravan. They didn't make it far before encountering something she would definitely not run into back home. A flock of sheep blocked the path ahead, forcing them to pause.

Wen nodded to the harried young shepherd trying vainly to shoo them along, then ducked his head close to hers. "Haven't weathered a sheep slowdown before, have you?"

"Can't say that I have. Guessing that happens a lot around here?"

He shrugged. "You get used to it."

A black sheep halted directly in front of them, locking gazes with Ali. "Am I crazy, or does that one look angry?"

Wen whispered out of the corner of his mouth, "Don't let her see the sausage on your plate. Might be her mother."

She snorted a laugh. "If she charges at us, I'm diving behind you."

He grinned. "Human shield, at your service."

Luckily, the angry livestock sauntered off with the rest of the flock. Ali's arms ached as they arrived at the caravan, and she sighed as she set down the loaded plates on the small table perched beside the lawn chairs out front.

"Thanks for the help, Wen. And your protection."

He put down the pitcher, then bowed deeply. "Always a great honor to defend a lady in distress."

She chuckled.

"So I hear you're planning to head out today," Wen said.

"That's right."

"Well, I'm sorry to see you go. It's been fun getting to know you, Ali." His eyes sparkled in the morning sunshine, his smile warm and genuine.

"Same here. It's been a pleasure." She smiled back, truly meaning it. Wen was a great guy, creative, kind, and invested in his family. She'd been so certain that Lio was an outlier among their race, but meeting Wen had shown her that truly wasn't the case. Perhaps it was time she lifted her self-imposed ban on courting nymphs...

"Suppose this is goodbye. Are you a hugger by chance? Because if you are, I wouldn't say no..." He threw out his arms and wagged his brows.

Chuckling, she stepped into the circle of his arms. "Goodbye, Wen."

"Bye, Ali." He held her a beat longer than she'd been expecting. And when they broke free, he met her eyes and said, "If you ever come back, don't be a stranger. I'd really love to see you again." Then his gaze lifted, catching on something over her shoulder. "Hey, Lio. Good morning."

Of course he's there. She turned around, her heart clenching. Lio stood in the doorway, his scowl firmly affixed.

"What's all this?" he asked gruffly, his gaze darting between them both and the food.

She wasn't sure if he was talking about the fact that he'd snuck up on them hugging, or breakfast, but she chose to address the latter. "I brought back breakfast from the square. Wen helped."

"Be glad you missed it." Wen leaned back on his heels and stuffed his hands in his pockets. "A murderous sheep stalked us. We narrowly escaped with our lives."

"Sounds like an eventful morning," Lio muttered.

She lifted the pitcher. "I better go wake up Echo."

"See you around, Ali." Wen grinned, walking backward. "You too, Lio."

Lio watched him go from the doorway, a muscle in his jaw ticking.

"Are you planning to stand there and glare much longer?" She lifted the pitcher higher. "This is kind of heavy."

He plucked it out of her hands. "You could've woken me. I'd have helped you."

She turned back and grabbed the plates. "I figured you needed the rest. You were the last one to go to bed." Giggles rang out from inside, alerting her that the girls were awake.

He grunted, holding the door open wide for her. Then she slipped inside, adding another item to her mental list to bring up with Lio when they had a moment alone. For a guy who once claimed she deserved privacy, he had a funny way of always intruding on it.

"Ooo, can I light the campfire? Pleeaase?" Echo clasped her hands in front of her chest, her eyes wide and eager.

"Sure, baby." Ali dropped an armload of sticks into a rock circle at the campsite they'd selected for the night. "Just let me get out of the way first."

They'd left Paradise Plains before midday and walked well into the afternoon. Echo had put up a bit of a fuss when she'd learned she wouldn't get another chance to see Tamas, but she'd perked back up when Tini offered to teach her a few new games while they walked.

The hours had passed swiftly while the girls giggled away. They'd pretended to be pirates, collecting tiny treasures—mostly glittering rocks and odd-shaped leaves—then, they'd moved onto a step challenge, where they took turns seeing who could walk the furthest while taking giant orc steps, or bouncing like rabbits.

Watching them had been a pleasant distraction, especially considering her only adult company had been even surlier than usual. Each time she tried to strike up a conversation, Lio only replied with short, one-word answers, unless he could get by with a grunt.

"Hurry up, Mom," Echo demanded.

Ali glared at her daughter over her shoulder. "If I don't stack them right, then the fire will die down."

Echo grinned. "No problem. I'll just blast it again."

She cast a sidelong look at her daughter as she continued to stack the logs. "Careful. You go blasting your magic all over the place, and you might run out."

"That can happen?" Her eyes widened. "Wait... you're just teasing me, aren't you?"

She stood and ruffled the top of Echo's head. "Yep. Had you going for a moment there, though, didn't I?"

Echo hit her with one of her sassiest faces, her voice dripping with sarcasm. "You're soo-ooo funny."

"Glad you know it, baby." She winked and gestured to the sticks. "Go ahead. It's all yours."

Her breath caught as Echo's hands rose, and fire streamed out. A wide grin broke out on her daughter's face as she watched the logs catch. Then she cut off the stream, dropping her hands to her sides.

"Perfect! You're doing so well, Echo." Ali beamed.

"Thanks." She lifted a hand again, her brow furrowing as she stared down at her fingers. "It's a little weird how that ritual just fixed my magic, but I'm not gonna complain. Did it happen like that for you, too?"

She nodded. "Spirit magic works wonders."

Echo glanced across the clearing where Tini stood, helping Lio set up the tents. "And that's what Tini has."

"Yeah. Pretty cool, huh?"

Echo slumped onto a boulder and stared into the fire. "Yeah, I guess."

"Hey." Ali sat beside her. "What's wrong?"

She sighed heavily. "Tini told me they want her to be the new hearthmother, but I don't want her to. We just became friends."

Her heart twinged. "Just because someone lives in a different village doesn't mean you can't still be friends."

Echo scowled. "Yeah, but it's not the same."

"It'll be all right, baby. You'll see." She smiled reassuringly and patted her shoulder.

"Hey, Echo," Tini called. "You wanna help me feed Cinder?"

Echo perked up instantly. "Okay!" Then she popped to her feet, bouncing off with a smile on her face.

If only her troubles would disappear so easily. *Speaking of trouble...* "You cooking tonight, or should I?"

"I'll do it." Lio dug into the supply cart, barely sparing her a glance.

Three words. Guess that's a step up from one. "You want some help?"

"No need."

And we're back to two. She strode to his side, lowering her voice. "Did I do something to piss you off?"

He shook his head sharply.

"Clearly something's bothering you. I've tried to be nice and give you space, but if you think I'm going to stay silent while you mope for the rest of the trip, you are sorely mistaken."

His jaw clenched, and he lifted his gaze to stare at the girls as they took turns feeding bits of meat to Cinder. "Not now. We'll talk later, when they go to sleep."

She let out an exasperated sigh and forced a smile. "Fine. It's a date."

Their gazes clashed, and Lio's was so intense, she would've given anything to be privy to his thoughts.

"What's for dinner?" Echo skipped up to her side. "Feeding Cinder always makes me hungry."

Ali tore her gaze away from Lio. "There's not much that doesn't make you hungry, is there?"

"Hope you're not tired of mutton already." Lio held up a skewer of cubed meat.

"Can I help you cook, Lio?" Echo asked. "Pleeaase?"

She tensed, prepared for him to shoot Echo down. Clearly, he wasn't in the mood to be social, and he hadn't been shy about telling Echo to stay away in the past. But once again, Lio surprised her.

"Sure." He waved her over. "Have you ever cooked over a campfire before?"

Echo shook her head. "Is it hard?"

"It can be when you're first learning. You up for the challenge?" He lifted a brow.

"Yeah. Let's do it!" Echo's excitement was palpable. She listened raptly to Lio's instructions, grinning from ear to ear when they successfully placed the skewers over the fire.

Her heart warmed. Lio might be gruff and standoffish, but he could also be extremely patient and kind. He didn't even get upset when Echo knocked a skewer into the fire. He just fished it out and told her he liked his with a little extra char—though she suspected from the way he scowled at the blackened meat when Echo wasn't looking that it had been a little white lie.

Echo handed her a skewer, her face lit with pride. "Here you go, Mom. *I* cooked for *you*. Bet you didn't think that was gonna happen, did ya?"

"I sure didn't." She took a bite. "Mmm, and it's good, too."

"Course it is. I'm a great cook." Echo plopped down beside her, wolfing down her meat so fast it was a miracle she didn't choke.

The girls dominated the conversation during dinner, and Ali was happy to allow it. But eventually the horizon darkened completely, the stars hidden behind the cloud-strewn sky, and Echo's yawns became too frequent to ignore.

"I think it's time we got you to bed." Ali stood, holding out a hand. "Say good night, Echo."

"Wait." Echo turned to Tini. "Can I sleep with Cinder tonight?"

Tini glanced Ali's way, waiting for her nod before she said, "Sure. I'll get her for you."

"Thanks, Tini." Echo grabbed Ali's hand and let her pull her to her feet. But then her fingers slipped free. She darted around the fire and flung her arms around Lio's neck. "Good night, Lio. Thanks for letting me cook dinner with you."

Good goddess... Look at that. Ali's heart warmed.

Lio patted Echo's back gently. "No problem," he said gruffly. "Good night."

Echo's hand slipped back into hers. As the tent zipper hummed in the air, Tini's boots rang out. "Here's Cinder, all ready for her slumber party."

"Not much of a party when it's just us." Echo cuddled the kitten close. "Ooo, can Tini sleep in our tent? Then it'll be a party!"

Ali waved a hand dismissively. "There's barely enough room for us in there, silly."

"Oh, right." Echo frowned. "What if you trade tents?" She gazed at Tini. "Think Lio would mind?"

Goddess, of all the inappropriate suggestions. Echo just wanted another chance to cozy up with her new friend, but that would absolutely *not* be happening.

Tini chuckled. "You should probably ask your mom instead."

"Mom?" Echo's nose wrinkled.

"Let's save the sleepovers for when we have a real roof over our heads, hmm?"

Echo pouted. "Dang it."

Tini yawned. "I'm going to bed, too. Make sure Cinder gets a good night's sleep for me, okay? See you in the morning, Echo."

"I will!" Echo climbed into her blankets, foregoing her usual cajoling to stay up just a little later.

"Good night, baby. Sweet dreams." Ali zipped Echo in, her heart racing. Now she could finally get to the bottom of Lio's terrible mood.

She found him sitting alone by the fire, his shoulders tense. It felt like a week had passed since the last time they had found themselves in the same situation, with the girls asleep in their tents. He'd been candid back then, more so than she'd ever expected, but she had no way of knowing if he'd be just as honest tonight. Would he own up to what was bothering him, or try to act like nothing was amiss?

She perched beside him on a downed log, keeping her voice whisper-soft. "All right. Time to spill. What was making you so cranky today?"

He shot her a sideways glance. "You sure you want to know? We might be out here for a while."

"I've got time. And I wouldn't have bothered asking if I didn't want to know."

"I knew something awful would happen if I took Tini back." His hands clenched into fists. "And it did."

Her stomach churned. "What are you saying?"

"Tini has no business being a hearthmother. She didn't even know what they were a week ago, and now she's got her whole life planned out for her. It's not right."

He had every right to feel blindsided. With how rare spirit summoners were, no one went into their ritual expecting to discover that was their talent. But it was a little odd that Lio seemed more upset about it than Tini did.

"It's a tricky situation, but she's handling it well. And she agreed to think everything over before making a decision."

"True." He sighed. "I just can't stop wishing we'd never come."

"Tini was bound to discover her talent eventually. Imagine what would've happened if the spirits had appeared to her one day out of nowhere." She shook her head. "You did the right thing."

"Doesn't feel that way," he replied glumly.

"You heard what she said last night. How she's seeing things more clearly than ever before."

"Yeah…"

"That's pretty amazing, don't you think? I'm sure it's not what you pictured for her, but maybe this is exactly what she needs."

He scrubbed a hand down his face. "I don't know what's wrong with me. I spent so long waiting for her to grow up so I could be on my own, but now that she's thinking about leaving, I can't stand the thought of it."

A string twanged in her chest. Had Lio finally realized the freedom he craved was in direct opposition to the one thing his actions had proven he valued above all else—taking care of his family? She didn't know if he realized how at odds his thoughts and actions were, but maybe the truth was starting to dawn on him.

"You could always move with her, if that's what she decides to do."

"And subject myself to those harpies day in and day out?" He scoffed. "No thanks. Besides, I have people counting on me in Everpass. I promised the old brigade chief I'd stick around."

"I'm sure no one would blame you if you found a replacement. Especially if leaving was the best move for your family." She flashed a crooked smile. "You know, I heard they don't have a glassblower in Paradise..."

His head jerked up. "And?"

"And maybe it would be good for Echo to live somewhere she'll actually fit in."

"That's what you decided? After visiting for a day?" He hopped to his feet and began pacing in front of the fire. "Goddess, has the whole realm gone mad?"

"Relax." She snagged his shirtsleeve and tugged until he sat back down. "I haven't decided anything."

"But you're considering it."

She shrugged. "I have to consider everything that could make a difference in my daughter's life."

"Great," he muttered, dragging his hands through his hair.

Instead of Lio being relieved at the possibility of a few friendly faces in Paradise, he was back to acting pissed, and she wasn't sure why. *As long as I've got him in a good mood...* "Since we're airing our grievances, there's something that's been bothering me."

He dropped his hands into his lap. "Yeah? What is it?"

"You've got to stop sneaking up on me. I forgave you back in the capital, but then I caught you listening in by the stream—"

"That was an accident. I had to wash up, too."

She gritted her teeth. "What about this morning, when I was saying goodbye to Wen, was that an accident?"

His nostrils flared.

"For a guy who once claimed I deserve privacy, you don't seem very inclined to allow it."

"What do you want me to say?" he choked out.

"An apology would be a good start. If we're going to be neighbors in Paradise—"

"Goddess's sake. I don't want to be your neighbor." His chest heaved. "And I sure as hell don't want you in Paradise."

Her heart dropped. "Oh. I-I"—she gulped, feeling like the realm's biggest fool—"I thought—"

"Ali, I can't stop watching you because... I'm drawn to you. Each time I hear your voice, or that damned distracting laugh, it reels me in like a siren's song."

Wait... Really? Her pulse sped. And when he lifted his gaze off the fire and met her eyes, her blood burned so hot it's a miracle she didn't detonate.

"That's why I came outside this morning. I heard you laughing, and I just couldn't help myself." He reached up, toying with a lock of her hair, his fingers grazing her neck. "If that fiery freak held onto you any longer, I would've torn his arms off."

"Lio..." She was just as mesmerized as before, but there were no children around to ruin the illusion. She could almost forget they weren't entirely alone, with her daughter sleeping—*Drat. Echo is here.* The thought made her tense, though she couldn't stop herself from drifting closer.

"So, no, I don't want you in Paradise... with Wen." He spat out the name, even as his hand glided tenderly from her hair to her jaw. "And I don't just want to be your neighbor."

"Then what do you want?" she asked softly.

His brow furrowed, his gaze holding her captive. "I'm still figuring that out... But I know one thing for sure. I've been dying to kiss you."

She felt like she'd been transported into one of her books. Suddenly, she wasn't an overwhelmed single mother trying desperately to do her best. She was just a woman sitting before a campfire, with a sexy as sin firefighter begging to kiss her.

"Then why haven't you?" She smirked, purposely goading him. "Are you waiting for an invit—" The word cut off on a gasp as he kissed the smirk right off her face.

Lightning zinged through her veins. *Yes, finally!* She wound her arms around his neck, dragging him closer, determined to make it last. After waiting so long, she refused to settle for anything less.

Lio seemed all too eager to deliver. His lips lingered, and she memorized the shape of them, reliving the ache of all the moments she'd longed for him but hadn't found the courage to give in to her desires. Ali hummed, loving his intensity. His *passion*. She shouldn't have been surprised that his kisses were just as multifaceted as he'd proven to be. Frantic and rough one moment, soft and thorough the next.

And goddess, his *hands*. Shivers wracked her frame as he traced her shoulders, her arms, then slid down to her waist. Then she gasped again as he tugged her out of her seat and dropped her into his lap, straddling his waist.

"Lio." She dragged her mouth away.

He chased her lips, delivering another drugging kiss. She groaned, nearly giving in and sinking into the sensation.

But she couldn't escape the gnawing realization that this wasn't one of her books. She *was* a mom, and her daughter was asleep nearby, with only a thin barrier separating them. And she wasn't about to get caught kissing a man who'd just openly admitted he still didn't know what he wanted out of his life.

She tore her mouth away again. "Lio, wait."

He froze, his chest heaving, his hands warm and heavy on her back. "What is it?"

"That was... wow." She pressed her forehead against his. "You should know, you're a fantastic kisser."

"Why do I sense a but coming..."

She smiled. "But we shouldn't be doing this when you're so conflicted about what you want out of your life."

He drew back, staring at her again just as intensely, and goddess help her, she wanted to kiss him again. She buried the urge, certain this had to be said. Now, before she let things get out of hand. If the feelings he inspired in her were any indication, they weren't far off from that point.

"If it were just me, I would happily kiss you all night."

He groaned, inching closer.

She pressed a hand flat against his chest, halting his advance. "But it's not. I have to think about Echo, too. I can't get close to someone—to let *her* get close to someone—who has no interest in sticking around and being a part of her life. I made that mistake once, and I won't do it again."

She held her breath, waiting, praying that he'd say the words she was dying to hear. That a kiss wasn't all he wanted from her—not even close. That he wanted them *both* in his life. That he'd do his best to be the man they needed, even if it wasn't what he'd pictured for his future.

Instead, his hands slid to her waist, he gently lifted her off his lap, and set her on her feet. "I understand," he said flatly.

She swallowed heavily. *That's it?* Though she wasn't entirely surprised, she couldn't help wishing for more. Sure, he probably wasn't ready to burst out with a love sonnet, but even a promise to think about what he wanted would've been more reassuring than the tepid understanding he'd offered.

"Good. Glad we got that, uh, out in the open." She forced a smile. "I guess I'm gonna head to bed. Good night, Lio."

And when she walked away, she didn't let herself turn back. Not this time.

She flicked the lantern on in her tent, keeping the dimmer switch turned down low. *Echo's fast asleep. Thank the goddess.* The last thing she wanted was to wake her up and be forced to explain why her eyes were brimming with unshed tears. Or worse—why her lips looked bee-stung.

But just after she crawled under her blankets, Cinder stirred and meowed once before settling back down. Ali shut off the light, her heart racing.

"Mom, is that you?" Echo asked softly in the dark.

"Yeah, it's me, baby. Go back to sleep."

Just when Ali thought she'd listened, Echo's voice rose again. "Do you think Tini will take Cinder with her when she leaves to become a hearthmother?"

"I don't know. That's a question for another day."

"I hope Lio keeps her. I think he'd make a good daddy, don't you?"

Ali unleashed a heavy sigh, her heart wrenching. "Yeah, baby. I think so too." *Too bad he wants nothing to do with the position.*

EXCUSES

Lio

"Home sweet home," Tini announced breathlessly as they stepped off the dirt road onto a cobblestone street. "I can't wait to sleep in my own bed."

They'd pushed hard during their second day of travel, the promise of home helping them arrive in Everpass shortly after nightfall rather than setting up camp again. He was certainly glad for it. If he had to endure another night by the fire with Ali, he'd surely be driven mad.

It was hard enough merely walking beside her. She'd been quiet most of the day, unless the girls included her in their conversation. He'd been no help. Not when he kept recalling how incredible she'd felt in his arms. And how sweet and pliant her lips had been under his.

His thoughts kept him on edge, and he'd kept his mouth shut, certain he'd say something even more idiotic than he had last night.

Goddess... Did I really have to tell her I'm drawn to her? Ali was probably itching for a chance to get away from him so she could have the privacy she craved. He'd come on too strong, and now she was full of regret. Why else would she be avoiding him as if he were diseased?

"Couldn't we sleep in the tents one more time?" Echo pouted, her steps flagging. "It's not fair. I like camping."

Ali rubbed Echo's shoulder. "We'll go camping again soon. Promise."

"It won't be the same." Echo sighed. "Cinder made it the funest."

"Hey!" Tini crossed her arms. "What about me?"

"You too, Tini." Echo grinned.

"You'll have to stop by for a visit soon then. See how Cinder is settling in." Tini tapped her chin. "What do you think, Lio? Can they come for dinner tomorrow?"

"That's fine with me."

"Can we, Mom? Can we?" Echo bounced lightly where she stood.

Ali's gaze flashed to his for what might've been the first time that day. But she was quick to look away, shooting Echo a soft smile. "I don't think so, baby. I have a lot of catching up to do at the shop."

Yep. Definitely avoiding me. And he only had himself to blame.

"But you still have to eat." Tini's gaze bounced between them, her eyes narrowing as she scrutinized his face.

"I appreciate the invitation, but now's not a great time." Ali bit her lip before ducking down to Echo's level. "Let's just play it by ear, okay? We'll set up a visit for you and Cinder soon."

He was beginning to suspect Ali had no intention of keeping her word. Or maybe she'd just arrange the visit with Tini when he was working.

Echo hung her head. "Fine."

Soon they turned down their street, and Lio dug into the cart, pulling out the first of his and Tini's things. Echo unleashed a massive yawn as they lingered on the road.

"I'd better get Echo home," Ali said. "We'll see you guys around."

"Wait! I need to say goodbye." Echo flung her arms around Tini, and Cinder meowed, clearly displeased at being squashed between them. "I'm gonna miss hanging out with you all the time, Tini."

Tini wrapped an arm around Echo's back and hugged her tightly. "I'm gonna miss you too, Echo. Don't forget, you're welcome to stop by and see Cinder anytime you want, okay?"

Echo scratched Cinder behind her ear. "I'm gonna miss you the most, Cinder."

Lio dumped the last of their possessions on the porch. But before he could straighten fully, a pair of arms wound around his waist. "Goodbye, Lio. Thanks for taking us to Paradise Plains. I had a lot of fun."

Surprise shot through him, just like it had the first time Echo had hugged him by the campfire. He hugged her back, while a dozen muddled feelings raged within his chest. "So did I. You be good for your mom, yeah? No more trouble?"

"Yeah, okay." She slid out of his arms and swiped a thumb beneath her eye. "Bye."

His heart twisted, the damned organ aching so badly he wouldn't have been surprised if it ripped in two.

Tini cleared her throat. "Goodbye, Ali."

Ali smiled warmly at his sister. "Bye, Tini." She dropped her gaze to the cobblestones and grabbed the cart. "Lio." Then she waved Echo forward. "Come on, baby. Let's go home."

Lio stood on the porch, watching them walk off into the moonlit night. Echo's braids bobbed on her head as she glanced back, sneaking peeks at them and waving every few steps. But not Ali. She didn't look back. Not even once.

The door banging open made him flinch. Lio whipped around, frowning as he spotted Tini glaring at him.

"Get in," she demanded, her voice hard. And when he bent to grab their things, she barked, "Leave them. We need to talk."

He strode inside, eyeing her curiously. In that moment, she reminded him so much of his mother. It was almost... eerie. "What is it?"

Tini deposited Cinder on the couch, then waited for the door to slam closed behind him before punching his shoulder. "What did you do?"

That's better. His mother had never pulled *that* move before. "I don't know what you're talking about."

She punched him again. "Liar. You clearly did something. Ali barely spoke a word all day. And you"—she sneered—"have the guiltiest look in your eyes. What." She punctuated each word with another jab. "Did. You. Do?"

"Goddess, would you stop hitting me?" He captured her fist as she drew back for another punch. "What the hell's gotten into you?"

"Me?" Her nostrils flared. "What about you?"

He released her hand. "Nothing's wrong with me."

"Not from where I'm standing." She crossed her arms. "Tell me, Stelios. What did you—"

Goddess, if she asks me one more time, I'm going to scream. "I fu—" He sucked in air through his teeth. "I messed up. There, you happy?"

"How?" Her voice softened.

He sank onto the couch. "Hell... I don't know. One moment we were kissing, and then—"

She gasped. "You kissed her? Really?"

"Yeah, really. But she stopped it." He sighed. "It was a mistake."

"Is that what she said?"

He dragged a hand through his hair. "Not in so many words."

"What words did she use?"

"She said she couldn't risk getting close to anyone who wasn't prepared to be a part of Echo's life."

She nodded. "I'm not surprised. And then..."

"Then... nothing. I told her I understood. Then she went to bed."

Tini picked up a throw pillow and clobbered him over the head with it. Repeatedly. Cinder dove off the couch and hid beneath it.

"I thought I told you to quit that." He caught the pillow on her fourth swing and stuffed it underneath his leg.

"I have to do something to get through your incredibly thick head."

He scowled.

"She wanted your reassurance, you idiot. Why didn't you tell her you're not going anywhere?"

"I wasn't about to lie."

Her brows furrowed. "What are you talking about?"

He muttered, "You might be moving."

"If I do, I wouldn't expect you to come with me." She scoffed. "You hated every moment we were in Paradise. I won't drag you to a village you can't stand."

"Why not? I've done the same to you."

"Sure. When I was little and moving was the best thing for me. But you're not a kid, Lio. And living somewhere that reminds you of the worst day of your life isn't best. Far from it." She sank down beside him. "I'm not a kid anymore either, you know. You're off the hook for raising me."

"We're still family. We've always stuck together."

She replied softly, "I know. And I'm really glad we did. But maybe it's time I struck out on my own."

"If that's what you want." As he forced the words out, his voice croaked and shock pulsed through his chest. He'd been positive that when Tini was ready for independence he'd be dancing in the streets. Not so choked up with emotion he could barely string a sentence together.

"What I want is for you to stop using me as an excuse to push that incredible woman away."

He scowled. "I am not."

She shot him a glare, a brow lifted so high it practically disappeared beneath her curls.

Is that what I'm doing? Hell, it wasn't even the first time he'd been accused of using Tini as an excuse.

"I love you to death, Big Butt. I really do. But I can't keep watching you give up your life for me. Do me a favor and tell Ali you're staying. Please?"

He sighed heavily. "I don't know if it'll do much good." Especially if Ali decided to uproot her life and move to Paradise for Echo's sake.

"Of course it will." She smiled. "Unless... that's not all you're worried about, is it?"

Damned spirit magic. She shouldn't be able to take one look at his face and see all his hidden fears staring back at her.

"Losing them"—he glanced at the portrait hanging over the mantelpiece—"it really was the worst day of my life. I don't know if I can live through another worst."

She clasped his hand within both of hers, her eyes growing misty. "I don't believe that. You're the strongest man I know, and I'm not just saying that because you're my brother."

He shook his head.

"Besides, you're the only one who makes a habit out of running into burning buildings. There's a pretty good chance they'll outlive you."

He shot her a glare.

She squeezed his hand. "You don't have to listen to me, Lio, but I really hope you do. I'd hate it if you let the fear of losing someone else stop you from opening your heart to love." She nodded at the portrait. "And I'm sure they'd hate it, too." Then she pulled her hands free. "Just promise me you'll think long and hard about what you really want. If I can do it, then so can you."

"I can do that."

"All right." She stood. "Now that we've got that settled, my bed is calling me."

He sat there long after Tini went to bed, mulling over her words. She'd opened his eyes to the deep-rooted worries he'd been too scared to face. But merely understanding what had driven him didn't make the fear fade. If anything, it just made it worse. Now that he wasn't actively ignoring all the warning bells chiming deep in his soul, they rang out loudly, deafening him.

Would Ali give him another chance after he mucked things up so horribly? Could he be the man she needed? Not just a lover... but a surrogate father for Echo, too. At least with that, he held a sliver of confidence. He'd certainly had enough practice, and he hadn't lied when he told her he couldn't imagine having a child, only to ignore them. But would Echo accept him in that role after their less than auspicious introduction?

Hell, even if everything went well, could he live with the persistent fear of losing them?

Maybe it was better just to forget it all. Ali could find someone better. A man who didn't risk his life running into burning buildings. Who didn't make her dizzy by shadowing her one moment and pushing her away the next.

Goddess... What am I going to do?

CHANGES

Ali

Stellar Spirit's front door swung closed behind her. "Nora? You in here?"

She'd spent a restless night tossing and turning before dropping Echo off at Mrs. Pilbeck's place. Then she'd hightailed it back across town, desperate for advice.

Nora's blue dress swished around her legs as she breezed in through the back door, a small stack of boxes balanced in her hands. She must be returning from her morning ritual, handing out leftovers from the night before to any hungry children that stopped by on their way to school.

"There you are!"

"Ahh!" Nora shrieked, fumbling the boxes. "Goddess, Ali. You scared me! I wasn't expecting you back so soon."

"Sorry. We got back earlier than expected." She grabbed half the stack, which amounted to two boxes. "Let me help you with that."

"Thanks." Ali crossed the floor and placed the rest on the bar top. "Slow day yesterday. I ended up with more leftovers than usual. Have you eaten yet?"

She shook her head, attempting to hand the boxes back.

"Dig in. Least I can do is feed you after I screamed your ears off."

"Thanks." She tore open the lid, grinning as the savory aroma of eggs and roasted vegetables drifted up to greet her.

"So how did the trip go?" Nora opened a box and placed it on the shelf next to Roo's nest. "How's Echo doing?"

Roo's big ears perked up, her nose twitched, and she wasted no time hopping out of her bed and into the box. Ali swallowed the urge to laugh as the tiny critter disappeared completely within the container.

"She's doing great, all things considered. And the trip went surprisingly well. I'm honestly a little shocked at how different Paradise Plains ended up being from my old village."

"Different good?" Nora asked, sliding a mug of cider in front of her.

"Yeah." She sighed.

Nora's brow furrowed. "If that's the case, then why do you look so down?" She leaned on the bar. "And why the early visit?"

"You know me too well." She forced a grin. "I need your advice."

"Happy to help. But you'd better start at the beginning. I need all the dirty details if you want the best advice out of me." Nora wiggled her brows.

"All right…" She drew a deep breath and started talking. By the time she'd recounted everything, they'd finished eating, even Roo. Nora's familiar had climbed back into her bed, licking her fur and observing Ali with her unusually intelligent eyes.

"So what do you think?" Ali asked.

Nora tilted her head. "About which part?"

"All of it." She rubbed her temples. "Especially Lio."

"Don't know if I can say. Think I'm gonna need more details."

"I already told you everything."

"Yeah, you told me what happened. But you left out the most important part. What are you feeling?"

Ali searched within herself, but all she found was a jumbled mess of conflicting emotions. "Too much," she admitted finally. "I don't even know how to sort it all out in my head."

"That's your problem." Nora leaned forward and tapped Ali's chest gently. "You're listening to the wrong organ."

She groaned, dropping her head onto the bar. "And if my heart wants the wrong man?"

"Maybe your heart sees something that your mind doesn't."

She shook her head, welcoming the hard press of wood rolling across her forehead. "I can't just ignore the facts. Not with Echo counting on me." She lifted her face. "He's made it clear what he wants time and time again. I can't keep being a fool who doesn't listen."

"I thought you said he admitted to being conflicted when you kissed?" Nora arched a brow.

"It's not enough. I can't let someone into our lives who isn't all in. Right?"

Nora smiled softly. "You don't have to convince me." She reached across the bar and grabbed her hands. "Me, though? I'm gonna try my damnedest to convince you to stay, just like you did when I was thinking about leaving."

Ali twisted her lips. "It could be good for Echo... living with people who accept her as she is."

"I won't argue with that. But there's something to be said for sticking around when times are tough. If you stay here, running your successful business and spending time with the friends who love you both, you'll show her how resilience pays off." Nora chuckled lightly. "Or you can run away. What kind of message do you think that sends?"

Ali's heart clenched. "Not a good one." She'd run from her problems before—leaving her village when the stigma of summoning fire became too hard to bear, then again after Echo's father left her—so it wasn't much of a surprise that she'd been considering it again. But Nora was right. She couldn't keep running. Not while Echo was watching.

"If you end up deciding to move, I'll hate it, but I'll understand. Just make sure you're doing it for the right reason." Nora picked up a rag and started polishing the bar. "Or you can stay just to make me happy. I won't argue with that either."

Ali chuckled. "At least someone wants me."

Nora clicked her tongue. "Strange thing to say when you have two guys sniffing after you. Maybe we should hunt for a love triangle romance for book club. Could put some things in perspective."

"Or I can just forget them both. Go back to living vicariously through my fiction."

"That's always an option." Nora grinned. "Speaking of books... I may have the perfect thing to take your mind off your troubles for a little while."

"I can stand for a distraction." She certainly wasn't any closer to working through her muddled emotions. "What is it?"

Nora bent behind the bar. "I'm finally ready to try writing to my sister. You want to stick around for moral support?"

She sat up straight. "Of course I will." In her opinion, Nora had put off the task for far too long. If Ali had found out she had a long-lost sister who she could contact with a charmed book, she would've written a message immediately. But they all had their own personal demons to battle. She'd certainly unearthed her share of the pesky beasts over the last few weeks. The least she could do was stick around while her bestie tackled hers.

Nora slid the black book onto the bar top. Then she plucked Roo out of her nest and placed her beside it before slipping her white crescent moon necklace off her neck.

"What did you end up deciding to write?" Ali asked.

Nora fitted the necklace into the matching indentation on the book's front cover. "Goddess, don't even ask. I can't tell you how many messages I've drafted in my head." She sighed as she tugged the front cover open and flipped to the first empty page. "Finally, I decided, the hell with it. No words will ever be perfect enough. I just need to write something and get it over with."

"Huh. Almost feels like you could've come to that conclusion on day one."

Nora's eyes narrowed. "Yeah, well, ask anyone. I'm too stubborn for my own good." She chuckled humorlessly. "Goddess... Am I really ready for this? What if she's dreadful? What if—"

"Stop." Ali covered Nora's shaking hand with hers. "She could be amazing, just like you. You won't find out if you don't give her a chance."

"You're right." Nora sucked in a deep breath, then set a pen to the page.

Ali sat in silence, listening to the soft scrape of ink on parchment.

Nora spun the book to face her after she finished. "What do you think?"

She glanced down, her gaze dancing across the page.

Hello,

You don't know me, but ever since I learned you existed, I've wanted to know you. I'm your sister, Nora, the proud owner of Stellar Spirits, a tavern in Everpass. I don't ask for anything except for a chance to speak to you. To finally meet you and discover the sister that fate hid away from me. I hope you'll write back, even just a few words.

Nora

"It's perfect." She smiled.

Nora stared at the page, her face grave.

"What's wrong?"

"I suppose there was a part of me hoping that she'd write back instantly. No such luck."

She clasped Nora's hand. "She'll write back. The fates wouldn't be so cruel to give you this chance just for nothing to come from it."

"I hope you're right." Nora closed the book softly. "You do give the best advice... I really liked what you said earlier."

"Hm?" She lifted a brow. "What was that?"

"When you said I won't find out if I don't give her a chance." Nora tapped the pen on the bar. "It's good to give the people in our lives a chance, don't you think? Maybe even... a second chance?"

Ali rolled her eyes. "Uh huh. Real smooth way to get your point across."

Nora chuckled. "It was your point, not mine. Just saying..."

With a sigh, she hopped off her bar stool. "I'll keep that in mind. Thanks for listening, Nor."

"Anytime." Nora smiled.

She left Stellar Spirits feeling marginally better than when she'd entered. Sure, her life was still a mess, and her emotions were just as tangled as before, but at least her belly was full. That counted for something. The rest, she'd figure out later.

DRAGGING

Lio

"Hey, beef—" Lio cringed when he spotted a blond man facing away from him in the smithy. "Sorry, didn't realize you had customers. I'll come back."

"Don't leave on my account, Chief." The man swung around, grinning.

Lio sighed and walked further inside. "Oh, Kieran. It's just you." He'd gotten to know the half-elf pretty well since Kieran joined the brigade over the winter. He was a bit of a joker when they had downtime, but he always took his job seriously when it counted, and that had been enough to earn Lio's respect.

Kieran lifted a wrist—showing off his scarred arm, minus the hand he'd lost in service to the Crown—and grinned. "Dav's making some adjustments to my prosthesis."

"Ah..." Lio had been the one to introduce Kieran to Davos and recommended the hook attachment on the day they'd first met. "Sure you don't want privacy for that?"

"If he did, he wouldn't have invited me to tag along," a deep voice said.

Lio's stomach clenched when he spotted the source. It was a miracle he'd missed him. If the burly half-orc hadn't been squatting to admire one of Davos's trinket cases, he'd have been impossible to miss.

"Gotta squeeze in our hangouts when we can, right Seth?" Kieran chuckled.

Seth straightened to his full height. "If you weren't shacking up with my sister, we'd have a lot more time on our hands."

"Aw, still missing me like crazy, aren't ya?" Kieran shot Seth a mischievous smirk. "That's why I brought you to meet Dav. You bachelors ought to stick together."

Davos glanced up, his hands still busy fiddling inside of Kieran's hook. "How did I get dragged into this? You're swinging a sword at the wrong foe." He nodded in Lio's direction. "Chiefy charmer over there is the one with all the village ladies chasing after him."

Lio's scowl deepened so much his cheeks ached.

Davos slanted his head. "What? It's true."

"Don't remind me. I just spent the last few days warding off a bunch of baby-crazed nymphs in Paradise Plains." He shuddered.

"How did the trip go?" Davos's eyes narrowed. "Ali was pretty tight-lipped when she lit my forge this morning."

Seth whistled. "I heard she was heading off on a holiday. You went, too?"

"Yeah." Lio crossed his arms. "You got a problem with that?"

"I didn't say that." Seth raised his hands in surrender. "Ali and I are just friends, so you can quit with the death glares. I had my fill of that at the dance."

Davos chuckled. "Really? Do tell."

Seth jabbed a thumb outward, pointing it in Lio's direction. "I kept catching him leveling these lethal stares at me. That got old real fast. Kind of hard to dance a jig when you're in fear for your life." He dropped his hand at his side, smirking. "I managed, though."

Lio gritted his teeth and turned his attention to Davos. "The trip was fine."

"Just fine?" Davos's eyes narrowed again.

He shrugged. "Most of it." He shook his head, regretting his decision to drop by. He'd just wanted Davos's advice, not to make his romantic blunders public knowledge. "I ought to come back when you're not busy."

"If you're about to ask me how to woo the girl, you'd be better off asking while I have some backup. I'm not exactly an expert on courting." Davos nodded at Kieran. "At least we have one success story present."

"Guilty as charged." Kieran puffed out his chest. "And since I'm currently shacked up with the object of your affection's best friend, if you don't fill me in now, I'm bound to hear what happened eventually."

Seth leaned against the wall, crossing his arms. "Nothing stays a secret long in small towns."

True, Davos didn't make a habit of courting. In the years Lio had known him, he could count the number of times he'd spotted Davos out with a lady on one hand. Maybe it would help to get some input from men who were a bit more familiar with dealing with the opposite sex. "Fine. Guess I could use all the advice I can get."

"So what happened on that trip that's got you so wound up?" Davos asked.

"Long story short, me and Ali had a moment where things got... physical. But she put a stop to it before it got far. Said she wasn't interested in taking things further with anyone who wasn't in it for the long haul. For her—and Echo."

"Sounds like something she'd say," Davos said as he continued to tinker. "I don't blame her. She's been abandoned by plenty of folks in the past who should've stuck around."

"What did you say when she told you that?" Kieran asked.

"That I understood."

"That's all?" Seth clicked his tongue. "Not very reassuring."

He scrubbed a hand down his face. "I know. It's just that none of this was part of my plans."

Kieran bobbed his head in agreement. "Been there. But plans change. Doesn't mean the change won't work out for the better. It did with me and Nora."

Lio sighed. "I can't help feeling like I'm being pushed into something I'm not ready for."

Davos nodded. "Hm. I think I see what's happening here."

"You do?" Lio asked.

Davos said, "When your parents passed and you took on the responsibility of raising Tini, you were caught off guard. Now Ali asking you to be a part of Echo's life feels like more of the same. Am I right?"

"Yeah," he admitted.

"Well, you're wrong. This is totally different," Davos stated matter-of-factly.

Lio blinked. "How do you figure?"

Davos explained, "Tini was family. You felt duty-bound to take care of her, and rightly so. I don't think any decent man in the same position would do any differently. But being there for Ali and Echo—that's a choice, and one you have no obligation to uphold. No one would fault you for cutting ties if that's what you really want."

Kieran asked, "Is that what you want?"

Stomach churning, he searched within himself. It didn't take long to find the answer.

He had to admit, things were so much better with Ali around. His feelings for her went far deeper than physical attraction. He got a thrill out of talking to her and looked forward to seeing her each day. She brought fun and laughter to his life that he'd been sorely missing.

Yeah, Echo had seemed like a deal breaker at first, but he couldn't deny how much she'd grown on him. She was silly, and genuine, and sweet. Like on the night when he'd been beside himself, worried over Tini's future, and she'd brought Cinder to keep him company. Sure, she got into trouble more often than was wise, but what kid didn't? If he let the fear of future obstacles stop him from pursuing a relationship with them, then he was robbing himself of potential happiness.

"No. I don't want to cut ties," he admitted gruffly.

"You really think you aren't ready to handle courting a woman with a kid?" Seth lifted a brow. "I don't know if you've noticed, but Echo's pretty great. And it's not like you don't have any experience."

"I thought I wasn't. But I've been starting to come around to the idea."

Davos tipped his head forward. "Thought so. If that's the case, then you ought to march next door right now and tell her exactly how you feel."

Seth chimed in, "Agreed."

He swallowed, his heart thudding heavily.

"Go on then." Davos set down his tool and made a shooing motion. "What are you waiting for?"

He knew their advice was sound. Nothing was going to change if he didn't find the courage to put his heart on the line. Yet despite that knowledge, his boots remained rooted to the floor.

Kieran eyed him shrewdly. "Think I know what your problem is."

"You do?" he asked.

"Yep. I recognize that look in your eyes. Had it myself not too long ago." Kieran leaned back on his heels. "You've got a little voice in your head telling you that you aren't up to the task. That she deserves more. She'd be better off without you. Sound about right?"

"I was there for that." Seth chuckled and jabbed a thumb in Kieran's direction. "Don't let yourself turn into him. I had to wade through a literal mess he made while wallowing in his misery. It wasn't pretty—and don't even get me started on the stench."

"Hey, that's my boss you're mouthing off to, numbskull." Kieran shoved Seth's shoulder with a smirk, then turned to Lio. "I'd tell you to ignore him, but he makes a good point. I wasted months thinking Nora was better off without me. It took Seth knocking some sense into me for me to realize that what she actually deserved from me was honesty."

Seth nodded. "It's natural to have doubts. Everyone does sooner or later, but what's important is working through them together. Keeping secrets from your partner is the fastest way to destroy a relationship." Seth's gaze went unfocused, and his expression suddenly turned grave. Lio couldn't help wondering if he was recalling something specific—and personal.

"He's right. As soon as I talked it out with Nora, everything got better. Yeah, it wasn't easy delving into my past and laying my feelings bare, but it was all worth it. Now I have her." Kieran leaned back, flashing the carefree smile of a man who'd landed the girl of his dreams.

A pang of jealousy struck him. He wanted that, too. And not just with some random childless beauty. There was only one woman he could picture filling that role in his life. He hadn't counted on her coming as part of a package deal, but that thought didn't bother him half as much as it once had. And while he wouldn't lie that he was thrilled about taking on the responsibility, he'd begun to open himself up to the positives that he'd forgotten about before their trip.

Another child meant more worries, but it also meant more fun. He'd finally give Tini the sister she'd always longed for. He'd have someone to tuck in at night when Tini moved away and left him on his own. Plus, he'd have another shot at having the close family he'd been missing since his parents passed. And all of it with the one woman who drove him to distraction, and felt like utter perfection in his arms.

"Stop dragging your feet, puddle brain. Go get your girl." Davos shooed him away again, a crooked grin curving across his bovine lips.

"All right. Think I will." He backed away, heading for the front door. "Thanks for the advice."

"Anytime, Chief," Kieran said.

Seth grinned. "Good luck!"

He blinked as his eyes adjusted to the bright morning sunshine before staring at the Open sign in Our Glass's front window. *Let's hope it doesn't come down to luck...*

Lio was finally ready to lay it all on the line. Yeah, Ali was frustrating as hell at the best of times. She never missed a chance to crack a joke at his expense. And she worked in a profession that guaranteed she'd always be susceptible to the danger he'd dedicated his life to fighting.

But as he stood there in the street, dredging up the courage to take the final steps that would bring him to her, all his worries paled in comparison to the future he knew they'd have if she gave him another chance.

Living a life by her side wouldn't be neat and tidy like he was used to. It would be chaotic and unpredictable, and he might even get burned once or twice, but he had no doubt it would be worth it. He'd rather be singed by her sharp wit a thousand times than spend an eternity in his safe, boring bubble without her.

Here goes nothing.

He inhaled deeply and marched to her door, only to be cut off as he reached for the handle by a tall stranger who seemed oddly familiar.

"Sorry, friend," the man said with a polite smile as he held the door open, setting the bell chiming and alerting Ali's assistant to their presence. "After you?"

"No problem. You go ahead." The last thing he wanted was to interrupt Ali while she had customers waiting. But with the bloke holding the door for him, he had little choice but to follow him inside.

Goddess, this is already going so well... Hopefully the awkward entrance didn't set the tone for the entire visit, or he might need that luck after all.

The teller, a young man with curly red hair and pale freckled skin he'd seen around but hadn't been introduced to yet, greeted the stranger. "Welcome to Our Glass. Can I help you find anything?"

"Not just yet. I'd like to browse, if you don't mind," the man replied. He scanned the showroom, his eyes widening as he meandered closer to the back wall, which was covered floor to ceiling in gorgeous lamps glowing softly with light magic.

"Sure, be my guest." The teller waved him forward with a smile, then faced Lio. "Hello, Chief. Anything I can help you with today?"

Lio approached the sales counter and cleared his throat. "I was hoping to speak with Ali. Is she in?"

"She's in the workshop. I'll get her for you."

Lio nodded. "Thanks." Then he heaved a sigh and stood there waiting as the teller disappeared into the back room.

His pulse ran rampant, his mind swirling with a thousand things he wanted to say. He clenched his hands into fists, turning to stare at the stranger to take his mind off the myriad ways their impending conversation might go wrong.

Where did he know that man from? He was dark-haired, with rich brown skin and a handsome face, wearing plain hand-spun clothes. But though he swore he'd seen him before, Lio just couldn't put his finger on where.

"Lio?" Ali emerged from the back room with a battered apron covering her clothes and a frown on her pretty face. "What are you doing here?"

He swallowed. "I was hoping we could talk. Do you have—"

"Alsira? It *is* you!" The stranger strode forward, stopping beside him. "I can't believe it!"

Ali's eyes popped wide. "Joffin. How—Where?" She blinked repeatedly. "Goddess, it's been ages."

Lio's heart stalled. He suddenly recalled where he'd spotted the man—during their trip to the capital, from across a crowded street. It was the same man who'd caused Ali to stop short and say, "*Just thought I spotted someone I knew a lifetime ago.*"

And what's worse, he'd overheard enough of Ali and Echo's conversation to recognize the name. Echo's father was back, staring at Ali like she was a lost treasure he'd been searching for his entire life.

Lio had the sudden urge to scream.

Ali turned to him, her face pinched. "Lio, do you mind if we talk later?" Then she glanced at the door, and he wasn't too dense to realize she wanted him gone.

He nodded blankly. "Sure." He'd rather gouge out his eyes than leave her alone with that prick, but he couldn't exactly insert himself into her conversation when she'd asked him again and again for privacy.

So he walked out of her shop, cursing himself for hesitating. It might have just cost him everything...

Try Harder

Ali

She watched Lio leave, his back ramrod straight, his head held high, hands tight fists at his side. *Why did I ask him to go? I should've begged him to stay.*

She'd been sorely tempted. If they'd left things even marginally better than the current state of uncertainty they were in, she definitely would've. But without knowing exactly where they stood, she didn't feel comfortable inviting Lio to stick around to hear whatever Joffin had to say.

What the hell is he doing here? She crossed her arms, staying behind the sales counter. She'd told Corbin to take a break when he'd ducked into the workshop and informed her Lio was looking for her, and now she was filled with regret. Not that she expected Joffin to do anything crazy, but it would've been nice to have backup ready to jump in, just in case.

There was always Davos. He'd come running in a heartbeat if she screamed for him. With that reassurance bolstering her spirits, she sucked in a deep breath and asked, "What the hell are you doing here, Joff?"

He stiffened slightly before flashing the disarming smile she'd once found so charming. Now, the sight of his pearly whites only irritated her. "Is that anyway to greet an old friend?" he asked softly.

She arched a brow and popped out a hip. "Funny. I thought for sure being friends was off the table when you left me in the lurch while I was pregnant with your child."

He glanced around as if searching for something—or someone. "Where is Echo?"

It was her turn to stiffen. "I'm surprised you even know her name."

He hung his head, the perfect picture of contrition—but she didn't trust it. She didn't trust *him*. Not for one heartbeat.

"I know I have a lot to explain, and a lot of mistakes to answer for. Can you just give me a chance? Please?"

Nora's advice about second chances rang in her ears. Yeah, she'd meant it for another man, but might as well put it to use now. "Fine. Explain."

"I should've never left you without a word. I was young and dumb and overwhelmed, but I know that's no excuse. My mistake has haunted me ever since. I lost count of how many times I wished I could go back and change that thoughtless decision."

"Uh huh." Pretty words, but who knew if they were true?

"I mean it, Ali." He reached across the counter, but she kept her hands firmly tucked under her crossed arms. "I'd left on a six-month voyage, and when I got back to Seahaven, the first thing I did was search for you. Both of you. That's how I learned our daughter's name. I tracked down the midwife you hired and begged her to tell me everything she knew." He flashed a crooked grin. "I had to bribe her with a ridiculous amount of coin to even get that much out of her. And she never told me where to find you."

A pang struck her chest. "She didn't know. No one did." Ali hadn't even known where she was headed, just that she couldn't bear another moment in a village full of so many painful memories. "It's not fun discovering someone you were counting on to stick around up and left, is it?"

"No, it's not." He sighed heavily. "I'm so sorry I put you through that. It was dreadful wondering where you'd gone. I searched for you at every port I stopped in for years until I finally gave up hope of ever finding you."

"How *did* you find me?"

He grinned. "That was you back in the capital, yes?"

So she *had* seen him... When their gazes met and he'd shown no sign of recognition, she'd been certain she was mistaken. Time had chiseled Joffin's features, and without his youthful softness, he was even more handsome, which had made it easy for her to doubt her recollection.

"At first, I was convinced my mind was playing tricks on me. But I couldn't stop wondering if it had been you. After a few days of driving myself crazy, I stopped in the shop I spotted you coming out of and asked the owner if she knew you."

"Ivana told you where to find me?"

"After a bit of convincing. At first, she was certain I was only interested in you so I could outbid her for your... unique product design." He smirked. "If I may say so, you're quite inventive. I'm impressed."

Her stomach dropped. "Um... thanks." Joffin was the last person she needed to know about her secret side business. Would he use the information against her, threatening her place in Everpass?

"I've been here for the better part of a week, waiting for your shop to open." He leaned back on his heels. "The village is lovely. It seems like a fantastic place to raise Echo. You chose well."

Her eyes narrowed. "We like it here."

"I do, too. I've been staying at the Golden Lark Inn, but I've been thinking about finding something more permanent."

Her mouth dropped open. "You are? Why?"

"Isn't it obvious?" He tilted his head, his gaze soft, his tone gentle and sincere. "I lost so much time with Echo. And with you. I want to be a part of your lives, the way I should've been from the start."

Goddess... can I trust him? She shook her head. "Joff... I honestly don't know what to say."

"That's all right." He shifted and looked away. "You weren't expecting me. And I know it's a lot to ask. But please think about it. Can you do that for me at least?" His eyes lifted to hers again, his gaze imploring.

She stood there in silence, utterly stunned. Not a single part of her had been expecting this. And not just today... *ever.*

Seeing Joffin brought so many memories swirling back. He'd been her first love. He was the father of her daughter. And here he was, begging for another chance to be a part of their lives, at the exact moment that she was so conflicted about what she wanted out of hers.

Wouldn't that be such a beautiful ending?

Old lovers reunited.

A family mended.

She could give her daughter the father she'd always longed for.

She'd always put Echo first, and she always would. Giving Joffin a chance to make amends and prove he could be the father he should've been from the start wasn't even in question. If she sent him away and destroyed Echo's chance of meeting him, that would be unforgivable. Not when she knew how badly her daughter craved that connection.

But no matter how much she loved her daughter, there was one thing she refused to bend on.

"I don't have to think about it." She drew in a calming breath and met his gaze directly. "Here's what's going to happen. I will tell Echo you're here. If—and only if—she wants to meet you, then we'll arrange a visit."

Joffin exhaled heavily and grinned. "Thank you."

"Don't thank me yet." She shot him a hard glare. "Echo's well-being is far more important to me than your feelings. If you hurt her, even once, I won't just cut off contact. I'll drag you to the edge of town and make sure you disappear—for good."

"Got it." He leaned forward. "You won't have to worry about dragging. I swear I don't want to hurt her. I don't want to hurt either of you."

"That's good to hear." Whether he really meant it, only time would tell.

"Does that mean you'll give me another chance? I asked around. Heard you're not married. Neither am I..." He flashed another disarming smile. "I just can't seem to get over my first love, no matter how hard I try."

"Joffin..." She finally uncrossed her arms and grabbed his hand. There were no tingles on her flesh. No flutter in her belly. Just the clammy hand of a man she'd once loved clasped in her grasp. "You're gonna need to try harder."

He squeezed her fingers gently. "You don't mean that... do you?"

"We're over. We have been for a very long time. Us getting back together will never happen. *Ever.* If you want a chance at being part of Echo's life, I need you to stop asking." She pulled her hand free. "Understood?"

It was all she could do to trust him enough to meet Echo. If she had followed her first instinct, she would've happily told him to get lost and never return. But Echo deserved a chance to know him, so she buried the urge.

Still, she knew she could never trust him with her heart. That ship had sailed the moment he sailed off without them.

Joffin sighed. "I'm sorry to hear that. But I understand, and I'll stop bringing it up. Though if you ever change your mind—"

"I won't." Her voice rang out, sharp and full of decisiveness. "I'll send word to the Golden Lark after I speak to Echo."

"All right." He straightened. "I'll be waiting."

She cleared her throat. "One more thing. You know that design you saw at Ivana's shop?"

"Yeah? What about it?" Joffin asked.

"Do me a favor and keep that between us. Please?"

Her pulse quickened. She'd been unsure until this very moment how much staying in Everpass mattered to her. Now that she'd been to Paradise Plains and discovered how easy it would be to pack up and start over, she shouldn't have been so worried. But the threat to her business, and to her place in the village that she'd made her home, where she'd met so many people that she loved, had scared her more than she cared to admit.

"My lips are sealed." Joffin backed away with a wave. "It was great seeing you, Ali. I'll see you soon?"

She nodded. "Goodbye, Joff."

After the door swung closed, she crossed the shop, locked the front door, and flipped the Open sign around. Then she rubbed her sweaty hands down her pants and slumped against the door. As soon as her assistant returned, she was giving him the rest of the day off. There was no way she could continue working today. Not with her head reeling from everything she'd just learned.

What would Echo say? At least Ali had already opened the conversation about Joffin when she'd told her the truth. Now Echo could go into their meeting with all the facts, and not be blindsided by his pretty words. But would she even want to meet him?

Anxiety thrummed through her bones. What would Joffin do if Echo said no?

All In

Lio

His boots echoed on the cobblestones as he paced between Davos and Ali's shops. His mind screamed at him to stare into Our Glass's windows, but he ignored the urge, determined to keep his word.

He had no doubt that idiot was inside, feeding Ali some sob story about their years apart. But he had no idea how she'd react to it.

Was she crying on his shoulder?

Had he wrapped his arms around her? Even... kissed her?

Lava coursed through his veins, burning so hot he knew if he summoned, only steam would escape.

A door banged open. "Lio?" Kieran asked. "What are you doing out here?"

He lifted his head, and whatever expression painted his face was enough to make Kieran gasp and Seth draw back in surprise, his mouth agape.

"Shit, something went wrong." Kieran snagged his elbow and hauled him inside the smithy. "Get in here before you murder someone."

Davos glanced up from the sales counter. "Did you forget—" His gaze landed on Lio, and he dropped the tool in his hand with a resounding crack. "Stelios, what the hell happened?"

When Lio didn't respond, Seth tilted his palms upward and lifted his shoulders. "We found him out front pacing a hole in the cobbles."

Kieran snapped his fingers in front of Lio's face. "Hey, are you okay?"

Lio blinked, forcing down enough of his maddening thoughts to choke out a reply. "No."

"Tell us what happened. Maybe we can help," Kieran said.

Lio dragged a hand through his hair. "Doubtful."

"Did she turn you down?" Davos asked carefully.

He shook his head.

"You chickened out?" Seth guessed.

Glaring, he spat out, "Hardly. We didn't have time to talk."

Kieran's brow furrowed. "Why not?"

"Her ex showed up, and she asked me to leave."

Seth gaped. "What ex?"

"Echo's father."

Kieran's brow furrowed. "I thought he wasn't in the picture? Nora said she's never seen him, and Ali doesn't even like talking about him."

Davos scoffed. "He's a piece of shit, if you ask me. Ran out on them the first chance he got." He glared at Lio. "Why did you leave her with that jerk?"

"I didn't want to." Lio rubbed his temples. "She could've asked me to stay." But she hadn't... Did she want to get back together with Echo's dad? What if she'd just been waiting for this opportunity all along?

"Stop," Davos insisted, his tone hard. "I can hear the gears clanking in your head. Don't turn a pebble into a mountain peak."

Kieran added, "He's right. Just because he showed up doesn't change a thing. Wait until he's gone and march back over there. She needs to hear from you." He clasped Lio's shoulder. "Trust me, if you don't tell her how you feel, you'll always regret it. I made the same mistake once, and I'm still kicking myself for it."

He drew a calming breath. They were right. He couldn't just sit back and let that fool drive a wedge between them. Ali needed to know that he was all in, and he wouldn't give up without a fight. "I plan to," he stated firmly.

Seth grinned. "That's the spirit!" He strode to the window and stared out at the street. "I'll let you know when he leaves."

Lio's heart raced. He still could hardly believe it. Why in the realm did the fool have to come back now?

"She won't take him back." Davos crossed his arms. "Ali's too smart for that."

His stomach churned. "I hope you're right." He sighed heavily.

"What is it?" Kieran asked.

"Ali's always going on about how she wants to do what's best for Echo. You don't think... Would she give him another chance, for her sake?" His hand tangled in his hair again, tugging at the roots. "They share blood. I can't compete with that."

As the words left his lips, shock reverberated through him. Just a few moments ago, he would've sworn he was still reluctant about taking a place in Echo's life, but now, he couldn't escape the realization that he'd been completely wrong.

Echo deserved so much more than being saddled with a father who would turn tail and run when things got tough. She should have someone she could count on through thick and thin. Someone who showed up, day in and day out, and chose her. If Ali gave him a chance, he'd happily spend a lifetime proving that he was the right man for the job.

"Family is more than shared blood. Ali knows that better than most." Davos rounded the counter and clasped Lio's arm. "You just have to remind her."

"He just left," Seth announced.

Kieran grinned. "Go on, Lio. You got this."

"Yeah, you do," Davos added.

"Wait..." Seth squinted out the window. "She just flipped the Open sign to Closed."

"Hell." He groaned. "What now?"

Davos waved at the back door. "Go out through the back. She won't leave without shutting down everything. She'll be in her workshop for a while yet."

"Thanks." He set off, each step making his nerves tighten. He'd barely worked out what he wanted to say earlier, but that was before her ex showed up. Now he had no clue what he was heading into. What Ali might have agreed to.

But no matter what pretty tale she'd just been regaled with, he was determined to speak his piece. Ali deserved the full truth, and it was beyond time he found the courage to share it. She was worth it. They both were.

He crossed the yard, his steps sure and solid. Then he lifted his fist, poised to knock, just as the door swung open.

"Oh, hello again." Her assistant flinched in the doorway. "Sorry, Chief, but we're closing early today."

"I need to talk to Ali."

The assistant lifted a brow and opened his mouth. But before he spoke, Ali's voice rose in the distance. "It's all right. Let him in."

"You're the boss." He stepped aside and called out, "Do you need me to stick around?"

"No." Ali appeared, her smile pinched. "See you tomorrow, Corben."

"Can I come in?" he asked gruffly as Corben headed for the back gate.

She sighed. "Sure."

Warmth wrapped around him as he stepped within reach of the lit furnace. "Are you all right?"

"Course. Why wouldn't I be?" Ali dragged the door closed.

He was surprised she hadn't cracked a joke to really sell the idea that she was okay. "Imagine I'd be pretty upset if someone who abandoned me showed up out of the blue."

"Caught that, huh?" She shot him a crooked grin. "The goddess loves sending chaos my way when I least expect it. Shocker."

And there's the joke... "Ali, I—"

"Look, I know you wanted to talk, but I have a lot going on. Can it wait?"

A smarter man would've likely agreed to her request. Better to rip out your heart and set it at someone's feet when they're in a good mood. But look how it turned out the last time he'd hesitated. "No, it really can't wait."

She crossed her arms, her smile fading. "What is it?"

All the carefully thought-out words he'd planned evaporated. Ali always seemed to have that effect on him. Normally, he'd run far and fast from anyone who evoked a similar reaction. But with her, he couldn't get close enough.

"I'm an idiot," he blurted.

Ali chuckled. "That's what you've been dying to tell me?"

He shook his head, his stomach churning. "No. I need to apologize."

She cocked a brow. "For what, exactly?"

"For our last night on the road. And that kiss."

Her eyes widened. "Oh."

Hell, he was bungling this horribly. He sensed it, but couldn't seem to stem the flow of dumb words escaping his lips. "Not the actual kissing. That part was great. Honestly think I forgot how to breathe while it was happening, and I'd love to do it again."

"Uh huh." Some of the tension in her frame lifted. "So what are you apologizing for?"

"I'm sorry for how it ended."

She picked at her sleeve, frowning. "Yeah. Me too."

He stepped closer, drawing near enough to touch her, but he kept his hands pinned to his sides. "You deserve to have someone in your life who doesn't make you guess where you stand. Someone who chooses you with confidence, not uncertainty. And not just you. Echo too."

"It's really nice to hear that." She smiled softly. "But really, Lio, you didn't have to explain or apologize. You said you understood then, and you're saying it now. We can go back to being friends. No hard feelings."

Goddess, you're bungling it again, Stelios. "Wait, that's not it at all. I mean—" He inhaled sharply. "I don't want to be friends."

"Ah… Tini decided to move?" She pursed her lips. "I get it. She was the reason you wanted to be friends in the first place, so now—"

"No." He grabbed her arms, keeping her in place when it looked like she was about to step back. "I want you. *Both* of you. And I'm sorry it took me so long to realize it."

WILDFIRE

Ali

She stood rooted to the spot, staring at Lio's face as shock reverberated through her bones. He wasn't a smooth talker, that was for sure. But she already had a taste of what life was like with someone whose pretty words amounted to nothing useful in the end. She'd take the bumbling confession of a man who stood by his word over the empty promises of a scoundrel any day of the week.

If she'd learned anything about Lio, it was that when he set his mind to something—like taking care of his sister, becoming fire chief, or showing up for the hastily made plans she'd sprung on him—he always followed through. Still, she was having a hard time believing her ears.

Why would a man who valued his freedom more than anything agree to give it up for her and her daughter?

"Um... Come again?"

"I've fallen for you, Ali. I want us to be together. For you, me, and Echo to be a family. And I wish I would've told you that after we kissed."

Her heart fluttered, the blasted thing acting like a caged bird desperate to take flight. But before she allowed it to soar, she had to know... "Why didn't you?"

"I already told you I was an idiot, didn't I?" The corners of his lips ticked up.

"I'm not debating that."

"As well you shouldn't." He stared down at the floor. "I had a lot of feelings I needed to work through. Some I'd been suppressing for years. It took Tini walloping me over the head about a dozen times to drag them back to the surface."

"What feelings?"

"Losing my parents the way I did..." He swallowed and lifted his gaze to meet hers. "I think a part of me has always been terrified that it will happen again. It was easier to dream about freedom than to admit to myself what I really craved."

She rubbed his arm softly, her heart clenching. "Which was?"

"A love like my parents had. And a family like the one I lost."

Her chest ached. "So you don't want to be free from the responsibilities of being a parent?"

He shook his head slowly. "For the longest time, I told myself that would be enough. That it was all I deserved. But then I met you." She stared into his eyes as her breath stuttered in and out of her lungs. His hand lifted, cupping her cheek. "Suddenly I was aching for all the things I'd denied myself. Closeness. Family. Love. I want it with you,

Ali. Only you. If you'll have me. Please tell me I haven't messed things up so badly that you won't give me a second chance."

I spoke too soon. The man can smooth-talk when he has a mind to. She blinked, utterly stunned that not one, but *two* men had just begged her for a second chance. And just like before, she didn't need to think very long to decide what she wanted. "Before I answer that, there's one more thing I have to know."

He leaned in, resting his forehead on hers. "Anything. Whatever you want, it's yours."

Her blood quickened, and she nearly rose on her toes and kissed him. It was impossible not to want to feel his lips on hers with his husky voice wrapping around her, full of so much wicked promise.

"Something Tini said has been bothering me," she admitted.

"What's that?"

"Nicknames. You give them to everyone you like best, right?"

He nodded. Swallowed. "Yeah."

"So where's mine?"

His lips curved, gracing her with the rarest gift—a full, unchecked smile. Her knees wobbled, her pulse kicking into overdrive. *Goddess, it's lucky he doesn't go flashing that thing around, or fending off rivals for his affection would become my full-time job.*

"I have about a dozen." He chuckled softly. "Sure you want to hear them?"

She nodded, biting her lip.

"Lately, I've been partial to"—he tipped up her chin with his thumb—"wildfire."

She grinned. "Not bad."

He dipped his head, and his breath tickled across her lips. "Had a couple come to me during that dance under the stars. What do you think of embermoon?"

She tilted her head. "Mmm, creative."

"Or my moonlit muse."

She wrinkled her nose. "Not so sure about that one."

"No?" He brushed his thumb across her lips, achingly slowly. "There is one I always end up coming back to."

Her arms wound around his neck, dragging him closer. "I'm dying to hear it."

"Temptress." As the word slipped off his tongue, she closed the scant space between them, pressing her lips against his.

Lio groaned, and his arms banded around her waist. She sighed against his mouth and sank into his embrace, seized by the sudden urge to pinch herself and make sure this was real. Had he really just marched into her workshop and offered her everything she'd secretly been craving?

It was too good to be true. Lio wanted her. He wanted them *both*. And she was so damned giddy, tingles spread across her skin, and heat thrummed through her belly. Or maybe that was just the effect of his kisses, which he'd wasted no time deepening as he caressed her back with long, soft strokes.

Then suddenly, she was weightless, being carried in his powerful arms. She gasped, pulling her lips free. "Lio what are you doing?"

He deposited her on the marver, with her legs dangling off the edge of the smooth steel-topped table. She had half a mind to chide him for it—she'd never in a million years imagined using her workshop quite like this—but his kisses were far too enticing. She pulled him closer instead, relishing each drugging swipe of his tongue against hers.

Only it didn't take her long to remember one important fact that could easily turn disastrous. She tore her mouth away. "The door. We need to lock it."

Just as she began to wiggle free, Lio smirked and lifted his hand. "I've got it." Then he blasted a stream of water across the room, and the jet spun the lock into place.

She lifted a brow, too impressed with his skill to be angry about the small puddle on the floor. "Aren't you just full of surprises?"

"I can think of a few surprises you'd *definitely* like." He leaned close, his breath whispering over her lips as his fingers traveled across her torso. "Are you ready for the next one?"

As she stared into his eyes, the answer was perfectly clear. With Lio, she'd have everything she always longed for. A true partner who stuck around, even when times were tough. One who was so kind and selfless, he'd dedicated his life to helping others. A man who was beyond beautiful, both inside and out.

She'd never been more ready for anything in her life. "Absolutely."

Lio was true to his word, just as she'd expected, surprising her with the depths of his intensity and passion. And as he stretched out beside her on the marver, she was certain nothing as magnificent had ever graced her table. None of her creations would ever compare to his sheer perfection.

They discovered each other slowly, marveling over every dip and curve as if they were the greatest works of art. Time melted away, only measured in breaths and sighs. And together, they created a master-piece wrought with pleasure, trust, and love.

After he took her breath away, she snuggled against his side as a delightful warmth spread through her chest.

"So you never answered my question." Lio cupped her face. "Are you going to give me another chance?"

She arched a brow. "Do you really need to ask? Even after all the *surprises*?"

He swallowed heavily. "Yeah. I do." He stared deep into her eyes. "For all I know, that could've been goodbye before you dance off into the sunset with Echo's real dad."

"Of course I will, Lio. Can't you tell that I'm crazy about you?" Her cheeks heated. "And you have nothing to worry about where Joff is concerned. Everything we had is in the past. I told him the same thing earlier."

His breath escaped in an audible whoosh. "Good."

"Don't tell me that was what drove you to share your feelings with me..."

He shook his head. "It wasn't. I was already here wanting to talk before he barged in, remember?"

She settled against his shoulder. "That's true."

"It did make me realize something, though." He toyed with her hair. "Echo deserves more than someone who'll run off at the first sign of trouble."

"I won't argue with that. But she has always wanted a father." How would he take the news that she'd invited her ex to be a part of her daughter's life—and, by extension—hers? "I told him I'd let her know he was here. Echo deserves the chance to meet her father if she wants to. I won't stand in the way of that."

He stiffened. "I won't lie and say I'm happy about that."

"Honestly? Me either." She sighed.

"Hey." He tipped her face toward his. "It'll be all right. And I want you to know I'm going to step up for her. Whatever she needs, whatever you *both* need, I'm your man. Okay?"

"My man, huh?" She smiled and snuggled closer. "Think I can get used to that."

"Good. Cause I have a big favor to ask."

She peeked up at his face and found him gazing back at her, with so much adoration in his eyes. When he looked at her like that, after promising to be there for her and her daughter, she was ready and willing to agree to anything. "Yeah? What is it?"

"Move in with me."

She giggled. "Wow. One romp on the marver and you're already begging to get me in your bed." But when he didn't join in with her laughter, only stared back at her unflinching, she blinked repeatedly. "Wait... You're not serious, are you?"

"Deadly."

She jerked up, sitting straight. "It's way too soon. You'll get sick of me—"

"No, I won't."

"Then you'll get tired of being woken up at the crack of dawn by a noisy ten-year-old."

He shook his head. "I'll sleep so much easier knowing you're both safe, not living above a fire hazard."

"We've been here for years, Lio. The apartment is perfectly safe."

He grabbed her hand and squeezed. "Is it? Pretty sure we wouldn't be here right now if I hadn't been upstairs putting out a fire a few weeks ago."

She pursed her lips. "That wasn't caused by living above my shop, and you know it."

"Not this time..." He held tight to her hand when she attempted to pull it free. "Please, Ali. Just think about it. It doesn't have to be immediately, though the sooner the better. But I hate the thought of the two people I care about most living in danger."

Her heart softened. It was absolutely too soon. And he was being ridiculously overprotective. But the memory of his family tragedy struck her as she gazed into his eyes, and she understood that his request had a lot more to do with his inherent fear of the past repeating itself than with reality.

Still, he had a point. As careful as she was, where there were flames, the chance of an accidental fire always existed. And there were the fumes... She kept her ventilation system constantly supplied with air magic, but surely it would be better not having to worry if the magic caught every vapor, or if some of it was escaping into the upstairs.

Was moving to his home—which was inarguably safer—really too much to ask to keep Lio from going out of his mind with worry?

She smoothed a hand down his biceps. "I'll talk to Echo about it, but I'm not making any promises."

"Come on. She'll be there in a heartbeat. I have Cinder, don't I?"

Ali swatted his chest. "Lio! That was your plan all along, wasn't it?"

He smirked. "Maybe. I had to stuff a few tricks up my sleeve to make sure I could keep you both."

"Tricks, you say? So there's more than one I need to be on the lookout for?"

"Maybe." He shrugged.

Her grin lengthened. "I really was right about you on the first day we met. I'd be better off with an imp."

He chuckled softly. "I'm going to enjoy proving you wrong, Wild-fire."

Freeing

Lio

"Hey Sis, you home? I have good news." Lio stopped short as Tini's bedroom door swung open. Her pack was wide open on her bed, but Tini wasn't taking items out—she was putting them in.

"I have news, too." Tini turned to him, a resolute gleam in her eyes. "I'm going back to Paradise Plains."

His stomach churned. "So soon?"

"Yep. I thought about it long and hard, just like you asked. And I decided this is the right move for me." She folded a shirt, avoiding eye contact. "I know you weren't expecting this, Lio, but I hope in time you'll understand why I'm leaving."

"I don't need time." He leaned against the doorframe. "I get it."

"You do?" She lifted a brow. "Wow, that's… surprising. I was sure you were about to demand that I stay."

"I didn't say I liked it. But I get it."

In a lot of ways, Tini was just like he'd been at the same age. She needed the freedom to choose her own path, and she was brave enough to follow her instincts and leave home to find it. As much as he hated the thought of her all on her own, he wouldn't stand in her way.

"Thank you." She grinned.

"So, when are we leaving?"

Her eyes bulged, and her words flew out, fast and frantic, tinged with a hint of panic. "Oh no. There is no *we*. I thought we talked about this, Lio? What about the brigade? And Ali, and—"

"Relax, Runt. I'm not planning on moving in with you. I'm just offering to keep you company on the road. It's not safe traveling alone."

"Oh." Her cheeks pinked, and she plucked a shirt off the bed, creasing it carefully. "Actually, I won't be alone."

"Really?"

She nodded, her voice calmer but still touched with a smidge of discomfort. "Sera is coming with me."

"Ah… I see." That explained the panic. She clearly didn't want him tagging along to be the third wheel with her sweetheart. "When did you arrange this?"

"Earlier today. I went to see her after I put in my notice at Stellar Spirits."

"Huh. Sounds like you've thought of everything."

"Don't worry." She dropped the shirt she'd been folding onto the bed and crossed the room to his side. "This isn't goodbye forever. I'll come back and visit. And you can visit me whenever you want.

But I need to do this. I want to learn more about my powers, and apprenticing with Nelida is the best way to do it."

He wrapped Tini in a tight hug. "I'm gonna hold you to it. I expect lots of visits in the near future." He sighed, soaking up the familiar warmth of his sister's embrace.

The moment he'd longed for had finally arrived, and he didn't even get to enjoy it. He ought to be shoving Tini out the door, not clinging to her. But even though he no longer craved solitude, he would be doing her a disservice if he refused to let her go.

He drew back, holding her at arm's length. "You're going to be an amazing hearthmother, Tini. I just know it."

She shot him a soft smile, her nose wrinkling. "Love you, Big Butt."

"I love you too, Runt."

Her head cocked sideways. "Hold on. You said you had news when you first showed up. What is it?"

"I took your advice. Had a talk with Ali today."

"You did?" Her eyes lit up. "And?"

"And... you were right."

She jabbed his shoulder. "Lio!"

"Jeez." He rubbed the spot, backing away. "Not this again."

"You can't just leave it like that! I need details."

"Fine, I'll tell you everything." Which he did, mostly—of course, he made sure not to mention the earth-shattering experience that took place atop Ali's workshop table. "So when you come back for your first visit, don't be surprised if the house is more crowded than when you left it," he finished.

"Goddess. I can't believe you asked her to move in already." She chuckled. "When you decide to commit, you don't hold back."

He shrugged. "Guess not."

"I'm thrilled for you, Lio." She sat on the edge of her bed. "I'm glad you finally took a chance on love. And I have a feeling Ali and Echo moving in is exactly what you need."

Sharing everything he'd been holding back with Ali had been so freeing. But there was still something eating at him. A question Tini had asked, which he'd put off answering to avoid dredging up painful memories.

He dropped her bag on the floor and sat beside her, his hands sweaty and heart racing. "Speaking of feelings... do you still want to know what really happened with Mom and Dad?"

She clasped his hand. "Yes. But only if you're ready to tell me."

"I am." He drew a deep breath. "On that night, I wasn't home. I'd snuck out so that I could meet a girl."

"Really?" she asked, eyes wide, voice hushed.

He nodded, his stomach clenching. Was she disappointed? Silently enraged?

"I ran back as soon as I saw smoke. I managed to save you, but I couldn't save them." He gritted his teeth. "I'm so sorry, Tini. I wish I'd been there. When I look back on that night, I'll always wonder if that would've made a difference. If I'd just been there, maybe I could've saved them, too."

Her eyes lifted, her expression turning almost... whimsical. "So that's what they meant..."

His brow furrowed. "What who meant?"

Her gaze snapped back to his. "You've been carrying that guilt around for so long. That's why you never asked me what Mom and Dad said to me during my ritual, isn't it?"

"Yeah." He slipped his hand free and rubbed the back of his neck. "I guess deep down I was worried they wouldn't be happy to see me."

Tini shook her head slowly. "You're dead wrong, Lio."

"How so?"

"They were happy, Lio. Dad said he was proud of you—twice. And Mom couldn't stop tearing up and beaming every time she glanced your way."

His heart skipped a beat. "Yeah?"

She nodded frantically. "But they told me one thing that I didn't understand. Not then. But now, it makes perfect sense." She grabbed his hand again and squeezed. "Do you want to hear it?"

He swallowed. "Tell me." He'd been too scared to ask. Even after that ominous stare Tini aimed in his direction during her ritual. But now he had to know. What message had his parents sent him from the grave?

"They said, tell Lio the answer to his question is no. And that the goddess sent him exactly where he needed to be." She paused, and he let the words sink in.

Did that mean... if I'd been there, would I have been caught in the fire?

She squeezed his hand, dragging him back into the moment. "They made me promise I would tell you when the time was right. They said I'd know when." She smiled serenely. "And I do. I can *feel* it."

Tears pricked at the corners of his eyes. "Hell, Tini." He scrubbed at his face with his sleeve. "They really said that?"

"They did." She laughed, a single peal ringing out in the quiet room and chasing away his lingering sadness. "I swear it didn't make a lick of sense until this very moment."

"Guess there's no denying you found your calling after that."

She nudged his shoulder with hers. "Nope. And I'm glad for it. Now you can move forward without wondering what if. Won't that be nice?"

"Yeah. Suppose it will."

"Just promise me you'll take it easy on yourself, okay? Allow yourself to love and be loved. I don't know anyone else who deserves it more than you, big brother."

He wrapped his arm around her shoulders and squeezed. "I can do that."

"Good." She patted his knee. "Got anything else you need to get off your chest, or can I get back to packing?"

He started to shake his head, but froze as a thought popped into his head. "Just one more question… about Sera. Were you ever planning to tell me I ought to stop wasting my time chasing away all the young lads in town?"

Tini giggled. "Nope. Then I'd have to deal with you scaring off the person I was actually interested in."

He shot her a crooked grin. "As long as you're happy, that's enough for me. And no matter what you choose to do with your life, or who you do it with, I'll always feel the same."

"Thanks, Big Butt. I never doubted it for a moment." She hopped up. "Now get out of here. I've got a lot of packing left, and you'd better get to work taking care of your new roommate."

"What roommate?" He rose from the bed, lifting a brow. "Ali hasn't agreed to move in yet."

"Not her, silly. Cinder. I had half a mind to take her with me, but that was before you decided to use her as a lure to convince Echo to put up with your grumpy butt day in and day out. I can't exactly steal her away now, can I?" She paced to the corner of her room and scooped the sleeping kitten off the floor. "She's partial to fish. Have fun deboning the trout I picked up for her at the market this morning."

Lio bit back a groan. "Thanks, Runt. I'll get right on that."

After he deposited Cinder on the kitchen floor, he found the fish on the counter and grabbed a filet knife. As soon as he opened the paper package, she twined herself around his ankles, purring and meowing incessantly. "It's coming, you little fiend. Don't worry."

If someone had told him a few weeks ago that he'd be racing to cut up a fish for a ravenous kitten and looking forward to inviting even more chaos into his orderly life, he would've laughed in their face. But honestly, he couldn't be happier with how everything had changed.

Of course, he was going to miss Tini, but he was also so damn proud of how brave, caring, and remarkable she'd grown up to be. Thanks to her, he could rest easy, knowing that his parents didn't blame him for what had happened on that awful night. And now, thanks to Ali, he could have the close family he'd lost again. He couldn't wait to spend more time with Ali and Echo—even if Echo was only interested in hanging around him so she could get close to his greedy little pet.

Yeah, it might not be easy—especially with her father back in the picture—but he was determined to win Echo over. And maybe one day, they'd even welcome another child into their home... Then things were sure to get wild.

Eh, who needs order anyway? Bring on the chaos.

CHANGES

Ali

One month later...

The door chimed, drawing Ali's attention away from the display case she'd been polishing. "Welcome to—" A grin graced her lips as a familiar green-skinned face turned the corner. "Seth, you here to pick up the bottles I made for Nora?"

"You have more? After I just carried a crate across town last week?"

"Yep. But it doesn't sound like that's what you popped by for..."

He ducked his head, narrowly avoiding whacking it on a glass chandelier hanging from the ceiling. "No, but I might as well take them with me when I leave. She'll only send me back for them once she hears they're ready."

Ali leaned back against the case, crossing her arms. "So what did you come for?"

Seth grinned. "Two reasons, actually." His grin faded, and he swallowed, seeming a tad... nervous all of a sudden. "First, I thought I might take you up on your offer and test out a few pairs of spectacles. If you're still up for it?"

"Sure, I'm happy to." She waved him toward a side room. "Follow me. I keep all the looking glass in here."

Seth whistled as they entered the cramped room, which contained little more than an oversized desk, a leather bench, and an enormous window. "Never realized this room was back here."

"I'm not surprised, since you've been stubbornly believing everyone else writes in chicken scratch and you don't have a problem with your eyesight." She chuckled, gesturing for him to take a seat.

"Well, I'm through with that now." The bench groaned as his weight settled on it.

"What made you change your mind?"

"Had a few documents I needed to read recently and earned one hell of a headache afterwards." He winced as if recalling the pain. "Figured it was time for a change."

"So you're not just itching to join our book club?" She dug in the dresser, pulling out a box of glass in varying thicknesses. Each piece was set into a metal frame with a handle, more reminiscent of a hand mirror than spectacles.

"No, but I might give a meeting a try if this works."

"Oh, it will. We'll make a reader out of you before you know it." She pointed to the far wall, at a book hanging open, displaying symbols written in fine print. "Tell me what you see on the bottom line."

He squinted and rattled off his answers, getting half wrong.

She held a piece of glass in front of his eyes. "Any clearer?"

He nodded. "Some."

She chose another. "Better, or worse?"

"Better."

She instructed Seth to close one eye, then the other, testing each individually with several thicknesses of glass. Finally, she crossed the room and flicked to the next page. Then she returned to Seth's side and held one of the glasses in front of his eyes. "Last line, please."

Seth sucked in a breath and rattled off the answers, getting every one right.

"We have a winner." Ali grinned.

"That's it?" Seth raised a brow.

"Pretty much. I'll make the glass as soon as you stop by the smithy and let Davos fit you for metal frames. We'll have them ready by the end of the week. Sound good?"

"Sounds great." He stood. "Now that we have that out of the way, I have a few other items I need to buy." He headed for the showroom. "Which of your lamps would you recommend for a first-time home-owner?"

She clapped her hands together and gasped. "You finally found a house?"

He nodded excitedly. "I did."

"That's wonderful news! I'm so happy for you, Seth. Tell me all about it."

"The house isn't much to brag about. Not yet, at least. But I figure it'll be fun to fix it up."

"Sure." She had no doubt he was up for the task. Seth was plenty handy. He'd made quick work of fixing Nora's shelves when they'd been destroyed last fall. And he'd even repaired the sagging roof at his mother's house.

"The land is what really drew me to the place. It's sitting on a huge plot, about an hour outside of town."

"A farmhouse, huh?"

"Yep. It's practically perfect." His smile faded around the edges. "Well, except for one thing."

"What's that?"

"Seems there's a bit of a property dispute with one of the neighbors. But I bet we can work something out." He puffed out his chest. "I'll just dazzle them with my charm. Shouldn't be too much trouble."

She chuckled. "I'm sure you will. Let me know when and where, and I'll stop by with a housewarming gift once you're settled."

"Of course. In fact..." He patted his pockets, and when one crinkled, he dug out a piece of parchment. "I've got the property map right here."

He unfolded the page. Ali glanced down, her pulse kicking up. "That's the Avalon Shallows, isn't it?"

"Yep." He pointed to a plot close to it. "I'm here, with just one farm between me and the lake."

"Is that the neighbor you're going to have to charm?" She tapped on the farmhouse next to the lake.

"You guessed it."

Hearty laughter bubbled out of her belly. "Oh, Seth. You poor, poor man."

His brow scrunched. "What?"

"Don't you know who your new neighbors are?" She chuckled again. "Best polish that charm until it shines like a diamond."

"Why?"

"That, my dear friend, is where your favorite witch resides with her mother." She clasped his shoulder. "You're moving in next to Paige."

His smile vanished. "Fantastic."

"Come on. Let me show you the lamps."

Seth followed along in silence as she pointed out his options, explaining the different sizes and colors. Once he'd made his selections, she strode behind the counter and jotted down his order.

"So is that everything?" she asked.

"For now." He sighed. "And I guess I'd better grab those bottles for Nor."

"Of course. I'll get them for you." She hefted the heavy box off the floor and deposited it on the counter.

"I've been meaning to ask, how's Echo doing?" Seth leaned against the counter. "She getting on well with her old man?"

Ali's heart twinged. "Surprisingly well, actually. It's definitely been an adjustment, but she certainly seems to love having two new father figures in her life."

"Don't forget, my offer still stands. If he ever steps out of line—"

She lifted a hand. "I really appreciate it, but so far so good." After sharing with her friends how Joffin suddenly reappeared, she'd quickly amassed several offers to teach her wayward ex a painful lesson if he ever acted out of turn around Echo. Not just from Seth, but Kieran, Davos, and even Maalik. If she'd still needed confirmation that she'd made the right decision to stay in Everpass, that would've done it.

"I'm glad to hear it."

"Yeah. Me too." She'd been extremely cautious at first, insisting on being present for their first few meetings. But after a couple weeks, she'd begun allowing them some time alone, at Echo's urging. And while she still wasn't comfortable enough to permit him more than a few hours with her daughter out in public, if Joffin continued showing up for Echo, she suspected he'd soon become a permanent fixture in her daughter's life.

She still wasn't sure how to feel about that. It was certainly hard allowing her daughter to spend so much time with a man who was practically a stranger to her. But as long as Echo wanted her father around, Ali was determined to deal with the discomfort. Perhaps in time, they'd even become friends again.

The front door jingled, and Ali's face lit up when her two favorite people strode inside.

"Mooooom. I'm starving!" Echo blurted in lieu of a proper hello. "Can we go to Stellar Spirits for dinner?"

Lio patted Echo's shoulder fondly. "What about Cinder? I thought you wanted to help me feed her tonight?"

"Oh, right." Echo bounded across the shop. "Can we go to Lio's then, my stomach—" Her words cut off on a gasp as her bouncing steps knocked a glass vase off its stand.

Luckily, Lio deftly caught it before it smashed into the floor. "Careful there, Trouble."

Echo winced. "I'm sorry."

"It's all right, sweetheart." Ali chuckled. "Just watch your step next time." She rounded the counter and pulled Echo into a hug.

"Oh, hi, Seth." Echo wiggled out of her arms. "What are you doing here?"

"Just picking up some bottles for Nora." Seth hefted the box easily in his arms.

Echo pouted. "I bet he'll get to eat before me."

Ali rolled her eyes. "How about we stop by Stellar Spirits on the way to Lio's, huh? We'll grab some food to go."

Echo clapped her hands. "Yay!"

"Come on, kiddo. Let's go out front where neither of us has to worry about accidentally breaking any of the pretties in here. You can tell me all about your kitten while your mom closes up." Seth led Echo out the front door, passing Lio with a wink.

Lio strode forward. "You need a hand with anything?"

Her heart raced. "Actually, I have a very important task only you can help me with."

He lifted a brow. "Oh really?"

She closed the space between them and balanced on her toes, bringing their lips flush. "Yep. I need some sugar."

Then they kissed, and it was everything she needed and more. Ali sighed happily, reveling in the embrace. Who knew the grumpiest fire chief in Everpass was secretly so sweet? When they first met, she'd certainly never have guessed it.

With a chuckle, he pulled away, holding out the vase. "Hold on, I still need to put this back where it belongs."

As he took a step away, heading for the stand, warmth rushed through her. Just a few months ago, her life was one big mess. Then Lio strolled in, and despite being walloped in the face with her problems—literally—he stuck around. And now, she was beyond grateful to have him in her life.

He'd spent the last month showing up for her, day in and day out, just like he'd said he would. He'd even rearranged his schedule with the brigade so he could pick up Echo after school. And while they hadn't moved in with him yet, they were planning to. Soon.

Yeah, it was still early days in their relationship. But as she watched him carefully set the vase back to rights, the truth sang out in her soul. Lio was right where he belonged. And she couldn't wait to see what the future held for their family.

Also By

The Palisade Trilogy

Shadows That Bind Us — Palisade Trilogy 1

Muses That Align Us — Palisade Trilogy 2

Lines That Drew Us — Palisade Trilogy 3

Palisade Trilogy – Omnibus Books 1-3 : an epic fantasy adventure

Sign up for my newsletter for a free standalone prequel novella that tells the story of how the Palisade was built centuries ago.

Fates That Entwine Us

You'll find the link on my website amberlwerner.com

Standalone Short Story

Somewhere In Between

The Blood Song Trilogy

The Odyssey Ring – A Blood Song Trilogy Prequel

Bloodfeather Lullaby — Blood Song Trilogy 1

Bloodfeather Heartsong — Blood Song Trilogy 2

Bloodfeather Symphony — Blood Song Trilogy 3

Fairvale Cozy Fantasy Romances

Magic and Mocktails

Sparking the Vibe

Upcoming Novels:

Ruling the Roost – coming soon!

Serenades and Steel

About the Author

A mber L. Werner loves to write about magic, monsters and mythical creatures. She lives in Norristown, PA with her husband and two children. The Palisade Trilogy is her debut series.

Follow her Facebook page Amber L. Werner
Or Instagram and TikTok as amberlwerner

Sign up for her newsletter and receive a free novella.
Find it here amberlwerner.com